VIMINY CROWE'S COMIC BOOK

FLYNN GOSTER
Viminy Crowe

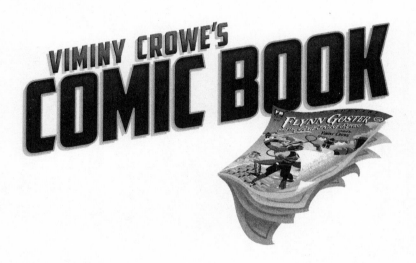

MARTHE JOCELYN &
RICHARD SCRIMGER

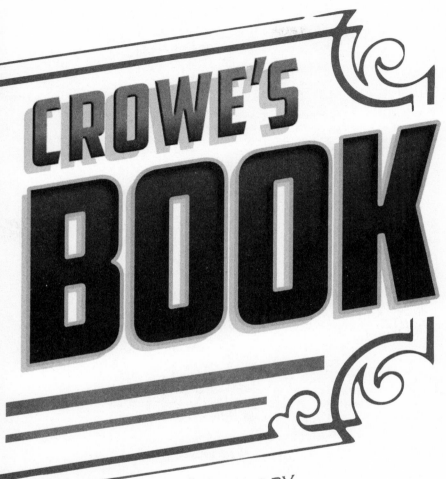

CROWE'S BOOK

WITH COMICS BY
CLAUDIA DÁVILA

TUNDRA BOOKS

Library and Archives Canada Cataloguing in Publication

Jocelyn, Marthe, author
Viminy Crowe's comic book / Marthe Jocelyn & Richard Scrimger;
with comics by Claudia Dávila.

Originally published: 2014.
ISBN 978-1-101-91893-7 (paperback)

I. Scrimger, Richard, 1957–, author II. Dávila, Claudia, illustrator
III. Title.

PS8569.O254V56 2017   jC813'.54   C2016-900996-3

eBook ISBN 978-1-770-49480-0

Published simultaneously in the United States of America by
Tundra Books of Northern New York, a division of Random House of Canada Limited,
a Penguin Random House Company

Library of Congress Control Number: 2013943886

Printed and bound in the United States of America

www.penguinrandomhouse.ca

1 2 3 4 5 6   22 21 20 19 18 17

TUNDRA BOOKS | Penguin Random House

To my father, who taught me to laugh—R.S.

For Henry, Thomas and Joseph. First listeners—M.J.

For Michael and Yolanda—C.D.

WYLDER
WALLACE

ADDY CROWE

FLYNN GOSTER

VIMINY CROWE

CATNIP

NEVINS

PROFESSOR
ALDOUS K.
LICKPENNY

ISADORA
FORTUNA

NELLY DAY

CAPTAIN
MCGURK

SERVIDUDE

SNAP

KRACKLE

After the best morning of his life, Wylder Wallace faced a big decision.

French fries or onion rings?

The good news was that he liked them both.

But which did he want right now?

The tall girl ahead of him in line at the food court was having trouble too. From the expression on her face, nothing looked good enough for her.

"Not that one," she said. "That doesn't look fresh. The one beside it, please." She pointed at a container of salad.

Of course, thought Wylder. A lettuce lover.

An announcement came over the loudspeaker. The Vampire King would be signing autographs at booth

1282 in five minutes. There was a lost child in the lobby. Would the owner of a car with license plate number AYYB-663 please move from the loading dock?

Wylder imagined biting into an onion ring. The sweet, sharp flavor breaking through the batter, coating his mouth in amazingness. Oh, yeah. But french fries were pretty good too. Little wedges of energy, so familiar, so satisfying. Eating a french fry was like coming home.

The tall girl took her container of lettuce and grated carrots and moved toward the cash register. Wylder's turn now. But before he could open his mouth, he felt a tap on his shoulder. Superman was standing behind him.

"Mind if I butt in here, sonny? I'm in a hurry."

The square jaw, the dark curl over the forehead, the muscles, the blue tights—he was perfect. His hand rested for a second on Wylder's shoulder. A man in line took a photo with his cell phone. Wylder tried to act casual.

"Sure, sure. Uh, go ahead. Is someone in trouble? Is it that lost child they were talking about over the loudspeaker? Is that what you're doing here?"

The Man of Steel smiled.

"Nah, I'm late, that's all. I have to be in Hall B in ten minutes so people can get their pictures taken with me. Tuna sandwich," he said to the lunch lady. "Put it on DC's tab."

"You got it, Clark." She tossed the sandwich over the counter.

"Shhh!" He shook his finger at her. "Don't give away my secret."

"Hey, Superman!" said Wylder. "Which should I order—french fries or onion rings?"

He turned in a swirl of scarlet cape. There was the smile again.

"Onion rings." The answer was definite. "You can get fries anywhere."

"Thanks, Superman!"

But he was already gone, dashing through the crowd.

What a guy.

There was only one empty chair in the whole food court. Wylder didn't notice who was sitting at the table until he was almost there.

"Oh, hi," he said. "Someone sitting here? Did you see Superman just now? He told me to try the onion rings. Pretty cool, eh? Like we were buddies, me and Superman. I think I'll get his autograph later. He had a tuna sandwich, by the way. I'll have to start eating more tuna myself. Want an onion ring?" he asked. "Good enough for the Man of Steel. What do you say?"

The girl shook her head without looking up from her comic.

Wylder shrugged out of his backpack. He wasn't going to have this wonderful day ruined by a girl with a mouthful of carrot.

The International Comic Book Festival—ComicFest—came to Toronto every other June. It was a huge show, taking up the entire downtown convention center and spilling over into the domed stadium where the Blue Jays play baseball. Thousands and thousands of people came. Two years ago, Wylder had come with his mom, his aunt Mary Lee and his cousin George. He'd had a pretty good time. *The Fist* poster—signed by both Bill Avery, who drew the comic, and the villainous Underhand himself—was one of Wylder's prized possessions and hung over his bed. But two years ago, Wylder had been ten years old. Now he was almost twelve. Old enough to go to ComicFest on his own, he'd told his mom, who had agreed—reluctantly. And what a time he was having! Already he'd picked up five brand-new comic books, a signed photo of Wolverine and a free video game introducing Phlegm—A Hero for Tomorrow!

He ate two onion rings in quick succession. They were brilliant. Superman was right, of course. Wylder's feet didn't quite reach the floor. He kicked happily against the plastic legs of his chair.

Wylder's cell phone vibrated. He sighed. Mom checking up on him again. The text read: **u ok?**

He wanted to text back: **i am fine. the same way i**

was fine a half hour ago. leave me alone. He texted back: **yes**

She worried about him all the time. Breakfast to bedtime, school day or holiday, she had to know he was there. She'd knock on his door or call up from the kitchen.

"Yes?" he'd say.

"Just checking, honey."

It was like she thought he would disappear if she wasn't in touch all the time. Or wander away and never come back. Wylder wondered if her anxiety had something to do with his dad moving out. That happened years ago—he couldn't even remember a time when Dad lived with them. Was Mom afraid Wylder would walk out too?

Another message came through right away: **luv u**

What were you supposed to say to that? Nothing, that's what. For a chatty guy, Wylder often had nothing to say to his mom. It was easier with Dad, who only texted to find out where Wylder wanted to go for dinner.

The more Mom tried to hang on to Wylder, the more he wanted to disappear.

The onion rings made him feel better, though. He settled back in his chair and let himself enjoy the hum around him. The air was full of energy, words and ideas crashing into each other like billiard balls. And something else too. The fantasy and mystery and power of comics. All the people who wrote and drew and believed in them … all that magic had somehow drenched the whole convention center.

"Do you mind?" said the tall girl. She smiled in a not-smiling kind of way.

"Huh?"

"You're kicking the table," she said. "Please stop."

She wore a T-shirt featuring a big question mark. Her jeans were tight. Her hair was loose. Her high-tops were undone. She probably wasn't any older than he was, but she sure acted it. Her smile was, like, thirty years old. She took out her phone and started messing with the screen. Of course it had one of those zippy waterproof skins on it.

Another fuzzy announcement came over the loud-speaker.

"Did you hear that?" Wylder said to the girl. "Was it something about—Hey! Hey!! HEY!!!"

He jumped to his feet and pointed down at the table, his mouth wide open. Her comic book sat faceup. All this time she'd been reading, he hadn't even noticed.

"That's the new Flynn Goster comic! The Summer Special! How'd you get that?" Wylder demanded. "I lined up for an hour, and they said all the copies were held up somewhere. But this is it, right?"

He grabbed it with trembling hands.

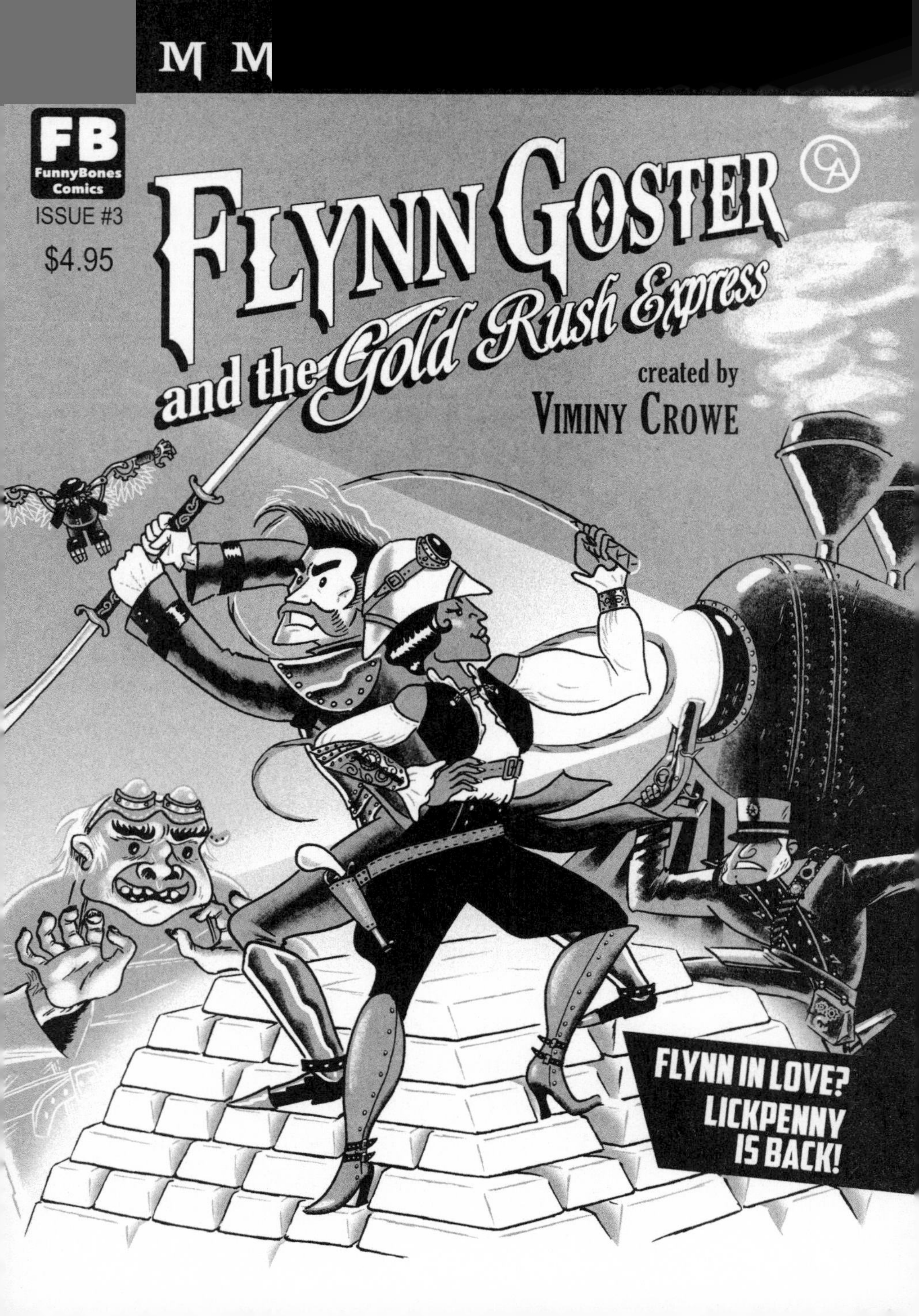
M M
FB
FunnyBones Comics
ISSUE #3
$4.95
FLYNN GOSTER
and the Gold Rush Express
created by
VIMINY CROWE
FLYNN IN LOVE?
LICKPENNY IS BACK!

"The guy who draws the comic—Viminy Crowe—has a booth here. I saw him. He's a funny-looking guy. Have you seen him? Like an ostrich or a palm tree or something. Or a celery stick, you know? I recognized him from that cemetery clip on YouTube. I've seen it a hundred times. I wanted to ask—"

"Please!"

The girl pushed her tray away and stood up, her chair tumbling backward. She held out her hand for the comic.

"Oh! Oh, sorry!" Wylder gave it back. "Gosh, sorry. I didn't mean to grab it from you like that. I'm a fan, that's all. I really like that Flynn guy. Thieves are cool. And Flynn can look like anyone. He's practically a shape-shifter the way he disguises himself. But always with the mustache. I read about this issue online. There's a big display here—a train engine that looks just like the online ad. Did you see it? Anyway, since you have a copy, I guess that shipment must have come in. I'll go to the booth right after lunch."

The girl opened her mouth to say something, shut it and opened it again.

"Don't bother. There are no comics there."

"Huh? But—"

"I don't know your name, but—"

"Wylder. Wylder Wallace. Nice to meet—"

"We're not meeting. I don't want to be palsy-walsy with you. I want you to be quiet so I can eat my lunch in peace."

The girl picked up her chair and put the comic back on the table. "Do you mind?"

Wylder was used to people telling him he talked too much.

"I can take a hint," he said. "You want me to shut up? I'll shut up. No problem. I do *not* have to be talking all the time. Not me. No, sirree."

He ate an onion ring.

And another.

The girl sat down and fiddled with her bag, looking inside.

Wylder stared at the tabletop. "Oh, hey there! Uh, listen. I don't know your name, but you might want to—"

"No."

"This isn't about being palsy-walsy. But I really think you—"

"No!"

He nodded. Drew his hand across his mouth in a zip-up gesture. But he pointed at her side of the table, which was swimming in salad dressing. The container must have spilled when she pushed her tray away.

She jumped back. Too late. Oily stuff was running off the table. There was a stain almost as big as a hockey puck on the leg of her jeans.

"Sorry," said Wylder.

She gave him a furious look and stormed off, shoulder bag swinging.

He popped another onion ring into his mouth.

The Summer Special was still on the table. "Wait!" Wylder called. "You left your comic!" He could see a flash of her dark hair leaving the food court. "Don't you want it? Wait!"

What began as a just fine day was fast sinking into sludge.

Addy had been eager to help Uncle Vim carry boxes of Flynn Goster back issues to the big comic convention. Total fun to be at ComicFest—plus, even a dribble of cash was always welcome. And there was no adult she'd rather hang out with than Viminy Crowe.

"If you want to bring a friend … ?" he'd said.

"Nuh-uh." Even to Vim, Addy wouldn't admit that she didn't exactly have any friends.

Her mother—who had to work, as usual—told Addy she shouldn't take Catnip along. But Addy, naturally, had smuggled him out of the house inside her shoulder bag, keeping nose and whiskers hidden during the whole carton-hauling interlude. Once they got to the convention center, disaster struck. First, she had to watch her uncle lose what little cool he had (and, really, *cool* he wasn't) when the giant train display for the booth began to malfunction. The way it was supposed to go, you "climbed aboard" by stepping up onto a little platform behind a windshield and—*whoopee!*—turning an oversized steering wheel. A glowing orange spotlight was supposed to beam out from the front of the engine. Pulling on a silk cord sounded an old-fashioned train whistle. Only this morning, the light didn't work, and the noise was more like a cow mooing than anything mysterious and steampunk-y to go with the comic.

Addy and Uncle Vim had dragged the display off the exhibition floor to the service area to await the repair team. Back at the booth, Vim raked his hair with his fingers, trying to figure out how to decorate without the cutout gold rush train. And *that's* when he realized that the ten thousand copies of the new Summer Special had not been delivered.

"Tomorrow?" he shouted into his cell phone. "What do you mean, *tomorrow*? I could be dead *tomorrow*! My own *blood* is in those pages! Blood *and* sweat—even a few tears. *Today* is the opening day of ComicFest. TO. DAY! Now! This minute! Before the toast pops up, you get it? Hordes of rabid fans are waiting to buy this issue! *Tomorrow* is not acceptable!"

He prowled back and forth in the aisle like a panther

in a crummy cage, ranting into the phone while the *hordes* watched.

Kind of loving the show, Addy thought. Except it wasn't a show.

Uncle Vim urgently needed this comic book to be a success. The first issue, *Flynn Goster and the Curse of the Diavik Diamonds*, had done okay. The critics hadn't really paid attention, but readers started to pass the word around that Viminy Crowe was an awesome new comic artist. The second issue, *Flynn Goster and the Emeralds of Green Gables*, sold like crazy. That's when Vim got a call from FunnyBones Comics offering to invest in Issue #3. *They*'d pay all the printing and distribution costs—in other words, *they*'d take all the risk—which was great, because Uncle Vim was at the very end of his money options. All he had to do was create the most brilliant comic book ever and guarantee that it would sell like buttered popcorn at the movies.

Those missing cartons held his *future*, even his *life*, as far as Vim was concerned. His older sister—Addy's mom—had been supporting him all this time, contributing money she saved from working two jobs. *She* knew her brother was a genius artist, but this was pretty much his last chance to prove it to the world. If the FunnyBones guys stayed excited and their investment paid off, maybe they would publish a whole series! But if the comic flopped … Addy's stomach did a small flop of its own. If it flopped, Uncle Vim was planning to move back to Saskatchewan and his former job at the Petalskin Soap Company, living a million miles away, letting his dreams of being an artist get sucked down the drain like old bath bubbles.

Addy's phone made its ding-dong doorbell sound, telling her there was a text from the person who slept on the living room couch.

all good? wrote Vim.

yep she sent back.

i have a break in an hour. u good til then?

yep she wrote.

Then, just when Addy finally got to a nice quiet table (she was pretty sure Catnip was expiring from lack of food and air), this dweeby kid sat down—with onion rings tormenting her nostrils!—thinking he was Addy's best friend, yakking away like an old lady you might get stuck next to on a train. He had the kind of round, freckly face that you'd see on a commercial for, say, phony homemade apple pie. He was round all over, actually, and his pants had those bulgy pockets, making him look even wider.

As long as he was sitting there, Addy didn't want to feed Catnip. You never knew who would object to the sight of a rat chomping lettuce in a public food court. She pretended to be enraptured by the sample copy of Issue #3, the Summer Special, a story she knew as well as her own toothbrush, since she had basically helped her uncle to write it. Well, maybe not actually *write* it, but she'd given him a whole lot of ideas. And no one could deny that Nelly Day, the young heroine and sneak thief, had Addy's eyes, her nose, her one dimple and her messy dark hair.

When Uncle Vim had clogged up the plot with too many complications, it was Addy who reminded him to "Keep it simple! It's all about the *gold*." He'd been so grateful for her input that he brought home an add-on rodent terrace for Catnip's ever-growing estate on the kitchen windowsill.

Plus, this kid? Wylder Wallace? (What mother names her kid Wylder Wallace unless she *expects* him to be goofy?) Addy didn't want to be mean, but he was having a major fan-attack about meeting Superman in the lunch line. While she had done her best to avoid the caped superdrip. True, Bob Fink did look the part. But holy cannoli, he might be the most boring dude ever! He'd showed up at Uncle Vim's barbecue last summer, on the back terrace of Addy's apartment building, one of dozens of people Vim had met through work. Half of them were actors who impersonated comic book heroes. (It was one thing, in Addy's opinion, to *create* a comic book. But to spend your life pretending to be *in* one? Come *on!*)

That night, Bob Fink got "overly fond of the beer," as Addy's mother put it, and started to sing, revealing the reason he was usually hired to stand around in tights and a cape with his mouth *shut*, instead of on a stage next to a microphone.

And now, Wylder Wallace had spilled salad dressing across the table, so Addy had to scram out of there with icky sludge all over her only pair of jeans. And when she got to the washroom, there was one of those annoying yellow signs dangling on the door: CLOSED FOR CLEANING. SORRY FOR THE INCONVENIENCE. PLEASE USE FACILITY ON LEVEL C.

Level C? Level C was all the way across the convention hall and up the escalator. The slimy orange gunk would probably have burned a hole through the denim by then.

Addy slipped a hand into her bag to stroke Catnip's head while she thought for a second. There was a staff-only restroom behind the food court, near where they'd hauled the broken train display that morning with Uncle Vim looking miserable. Addy had felt a lurch of pity for him.

"No comics," he'd said. "*And* the display is broken. I want it fixed by the time I take it home."

"I'm sure my mom will love that." Addy rolled her eyes. "Not."

A floor-to-ceiling curtain hid the scruffy "backstage" of the convention center and the staff washroom from the general public. Addy slipped through a break in the curtain and bumped smack into the broken train display, right where they'd left it. A flash of light bounced off the ladies' room door but then went dark at once. Addy reached into the engineer's cabin to toot the horn. *Moooo.*

Never mind. Poor Uncle Vim.

The door with WOMEN/FEMMES in fat black letters was luckily not locked. But the lights were out. She flicked the switch—on the wall outside the door—and the lights blinked dramatically with an amber glow. There was a noise, a sort of clicking and huffing at the same time. Seriously creepy. Addy would make this quick.

She snatched a towel from the stack beside the sink. Nice that it wasn't paper—wet cotton wouldn't shred all over her jeans. The lights kept flickering as Addy dampened the towel and scrubbed at the salad dressing. She looked around to see if there was one of those air-blowy things to help dry the big spot on her pants. No dryer in sight, so Addy waved her hand over the spot and blew on it, as if that would do anything.

The floor began to shake. Addy clapped a hand over the top of her bag to protect Catnip if she lost her balance. Was it an earthquake? The door sprang open and a girl came in, slamming it quickly behind her and then pressing her ear against it, listening. Even in the dim light, Addy could see that she was an actor in costume—a familiar character but not a superhero. She was wearing clunky laced-up boots, striped leggings and a cool utility vest with loads of pockets.

"Um, hello?"

"Aahhh!" The girl jumped and swung around, raising her fists as if ready to punch Addy in the nose.

"Whoa!" said Addy. "Didn't mean to scare you."

The ground shook again, and the lights dipped to nearly black.

The girl whispered from the shadows, "Keep your grimy hands off me, you mud-licking squit!"

"What?" Addy couldn't believe she was being snarled at. "I have a right to be here. I'm with the Goster booth. Number 418."

"I've watched every person on board," said the girl. "I only slipped in here to avoid the creeping brat who trails around after the suspicious professor. I've not seen you before, so I'm thinking *you're* fishy too. You're no friend of Aunt Isadora's. You're not a Rider. I've memorized everyone, so I know you haven't got a proper seat."

Holy cannoli! Addy should have recognized the character at once. Her words got all mixed up spilling out: "But-Isa-baba-Unca-Vim-fa-Rider-da-gold-rush ... ON BOARD WHAT?"

She paused to breathe and got a clear look at the girl's face. "Who *are* you?" she said.

They stared at each other.

"Who are *you*?" said the girl.

As if both their necks were on the same hinge, the girls turned to gaze into the scratched-up mirror above the sink. Two pairs of gray eyes stared back in surprise, before snapping around to face each other.

"I'm impressed," said Addy. "How did they find someone who looks even more like Nelly Day than I do?"

"I am Nelly Day," said the girl.

"You don't have to worry about keeping in character. I'm not some crazy fan who needs to believe that you're real."

The girl narrowed her eyes. "I *am* Nelly Day," she said again. "Who are *you*?"

"It's okay," said Addy. "We're in a washroom at the Toronto Convention Centre. You're not destroying some childish fantasy that Santa Claus or Superman or Flynn Goster actually exists."

The ground continued to rumble under their feet. The flickering light added to an unpleasant feeling of motion.

"Are we having an earthquake?" said Addy. "I've never heard of Toronto getting earthquakes. And what do you mean, *on board*?"

The actor squinched her eyes at Addy. "Are you loco?" she said. "How did you get here if you don't know? What kind of a sneaking rat are you?"

Addy slipped a hand into her bag to check on Catnip. Nothing wrong with rats, in her opinion. Rats were supreme beings, with a family heritage going back beyond ancient Egypt, while Nelly Day had been invented by Addy's uncle six months ago.

Things were getting a little too weird. Addy had no intention of standing around listening to insults from an actor! She nudged the other girl aside and opened the door.

She slammed it shut again—*BANG!*—her stomach turning upside down.

Instead of the empty, beige-curtained corridor of the convention center staff area, Addy had seen a row of grimy windows. And beyond the mud-spattered glass was an unfamiliar wilderness, rattling past the way it does when a person is sitting on a—

It was impossible.

Addy was on a train.

W hat a crazy girl, Wylder thought. Didn't want to talk to him, spilled on herself and dashed off without her comic. Just—*poof!*—gone. A salad eater. She needed to find a sense of humor. Must be hard to be cool all the time.

He still didn't know her name.

Wylder sat back down, ignoring the pool of salad dressing across the table. He bit into another onion ring. Chilly but still very good. The perfect accompaniment to reading. He stared at the cover of the girl's left-behind comic.

"Fancy meeting *me* here!"

A man with a crooked mustache tapped the tip of his sword on the table next to Wylder's hand. Wylder recognized the line. Flynn Goster said it all the time. This guy was dressed to look like Flynn—as much as he could, considering that he was short and fat and Flynn wasn't. Flynn didn't squint either. And his sword wasn't plastic.

"You are holding the new Goster comic, yes?" The man had a bit of an accent. "The Summer Special, yes?"

"Yes."

"I have been seeking this issue and not finding it. No one has a copy. And then I hear you and the girl talking. Your girlfriend, yes?"

"Yes—I mean, no."

Why was Wylder blushing?

"Not at all. I don't even know her name," he said.

"But she gives you comic, and now is yours. You will sell to me, yes?"

The man's tray held a cheese sandwich, a pickle and a paper cup of coleslaw. Wylder tried not to shudder.

"I am Flynn Goster's number one fan," said the man. "I live my life like him. I carry his collapsible sword with the concealed second blade. I look good like him, yes?"

"Uh ..."

"I have many copies of first two issues, with autographs. I have poster from Comic Con in New York last year—*Flynn Goster and the Emeralds of Green Gables.* You will sell to me new one, yes? I have much money."

The man's mustache slipped a little. Wylder was getting the creeps. He put the box of leftover onion rings in his backpack and stood up. "I have to go now," he said. "My mom wants me."

The man put down his tray and pressed the button on his sword so the second blade slid out of the handle. He held the weapon in two hands, like Flynn did, and whirled it with a flourish over his head.

"It's smiting time!" he bellowed—another Flynn line. The food court was crowded. Wylder wasn't the only one who ducked.

There was some applause from across the court. The man turned with a smile and a bow, and Wylder grabbed his chance to hurry away.

My mom wants me. Yeesh.

The hall was full of booths and people and fun. Wylder slowed down and took it all in, keeping watch for the tall girl. Ahead of him was a little kid dressed normally except for a blue cape. He tore around his parents like a dog on a leash—round and round, pumping his elbows, making the cape flutter. His smile was bigger than his face.

Down the hall on the left stood a padded ring where people fought with foam swords and spears and hammers. LARPing, it was called. Wylder got in line. Two years ago he'd wanted to do this, but his mom had said no, too dangerous. Now he'd give it a try. He was feeling dangerous.

Time to look at the comic. FLYNN IN LOVE? said the teaser on the front cover. Wylder wasn't sure he liked that.

The opening page, under the caption *VANCOUVER STATION, 1899*, featured an old-timey train with a smokestack and a cowcatcher, but other details showed this wasn't exactly real history. Not even close! Moving ramps allowed passengers to glide onto the train, and what looked like garbage cans on wheels carried baggage in extra-long rubber arms. Behind the engine and the coal car sat a flatbed carriage covered with a striped canvas labeled HOT-AIR BALLOON. Coupled to that was a car of burnished metal, like a giant safe. The League of Best Western Red Riders stood on guard, blunderbusses at the ready. An inset showed stacks of gleaming gold inside the armored car.

OPEN INVITATION TO TRAIN ROBBERS, IF YOU ASK ME, one Rider said to another.

So that's what was going on, thought Wylder.

There were so many details in the drawing. He knew he'd have to come back to it. He turned the page. The train was on the move now. The next panel showed a short guy with a comb-over, bulging eyes and monogrammed luggage: A.K.L. Wylder recognized him from the first Flynn comic—Professor Aldous K. Lickpenny, criminal mastermind. He and the geeky kid next to him held what looked like video game controllers.

NEVINS, YOU INSECT, USE THE BLUE BUTTON! snarled the professor.

Y-Y-YESSUNCLE, said the kid.

The next panel showed two huge guys with beaky noses and bowler hats lurching along. Robots? thought Wylder. Is that what the controllers are for? He turned the page.

His phone vibrated again.

u ok?

He was typing **still fine, mo—** when the first panel of the new page caught his eye. He slid the phone back into his pocket without finishing.

They both looked like the girl from lunch. Weird or what?

It got weirder. In the next panel, one of the girls wore a steampunk getup. The other girl wore jeans and a T-shirt with a question mark on the front of it. *Exactly the same* as the girl from lunch. Same hair, same green shoulder bag, same funny dimple in her cheek. She *was* the girl from lunch. Salad Girl. Only she was *inside* the comic.

Her speech bubble was the weirdest thing of all.

The man in line behind Wylder wore Dracula fangs. He was taking photos of the two LARPers smashing each other over the head. Wylder showed him the comic.

"Goster," said the man. "I don't read it. Not enough gore."

"Do you think the one in the jeans looks wrong?" Wylder asked. "For the comic, I mean?"

Dracula shrugged. "No gore," he said. "*That's* what's wrong. Unless …" He peered a little closer. "Is that blood on her pant leg?" he asked.

Wylder had noticed the stain too. "Salad dressing," he said.

"Too bad."

Wylder's mind whirled. It wasn't just some crazy coincidence, a picture of someone who looked like her. It *was* her—the girl who had told him to stop talking and then spilled salad dressing on her jeans and stormed off. *To end up in this comic.* But how? He read her speech bubble again: WE'RE IN A WASHROOM AT THE TORONTO CONVENTION CENTRE.

The other girl—Nelly, she called herself—looked suspicious. For half a second, Wylder considered the idea that Salad Girl was some kind of interplanetary alien. But the look on her face ... she was human all right, and she knew something was wrong.

Was she scared? Looking at the picture, he couldn't tell. He ran a finger down the page. ARE WE HAVING AN EARTHQUAKE? she asked. Wylder rolled the comic and held it tight.

"I have to go," he said to Dracula.

"Don't you want to play? It's almost your turn, man."

"I think I've got another game someplace else."

Wylder trotted off to look for the bathroom, thinking hard. He didn't think he'd be scared in Salad Girl's place. Imagine being in a story. Imagine meeting Flynn Goster in person! Hard to get cooler than that. Unless things weren't real in the comic. Maybe it was flat, in two dimensions, as if you were lying down all the time. That would suck.

But Salad Girl wasn't saying, WHY AM I LYING DOWN? So the comic must look like real life.

Wylder found himself outside an almost empty Hall B. Inside was a familiar figure in royal blue tights, standing by himself, yawning. He saw Wylder and waved. Actually waved.

"I need a bathroom, Superman!"

That's not something you get to say every day, Wylder couldn't help thinking.

The Man of Steel smiled down at him. "Sure, sonny, I owe you a favor from lunch." He lowered his voice. "Don't tell anyone, but there's a staff bathroom down a ways on your left. Near the big Flynn Goster train display."

"Train display? Isn't that at the booth?"

"Yeah, it's broken. Last I saw, the maintenance guy was trying to fix it. Look for the whacking great train, and duck in behind it. That's where you'll find a service hall with bathrooms."

Sure enough, Wylder found the cardboard train engine lying on its side, a bit squished. A man in a green uniform and a tool belt was fiddling with the casing over the headlight, watched by a little girl and her dad.

"I don't *know* what's wrong, kiddo," said the repair guy, reaching through the conductor's window. "The spotlight is supposed to go on when the steering wheel turns, but it's *mal*-functioning. It blinks on for a second and goes off again. Some kind of faulty connection. I replaced the wire and the switch, but the light is still unreliable. You want a try? Go ahead. Turn the wheel."

Wylder slipped past them down a dimly lit hall. The comic was in his hand. Behind him, the maintenance guy laughed. "Bingo! Look at you! You have the magic touch, kiddo! Shining right there on the door! But I don't think it's going to last ..."

Wylder's phone buzzed. Another text from Mom.

WHY NO ANSWER? U OK?

Wylder wanted to laugh. Okay? Way better than okay.

amazing he texted back.

In front of him was a door marked MEN/HOMMES. He paused for a second. He was going to do this, right? Well, yeah. How many chances did you get to go where no boy had gone before? He took a deep breath, and one more for luck. If he didn't walk through that door, he'd think about it for the rest of his life.

But the bathroom was completely, boringly normal.

"Hello?" His voice echoed off the tile walls. *Ello-o-o?*

Wylder looked at the urinals.

"Idiot!" he said aloud. No girl would be in here! He hurried down the hall and turned the handle on the door marked WOMEN/FEMMES.

4

Addy spun around to stare at Nelly Day, her heart thundering like a ... well, like a steam engine.

"We're on a train!" she gasped.

The other girl's gray eyes narrowed. Addy had the odd feeling of watching herself look suspicious.

"I been telling you," said Nelly Day. "You been not listening."

Addy grasped the door handle to balance herself on the shuddering floor. Either she was having a nightmare and would wake up any second, or—*fffttt!*—her brain had snapped and she'd gone crazy.

"This door leads to the corridor of a train?" she said. "And ... other people are here too? You're not alone? Am I part of *you* going crazy, or is it the other way around?"

Nelly went pink. "Don't know why I'm talking to you. Place is full of other people. People *and* ServiDudes. It's a *train*, isn't it? Go look for yourself if you don't believe me."

Look for herself? Duh! *Think on your feet, Addy!* Why had she been standing around waiting for permission?

"Oh," Addy said. "You're still here."

The girl glaring at her was actually Nelly Day! Addy was really, truly between the pages of Uncle Vim's comic.

"You've only been gone a minute," Nelly said. "Did you happen to see a nasty boy with ferret eyes and a mouth so mean he spits black pepper?"

"You mean Nevins?"

Nelly squinted at her. "I never heard his name. I only heard him called Insect or Scum-puppy. How do *you* know what it is if you're not friendly?"

Addy shrugged. Because she and Vim had named him after a kid in her school who thought it was funny to trip people when they were carrying their lunch trays. "Isn't he the one you were following?" she said.

"How do you know *that*?"

"My uncle invented you," said Addy. "Viminy Crowe?"

"You *are* loco," snapped Nelly. "One look at your ... your pantaloons should have told me that. I don't know any uncles. I have only my aunt, Isadora Fortuna, balloonist and lady adventurer."

"Yeah, yeah," said Addy. "More like lady thief with vengeance on her mind, although you won't have figured that out yet."

Nelly raised her fists, her scabby knuckles practically touching Addy's face. "You take that back!" she snarled. "You take back saying my aunt's a thief, or I'll pop you one right on the noggin."

Addy took a breath. Off on the wrong foot, as usual. No wonder most other kids thought she was prickly and unfriendly. She even annoyed fictional characters! Why was she taking this girl seriously? She had watched her uncle draw Nelly Day at the kitchen table on Balsam Road while banana-cinnamon bread baked in the oven and Addy tackled her homework.

"Hey," she said. "I shouldn't have said that about your aunt. Not that she's really your aunt— *Whoa!*"

Nelly's fists were dancing.

"The thing is," Addy hurried on, "I have this ... this ... *knowledge* from this other place, and—"

"You're a demon, aren't you?" said Nelly. "That's why you look like me. A spirit sent by my dead mother on the Other Side to torment me for bad deeds or rude talk. Or else you're dead yourself! A walking corpse with an unsteady soul—"

She lowered her fists and turned to a small device set into the wall, a metal plate that looked something like a cheese grater with a red button under it. Nelly banged vigorously on the button. A faint buzzing noise came out.

"Help!" she cried, her mouth right next to the holes. "I'm"—her finger traced a number over the mesh rectangle—"in station 28, the water closet. Please notify Isadora Fortuna, stateroom 2! I am in the grip of a demon! Come at once!"

"Holy cannoli," said Addy. "The BuzzBox *works*?"

When Uncle Vim decided to make the train employees robotic, he'd installed a BuzzBox in every car so the passengers could summon assistance. And here it was! The artist thought something up, he drew it and it *worked*!

"Where is this train going?" asked Addy.

"Toronto, of course. Isadora Fortuna will perform a stunt with her hot-air balloon that—"

"But"—Addy heard her own voice rise, matching the panic that hummed in her chest—"I was *in* Toronto, like, half an hour ago."

"First you know too much, and then you know nothing," said Nelly.

Addy leaned against the wall, head woozy. What was happening?

Uncle Vim! He would know!

She pulled her cell phone from her jeans pocket.

When in trouble call home, right?

Nelly cocked her head and took a step to get a better look.

Addy turned away from prying eyes. The home screen lit up, a close-up shot of Catnip's pointy little rat teeth around her own finger. She speed-dialed Uncle Vim.

"What you got there?" Nelly edged nearer.

Addy jerked the phone away. "Back off. This is my *cell phone*. It's ..." How to explain? "It's like a BuzzBox you carry around." She sighed. "Only the call isn't going through." She shoved the phone back in her pocket. The roaming charges would be ridiculous anyway. Her mother would have a total conniption.

The door handle jiggled, and the door opened a crack. Addy banged it shut. Had Nelly's cry on the BuzzBox actually summoned help? Or was it the ticket-taking ServiDude? In either case, *not* welcome.

"Ow!" said the person in the corridor.

"Aunt Isadora?" called Nelly.

"Hello?" A plaintive-sounding voice leaked through. "I'm looking for the girl I met during lunch? This is—"

It was that kid! What was *he* doing here?

"Wylder Wallace," said the voice. "I've got your new Flynn Goster comic and ... uh, something weird is going on, right? Please ... uh, please let me in." The voice faltered and started up again, along with more door-handle shaking.

If Wylder Wallace was there outside the door, Addy

35

must be in Toronto, right? Except … Nelly was still there, fists at the ready.

"It's okay," Addy said to Nelly. "He won't hurt us— he's just irritating."

To prove her point, the boy kept talking.

"Can you hear me? Because I'm staring at the comic and … well, you're inside it. In the … uh, *bathroom*." He whispered the last word, as if Addy might not be a human who had to pee every day of her life. "With another girl who looks exactly like you."

"How does he know that?" Nelly whispered. "Is the whole train possessed by demons?"

Addy turned the door handle and peeked through the crack. Wylder's worried face lit up the instant he saw her. Addy felt a strange whoosh of relief. But beyond the hunch of Wylder's backpack and the mad flapping of the comic book in his fist, she saw blurred trees dashing by soot-smeared windows.

"Hey," said Addy, "where are you?"

Wylder's eyebrows came together. "I'm right in front of you. Let me in." He waved the comic again.

"Look to your left," said Addy. "What do you see?"

Wylder turned his head, but then his eyes snapped back to meet hers with a look that shouted, "Are you *nuts*?!"

"There *is* something weird going on," she said. "It's really, *really* important that you tell me what you see out there."

As if Addy were a small child, Wylder enunciated every syllable of his description. "I see a long hall with a beige curtain hanging from the ceiling. A row of doors. A stack of Spiderman posters leaning against the wall. The broken train display for the Goster Summer Special, with a flickering headlight. A janitor's bucket with a crusty old mop. And—"

"That's enough." Addy allowed the door to swing open. The kid grinned again, let his backpack slide off one shoulder, put the comic book inside and stepped into the room.

Nelly squealed and bumped smack into Addy, knocking her shoulder bag to the floor. Catnip spilled out from where he'd been sleeping.

"Whatever is this hullabaloo?" A new voice rippled the air.

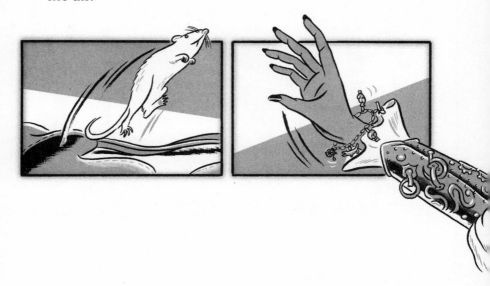

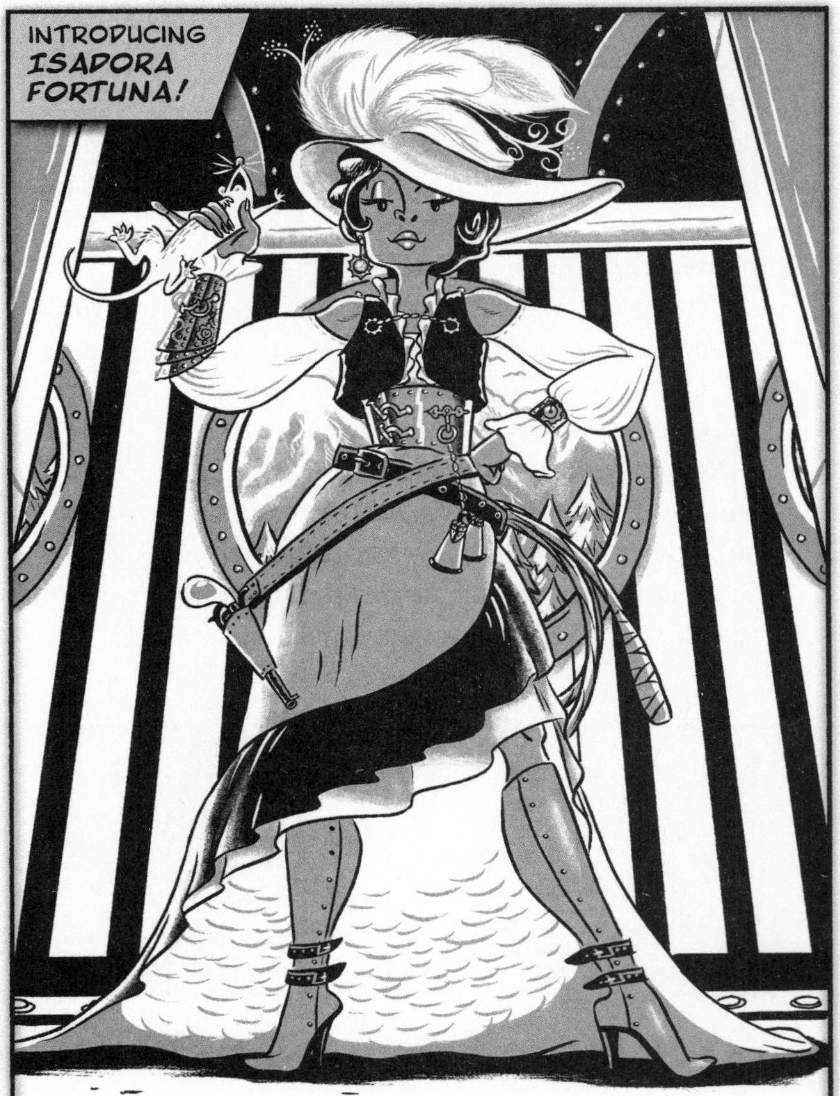
INTRODUCING ISADORA FORTUNA!

This. Was. Awesome. Wylder Wallace was *inside* the comic book.

It was all so real! The swaying floor, the clickety-clack of the wheels on the track, even this cramped bathroom with its smells of smoke and dust and some kind of perfume.

And now this totally cool woman—with a huge jeweled earring and a pistol—had caught a *live rat* in her *bare hand*! As if someone had tossed her an apple! How awesome was that?

The rodent balanced on her palm, flicking its long hairless tail.

The woman raised an eyebrow. "I believe this creature belongs to you?"

"Yes," said the girl from lunch. "This is Catnip. Sorry about that. He gets excited." She tickled the animal and let him roam up her arm to settle on the back of her neck.

Wylder didn't like rats normally, but there was nothing normal about being in a comic book. Deal with it, he told himself. All part of the adventure.

"Catnip—what a quaint name." The woman extended a hand. "May I ask who you are, young lady?"

"I'm Addy. Addy Crowe."

Addy. The name suited her, thought Wylder. Smart and maybe a bit odd. The sort of girl who might keep a rat in a shoulder bag.

"I'm Wylder Wal—" he began, but Addy interrupted.

"And you are Isadora Fortuna."

"You've heard of me? That *is* gratifying! And are you coming to Toronto to watch my balloon ascent?"

Addy hesitated. "Well … I'm *from* Toronto," she said.

"I'm from Toronto too. My name's Wylder. Hi!"

No one seemed to care. The girl in the funny clothes pushed past him to stand next to Isadora in the corridor.

"Auntie, watch out for these folks," she said in a low voice.

"Nelly, I remind you not to whisper about people. Not so they can hear, at any rate."

"But they're demons! That girl's wearing boy clothes. She knows things she couldn't know! And … and … she

40

looks like *meeee!*" The girl named Nelly was pouting, big time.

"Now, now." Isadora patted her. "You've allowed yourself to become entirely exflunctuated! But I own I am intrigued by the similarity. You girls are as alike as two buttons on a shirtwaist. It's enough to make a person wonder whether you might be related."

"You might say that," said Addy. "But not in the way you mean."

A red metal garbage can with a bunch of arms rolled up and stopped. The lid popped up and down when it spoke.

"SERVIDUDE AT YOUR SERVICE," it announced. "IS THERE A PROBLEM? MAY I CARRY YOUR BAG? SHALL I CALL A JANITOR OR MEDICO OR DISPOSAL UNIT? THE DINING CAR IS NEXT DOOR."

"No assistance is required," said Isadora.

The mechanical thing skittered away, voice receding. "SERVIDUDE AT YOUR SERVICE!"

Nice, thought Wylder. If he had one at home, he'd never have to tidy his room.

He realized that he had not heard from his mom in a while. He checked to make sure. No signal. He was out of range. He slid the phone into his backpack.

Out of range. The thought made him smile. No kidding! An entire world out of range!

The train swung round a curve and straightened out again. Wylder found himself balancing easily, adjusting to the roll and sway. He was getting used to this place.

"And who might you be, young man?"

Isadora was smiling at him. Somebody cared about him at last.

"I'm Wylder."

"Wilder than what?"

"Huh? Oh no, that's my name. Wylder Wallace. I'm not really very wild."

She laughed—a wonderful sound, like a tinkling fountain.

"I'm Isadora Fortuna, and this is my niece, Nelly. Now that we're acquainted, would you and your friend like to join us for tea and cakes? Nelly, please find us a table for four in the dining car."

Wylder wasn't sure about tea, but the cakes sounded good.

"Thanks!" He slipped past Addy into the corridor.

Nelly dragged her boot toes along the aisle ahead of him.

"Maybe we'll see Flynn Goster," Wylder went on. "In person. He's got to be here somewhere. Wouldn't that be cool?"

"I beg your pardon?" Isadora tipped her head, listening intently.

"Is that a real pistol on your belt? It looks real."

"Did you say Flynn Goster?" Her fingers briefly touched the sparkling blue earring.

"Do you know him? He's pretty famous. This is his comic—" Wylder caught himself. "I mean, he's going to be on this train. After all, there's a lot of gold here, right? Flynn is a kind of a thief. So he's going to be— What?"

Addy was shaking her head rapidly.

"What?" he repeated.

Isadora pulled him along, and he had to wrench his neck to look back at Addy.

"You are a fascinating young man, Wylder Wallace," said Isadora.

"I am?"

"Tell me more about Flynn Goster."

The windows in the train were circular and bulged outward so you could see all around. The countryside was impressive—mountains and gorges and bare rock. It seemed that the train was climbing to the sky. And everything was so darn real.

"Wait!" Addy came up behind them. "Sorry, Ms. Fortuna," she said. "Wylder and I can't join you for tea."

"Whyever not?"

"Yeah, why not?" said Wylder.

"Because," said Addy, "we have to go somewhere else. We. *Belong*. Somewhere. Else."

"No, we don't. We're— *Ouch!*"

Addy had dug her fingers into his arm.

"That hurts," he said. "What are you doing? Ms. Fortuna might— *Ouch!* Stop pinching!"

"Children!" said Isadora. "I insist that you join us for tea. There are tasty tidbits to discuss."

"We're going to go check with our parents," said Addy. "We'll come and find you."

Wylder was about to deny this, but she grabbed one of the straps on his backpack and pulled him away before he could open his mouth.

"Lovely," said Isadora. "We'll expect you momentarily. Toodle-oo!"

She sashayed away down the aisle, her skirt rustling and her pistol swinging at her side.

"Now just what—"

"Shut up, Wylder!" Addy still had him by the strap so he had to walk backward.

"You shouldn't have mentioned Flynn!" she said. "He doesn't get on the train until Banff, and we're not there yet." She glanced out the window at the snow-capped peaks of the Rocky Mountains.

"Why would Isadora care about Flynn? Unless … Oh gosh, is she the one he falls in love with? I bet she is. She's pretty cool. Did you see her pistol? But I hope they don't get together. That romantic stuff drives me crazy. If she's all, *Oh, darling, I love you more than anything*, and he's like, *No darling, I love you more!* I may be ill. Flynn doesn't need anyone else. And why did you lie about our parents being here? That's the coolest part—that they're not!"

"Stop talking. You are the—" Addy took a deep breath. "Have you thought for a single second about how freaky it is? We don't belong here. This is a *story*! We have to get out."

She raked her fingers through her wild hair.

"Okay," she said. "Starting over. Hello, Wylder, I'm Addy. Nice to meet you. Now let's see if we can work out what's going on. You saw me inside the comic book, right?"

People were giving them odd looks. Addy was the only girl wearing pants on the whole train. Maybe they should find seats.

"Yes," he said. "Right near the beginning. But I don't see—"

"Show me. Maybe there's a clue about how to get back to ComicFest."

"I don't want to go back. I want to have tea with Isadora. And meet Flynn."

"It's my comic! Give it to me."

"No."

"Okay." She held up her hands in surrender. "Okay. Remember when I said it was nice to meet you? Just now? We-ell … I lied."

In a series of quick moves she spun him sideways, tugged his backpack off his shoulders, leapt into the bathroom and slammed the door shut.

Wylder looked around. Fifty passengers were staring at him. He gave a weak wave.

"Addy, come out!"

He knocked. The door was already opening.

"Sludge balls!" She slumped against the doorway, the comic book in her hand. "I was hoping that you'd be back in the ComicFest hallway, the way it happened before."

"Can I have my backpack now?"

She kicked it over to him and came out of the bathroom.

"Follow the logic." She pointed to the right-hand page of the comic. "See?" she said. "There we are. Isadora and Nelly have gone off to the dining car, which is weird because there is no scene in the dining car in the original story. And here comes a—"

"SERVIDUDE AT YOUR SERVICE!"

With two sensors on the side of its lid, the little garbage can looked like it had a cheery red face to match its cheery voice.

"ServiDude is such a great name."

"Thanks." Addy actually looked pleased for a second.

"IS THERE A PROBLEM? MAY I CARRY YOUR BAG? SHALL I CALL A JANITOR OR MEDICO OR D—"

"We don't want any service," she told the ServiDude.

It tipped its red cap and rolled slowly away—the floor tilted as the train headed uphill.

"We have to go, Wylder."

"What's the rush? Let me look at that comic again. Just for a second."

Addy narrowed her eyes, but—amazingly—she let him hold the comic book.

Wow. He was really here. Addy snatched back the comic but who cared? It was time for some cake.

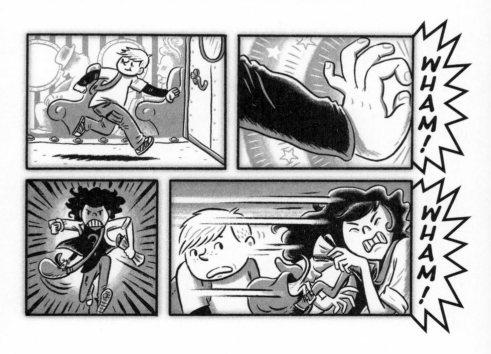

What?

Addy held up the comic to stare at the page they were on. With his eyes on his own character, Wylder lifted his hand—the Wylder in the comic changed a second later—and bumped against the force field or whatever it was. The border of the panel.

The *last* panel on the page. Did that have something to do with it?

"Oh!" said Addy. "Lightbulb!"

"Huh?"

"You know? In a cartoon, when a character has an idea, there's a—"

"I know about lightbulbs," he said. "So what's yours? The end of the page?"

"Don't you think? We started up there and now we're down here in the last panel. Stuck."

It all made sense.

"There's one thing we can do." Wylder reached over her shoulder to turn the page.

"Wait!" cried Addy. "*Wait!*"

6

"No!" Addy yanked the comic away and hid it behind her back.

"Why not? I want to see what happens next!"

What happens *next*? Addy had to figure out what was happening *now*, not what the *next* crazy thing would be!

"Let me think!" she said. "Give me one second before we do anything we can't *un*do, okay?"

Would it make a difference to turn the page? If they were being stopped by a force field, there must be a reason!

The train seat next to them was empty. Addy slumped down, and Wylder slid in next to her. She held the comic on her lap, chewing on her lip. Catnip crawled out of her bag and nestled for a moment in the crook of her arm before sniffing his way to her shoulder and curling up under her hair. She could sense Wylder twitching at the sight of the rat, but *ha*, get over it! She gazed out the round window for a few silent minutes. Mountains, mountains, mountains.

"What I want to know is, how did we get in here?" said Addy. "One day Uncle Vim is drawing a picture with an ordinary pencil on an ordinary flat piece of paper. And the next day—well, not the next day, because it had to go to the printer and everything—but you know what I mean. Somehow, we're *inside* it, like it's a whole 3-D world. It just doesn't make any sense."

Wylder stared at her. "Your name is Addy *Crowe*! I'm so stupid. Viminy Crowe is your uncle?"

"Yeah."

"Wow," he said. "Excuse me, but I have to say: THAT'S INCREDIBLY COOL!" His mouth actually fell open. "Viminy Crowe is your *uncle*?"

"I just said that, didn't I?" But Addy couldn't help smiling a little. She didn't get to gloat too often. Her mom would say that gloating was unkind, a way of making other people feel small. But if a person was *already* smaller—shorter, anyway—maybe it only made you feel bigger?

"That's how you know what the story is! He probably told you stuff going along, right?"

"He lives with us, my mom and me."

"What about your dad?"

"My dad … isn't there. Anymore."

"Mine neither," said Wylder, quietly. "He moved out when I was a little kid." He wasn't so smiley now.

"We were the ones who had to move out," said Addy. "My dad got a girlfriend last year, so now he lives with her instead of us."

"Yuck," said Wylder.

"So my uncle Vim moved in—you know, to help my mom during the crisis and stuff. And because he left his job and didn't have any money. It's a small apartment, so Vim sleeps on the couch. He uses our kitchen table as his so-called studio."

"That's why Nelly looks like you!"

"Yeah."

"So you're, like, *famous* now!"

"Uh, no."

Wylder seemed weirdly excited to discover this new fact about her. "Hey, is it true—the story on the Internet? That the red parts are all printed with blood?"

Addy rolled her eyes. "Seriously? You believe that sludge? Some fans are so crazy they've offered to donate their own blood."

"So *that's* why yours is the only copy of the Summer Special!"

"Well, plus my uncle's own sample." Her stomach turned over. "All the others are waiting for shipping documents or something. But Vim has a meeting this afternoon with Magnus Snayle, the president of FunnyBones. He

51

was going to give him this"—she waved the comic book—
"with an autograph, as a thank-you present. He's going to
kill me for taking it and disappearing onto another planet."

"It's not another planet," said Wylder. "It's more like
time travel. We're still in Canada, but in 1899."

"Uncle Vim's demented fictional version of 1899," said
Addy. *Inside a comic book!* It's impossible."

"Yeah, but cool!"

Addy's eyes prickled. "I just hate feeling like I'm
messing up my uncle's whole career."

Catnip woke up and nuzzled her neck for a moment,
almost as if he knew she needed soothing. Then he scuttled down her arm and into the shoulder bag bunched
on the seat.

"You've read the whole thing, right?" Wylder tapped
the comic.

"Like two hundred times."

"So you already know what's on the next page, right?"

"I guess so, if I think about it. Except that the page
we're looking at is not supposed to finish with two kids
from the twenty-first century slammed up at the end of
a train car."

Wylder wiped his forehead, which was beginning to
show teeny drops of perspiration. Addy tried not to be
grossed out. She didn't spend much time this close to
boys, especially sweaty ones.

"What was the next thing that was *supposed* to happen?" said Wylder. "Before we came along?"

Addy ran her finger lightly across the panels, telling him about the characters.

Isadora Fortuna, Lady Adventurer, was on the Gold Rush Express as part of a publicity tour for her upcoming stunt, when she planned to sail a hot-air balloon from Toronto Island all the way to the brand-new city hall on Queen Street.

"Oh," said Wylder, "and Nelly's a niece because you are too!"

"Isadora isn't really her aunt."

Addy had liked being Uncle Vim's model for Nelly—until she'd met her face to face. "Isadora caught Nelly trying to pick her pocket, but then she sort of adopted her and brought her along on this train ride. Isadora's such a great character—she cracks her whip like a lion tamer, shoots stuff blindfolded *and* is a certified surgeon! The FunnyBones guys think she deserves her own spin-off series, and there's going to be a video game."

"All I saw was the part with the Red Riders and the gold," said Wylder. "And the bit when the villain is yelling at some geeky kid. Same villain from the first issue, right? Lickpenny?"

"Yeah," said Addy. "His evilness is a little exaggerated, but wait till you read on. The grimmer the better, right?"

"Definitely! And his two … um, what are they? Giant robots?"

"Shh." Addy glanced down the train car. She could see them from here, two heads with bowler hats, sticking up above the other passengers. "Mechanizmos," she said. "*Serious* trouble, trust me."

"And then I turned the page, and you and Nelly were both in the bathroom."

"Nelly is only supposed to be in there for a single panel," said Addy. "When she leaves, she overhears Lickpenny telling Nevins what he's supposed to do to get ready for the gold heist. Then Isadora comes to find Nelly, and we switch to ..."

"To what?" asked Wylder. "Is that where we meet Flynn?"

"This blah-blah is a waste of time." Addy stood up, slipping her hand into her bag to check on Catnip. "My uncle will be going hairy bananas." She nudged Wylder's knees—like, *move!*—but he just sat there.

"I bet we meet Flynn on the next page, right? That's why you're suddenly all 'Time to go.'" He said "Time to go" in a squeaky, prissy voice.

"We. *Don't*. Meet. Flynn." Addy glared at him. "We. Go. Home."

"Ha!" Wylder grabbed the comic right out of her hand and—*THWIP!*—flipped the page quicker than you could say "sludge."

It was like losing your balance and falling up instead of down—like being flipped over, jiggled around and tossed to the ground with a soft thunk.

For a second, Addy thought she was going to throw up, but—*whew!*—she didn't. Wylder lay next to her, moaning. Served him right. They were leaning against the foot of a bed. Light poured through billowing muslin curtains that covered windows as high as the ceiling.

BRRRRING! A telephone! An old-fashioned trill, not a musical ringtone.

Right over their heads, someone moved beneath the covers. Addy locked eyes with Wylder. They both ducked lower.

BRRRRING! A shuffle and a bang as the person's hand felt for the receiver.

"*Phwa*-llo?"

ADDY HAD NEVER HEARD THE SLEEP-DRENCHED VOICE, BUT SHE KNEW EXACTLY WHOSE IT WAS.

"Thank you for the wake-up call, little lady. Since I have you on the line, I'd like to order breakfast. Four eggs, sunny-side up, a bison steak and a quart of tomatoes sliced and salted. And please have the ServiDude bring a newspaper, would you?"

Addy caught sight of the comic book under Wylder's thigh. She slid her fingers across the carpet. She knew that the front page of the newspaper would have a photograph of Isadora Fortuna waving at a flock of admiring pilots-in-training. That photograph would get Flynn Goster moving around the hotel room like a bee in a jar.

"Oh, and griddle cakes for dessert. Thank you."

They heard the sound of the phone being hung up and a bright whistling as the bedcovers were thrown back. He was getting up! He'd see them! Worse than that, Addy remembered what Flynn Goster wore to bed, and she didn't care to witness such a spectacle.

She tugged the comic book from under Wylder's leg and—*THWIP!*—turned the page back.

Wylder grabbed her arm, but the horrible tumbling was already happening. This time, the landing wasn't so soft. Addy banged her head on the edge of a seat as Wylder's lurching body knocked her sideways. They were back where they'd been two minutes ago, next to the door to the dining car.

"Why did you do that?" Wylder yelled. "That was Flynn!"

"No kidding," said Addy. "And in five more seconds, he was going to find two kids gaping at him in his skivvies!"

Wylder laughed. "Really?" he said. "Your uncle drew Flynn wearing ... er, boxers or briefs?"

"He's got one of those ... I think they're called union suits. Red. All one piece." She gestured, neck to knees, to show what she meant. "Button up the front and, you know"—she waved a hand behind—"a *flap* at the back."

"Let me see!" Wylder reached for the comic again, but she swung away, bumping her bag against the seat.

"Haven't you learned your lesson?" said Addy. "Stop trying to grab the comic! Holy cannoli! We don't have time for this!"

But Wylder wasn't listening. He wasn't listening because he was shrieking. He was shrieking because Addy's rat had nosed his way out of her bag and raced up Wylder's leg before leaping to the luggage rack above their heads.

"Catnip! Come back!" Addy lunged, but the rat was too quick. He executed a magnificent flip and landed in the center of the aisle before zigzagging under the seats several rows ahead. Addy's final view was the flourish of a long tail just before it disappeared from sight.

7

A rat was the perfect pet for Addy Crowe. And trust her to insist on not going anywhere until they found it. Was her uncle like this? Wylder hoped not. Viminy Crowe had to have a sense of humor and a real love of the world he had created. All Addy wanted to do was leave it. And she would *not* listen to anyone else's opinion. Her mouth set like concrete.

"It's only a rat," he told her. "I don't want to look for—"

"I'll start at the far end of the car. You start here, and we'll meet in the middle. Don't be scared, little boy."

"Who are you calling little? I bet I'm the same age as you are. I'll be twelve in October."

She was already walking away.

"And who's scared?" he called after her. "You think I'm scared? I was surprised, that's all. Your stupid rat surprised me."

She turned to look over her shoulder.

"You screamed. I turned twelve last month. And he has a name."

And off she went. *So* annoying. Wylder would have run in the opposite direction, except that he'd bump into that invisible wall again. He needed to get to another page. Could he grab the comic from Addy? It wasn't a nice thing to do—twice—but she wasn't being nice either.

He pretended to look for the rat under the nearest seat. A woman across the aisle glared at him. Mean old thing with her hair up and her eyebrows down. Wylder stuck out his tongue at her. He was angry at Addy and could pretend this woman was her.

"Come on, Catnip!" Addy pleaded from the other end of the car. She was on all fours with the comic rolled up in her hand. "I have some lettuce for you, Catty-pie."

Wylder looked out the windows on the left-hand side of the car, where the snowy mountainside climbed up to the sky in a two-pronged peak. A snowboarder carved along the mountain beside the train. An engine on the back of his board allowed him to keep pace with the locomotive! He hit a snowy bump and flew through the air, staying airborne for long seconds. What a sport—jet boarding! The guy's head turned—he was checking out the train, getting ready. He angled himself so he was pointing downhill, and at the next mogul he took off and flew right *over* the passenger car, landing on the other side of the train. For a second, he was almost close enough to wipe the window with his mustache, before he zipped away down the mountainside. Wylder wasn't the only one in the car who went "Ooooh!" The motor on the back of the board trailed a pure white jet of steam.

Wylder felt a thrill of recognition. It had to be Flynn, right? Who else? Checking out the train he was going to rob. Yes, he was in a hotel room on the next page. But you never knew when or where Flynn would pop up. That was the fun of the comic.

Wylder pressed his face into the curve of the window, hoping to get another glimpse, when a jolly voice spoke from down around hip level.

"DISPOSAL SERVIDUDE. PLEASE PLACE TRASH IN RECEPTACLE. THANK YOU."

This ServiDude was a short, wide cylinder. Near the top was a round opening with a flap that popped up and down when the ServiDude talked. The man beside him tossed a newspaper into the mouth. Munching noises, and then a belch and a roar as the newspaper was consumed. A wisp of smoke escaped the flap.

Wylder moved on. Those robot guys with the bowler hats were in the next seat. Jeez, they were big.

They looked like twins, with the same beaky noses and the same moles on their faces—small black spots at the hinge of the jaw. Or—wait! Wylder took a second look. Those weren't beauty marks. Those were the screws holding their mouths together.

Wylder stumbled down the aisle to Addy, who was peering under an empty seat.

"Did you *see* those giant robots?" he whispered.

"I told you." She twisted round. "They're called Snap and Krackle—like the cereal, you know? They're part of Lickpenny's plan to get the gold."

"They must be eight feet tall! I'm surprised they haven't broken the seats."

Addy sighed, reminding Wylder of his mother. Not in a good way.

"Did you or did you not find Catnip?"

"Not."

"Well, keep looking!"

The comic was still in her hand. Could he grab it?

"Hey! What are you two demons up to?" Nelly stood beside them. "You were supposed to be joining us for tea. Not that I care if you're rude enough to miss tea when you've been invited. But my aunt sent me to find you."

"We're looking for my pet," said Addy.

Nelly narrowed her eyes. "Are you referring to that pink-eyed beast that attacked us back there in the water closet?"

"Catnip is as cuddly as a kitten," said Addy.

The comic book was in reach. Wylder planned his move. *Ready ... set ...* But before he could think *go*, someone screamed at the far end of the carriage.

An old lady stood in the aisle, the ruffles on her dress bouncing as she jumped up and down. For a tiny person, she had enormous lungs.

"HELP! VERMIN! VERMIN!" She pointed at her seat.

"Holy cannoli!" Addy was alert at once. "Catnip!"

She ran down the aisle, Wylder and Nelly close behind. By the time they reached the spot, other passengers had gathered. A man with a hedge of whiskers and a monocle had given up his seat to the old lady. A younger woman wearing a considerable hat patted her hand and soothed, "There, there."

A ServiDude spoke in a brisk, no-nonsense voice. "MAY I CARRY YOUR BAG? SHALL I CALL A JANITOR OR MEDICO OR DISPOSAL UNIT? THE DINING CAR IS NEXT DOOR."

A cloth handbag sat open on the old lady's seat. Peering past the ServiDude, Wylder saw a pink nose and twitchy whiskers poking out.

Nelly grabbed a closed parasol from an empty seat and lifted it like a club. "Shut your pipes, ma'am," she said to the flustered old lady. "I'll get rid of the rat!"

"No! No! Leave him alone!" Addy was dancing in frustration, trying to get past the ServiDude. She tossed the comic to Wylder and jumped onto the seat. Catnip leaped and climbed out of her reach.

The carriage door opened and in strode Captain McGurk of the Best Western Red Riders, his face as red as his uniform. Flynn had foiled him in both of the earlier adventures. Wylder recognized him at once.

HO-HO! SO IT'S RATS, IS IT?

The tremendous explosion reverberated in Wylder's ears. Maybe throwing the comic book wasn't the smoothest move, but at least the captain's bullet had gone into the ceiling instead of the rat! But now the fluttering pages were making the train car spin in slow motion, whooshing the comic back toward Wylder. He and Addy fell over each other, ending up on the floor with the comic beneath them.

Wylder looked up. Where were they now?

Somewhere *far* from the Gold Rush Express.

8

S ludge balls! Inkhill Mountain was a *bad* place to land!

The stone floor under Addy's butt was really cold.

A thick glass pot on a burner produced a torrent of steam, along with a smell like a tuna sandwich left all day in a hot car. Addy stood up for a second to take a quick survey. A wooden countertop was cluttered with test tubes and beakers and small porcelain trays, each holding something gray and squirmy. The only windows were tiny slits up next to the ceiling. Suspended between them was a clothesline with strips of drying … Addy shuddered. Was that what she thought it was?

Wylder sat next to her, holding the comic book. But where was Catnip?

"What *is* this place?" Wylder's voice echoed oddly.

"*Shhh!*"

The last thing they needed was for Mr. Chatty to open his yippety-yapper in Lickpenny's laboratory. Not that any of this could really be happening. Was Addy dreaming? Was she making a guest appearance in Wylder's dream? *Nothing* made sense!

Focus, she told herself. Find the rat, keep Wylder quiet, get out.

She signaled for him to follow as she inched back into a nook between a giant metal barrel and a shelving unit that held dozens of labeled jars.

"Why are we hiding? There's nobody here, wherever *here* is, and—"

"Just. Be. Quiet. There will be someone here soon. A bad someone. Meanwhile, help me find Catnip. I can hardly see in this sludgy steam."

"Oh, jeez. Catnip again?"

"Yes, *Catnip again.* I had a good hold on him just as the shot rang out, but he went flying when we crash-landed here."

"So this isn't the next page? Did we go forward or backward?"

"Flashback." She put her hand over his mouth to shut him up. Just in time. With a screech of metal wheels, the heavy laboratory door rolled aside. Wylder's eyebrows climbed high. She took away her hand.

"Sorry," he whispered.

A gust of air from outside dispelled the clouds of steam. Professor Lickpenny limped into the room, his head bent over a gleaming gadget held in both hands.

"Oh, gosh! Is that—"

Addy glared and Wylder finally shut up.

Why was Lickpenny a professor? She had asked her uncle. Don't professors teach? He needed a title, Vim said, and "professor" sounded brainy and eccentric at the same time.

"The villain has to be just as clever as the hero," said Uncle Vim. "It makes the conflict stronger—more realistic—if they're evenly matched."

The professor's physical appearance was even nastier than she had imagined. Uncle Vim, sketching quickly, had asked Addy for the three most hideous features she could think of.

"First?" she'd said. "Nose hair. You know how it gets on some old men." Yes, Lickpenny looked like he had a dirty broom stuck up there.

"Next, a comb-over." Too much hair in the nose and not enough on the head was seriously awful. Vim had drawn long oiled hairs stretching across a pink scalp from one ear to the other.

"Third, bad teeth. He should look as if he rips apart baby squirrels for breakfast," Addy said. "And sucks on the tails."

She could now report that Viminy Crowe had succeeded in creating a mouth practically foaming with decay. Addy was pretty certain she could smell Lickpenny's breath from the not-so-safe hiding place where she sat huddled a little too snugly next to Wylder Wallace. She remembered how she and Uncle Vim had painstakingly printed tiny labels on the jars that now stood next to her on the professor's shelves: BABIES' EYEBALLS, PREMIUM MUCOUS, DIAPER EXTRACT, OFFICER ALLEN'S NOSE. That last one was revenge against the policeman who had stopped Uncle Vim for speeding on the Don Valley Parkway. The fleshy, mottled shape in the jar had enormous crusted nostrils. *Ew.*

"What's he holding?" whispered Wylder.

"Controller," mouthed Addy. "This happened six months ago." She pointed to a row of metal lockers along one wall. "That's where—"

CLICK!

No need to explain. Professor Lickpenny had pressed a button to open the locker marked SNAP. Wylder gasped as a familiar creature emerged from the narrow space, revealing a broad torso, an oversized head wearing a bowler hat, and long, stiff legs with shoes nearly as big as watermelons. It was as if he'd been folded like a coat and then expanded as soon as he stepped into the laboratory. A slight tremble caused all his metal parts to clatter before he settled, still as a statue.

Addy scanned the room for Catnip. He had to be

close by, but where? A second click and the next locker, labeled KRACKLE, sprang open.

Professor Lickpenny jabbed the air with the controller, repeatedly pressing one of the buttons. The mechanical man named Krackle didn't move.

"Scum-puppy!" shouted the professor. "Hurry up with the catalyzer! You good-for-nothing, lazy glob of putrid phlegm!"

Addy couldn't help smiling. That was her line.

"There's a new comic superhero called Phlegm," whispered Wylder.

"Shh!"

Lickpenny had hold of an ear and was using it to haul a howling boy into the room. Nevins! Even scrawnier and more pathetic than on paper.

"How many times have I hammered this into you? *Nothing* should prevent you from replenishing the supply of catalyzer serum. Not an earthquake, not a revolution, not *Flynn Goster* himself! There must *always* be catalyzer serum! DO YOU HEAR ME? Every morning! Be*fore* you eat your plateful of kippers, be*fore* you slurp your cupful of brewed chicory, what *should* you be doing?"

"C-c-catalyzer."

"If you fail to perform this one essential task, the mechanizmos do not function. Catalyzer is like the blood in their veins. If the mechanizmos do not function, they cannot penetrate the armored car on the

Gold Rush Express and abscond with the magnificent gold! If the mechanizmos do not function, *you* will not continue to function. DO YOU HEAR ME?"

"Y-y-yessuncle."

"There is *nothing* I'd like more than to turn your skin into the nice new covering for a mechanical piggy. ARE YOU LISTENING? Or do I need to pull your ear *off* for a direct line to the hole where your brain is meant to be?!"

He gave Nevins's ear an energetic twist, then let go. The boy flopped to the floor in a heap and bounced right up again, clutching his head with grubby fingers. He gave a terrified look at the drying shapes on the rope above. Addy knew why he was so scared. And she totally understood. Seeing those twisted strips in reality and up close was pretty terrifying.

Lickpenny raised a hand to squelch the piercing wail pouring from the boy's lips. "If you weren't my own sister's unfortunate offspring, I would have used you for kindling by now," he growled.

"Y-y-yessuncle," sniveled Nevins.

"Why are you standing there like an old umbrella?" bellowed the professor.

PREPARE THE SIPHON AT ONCE!

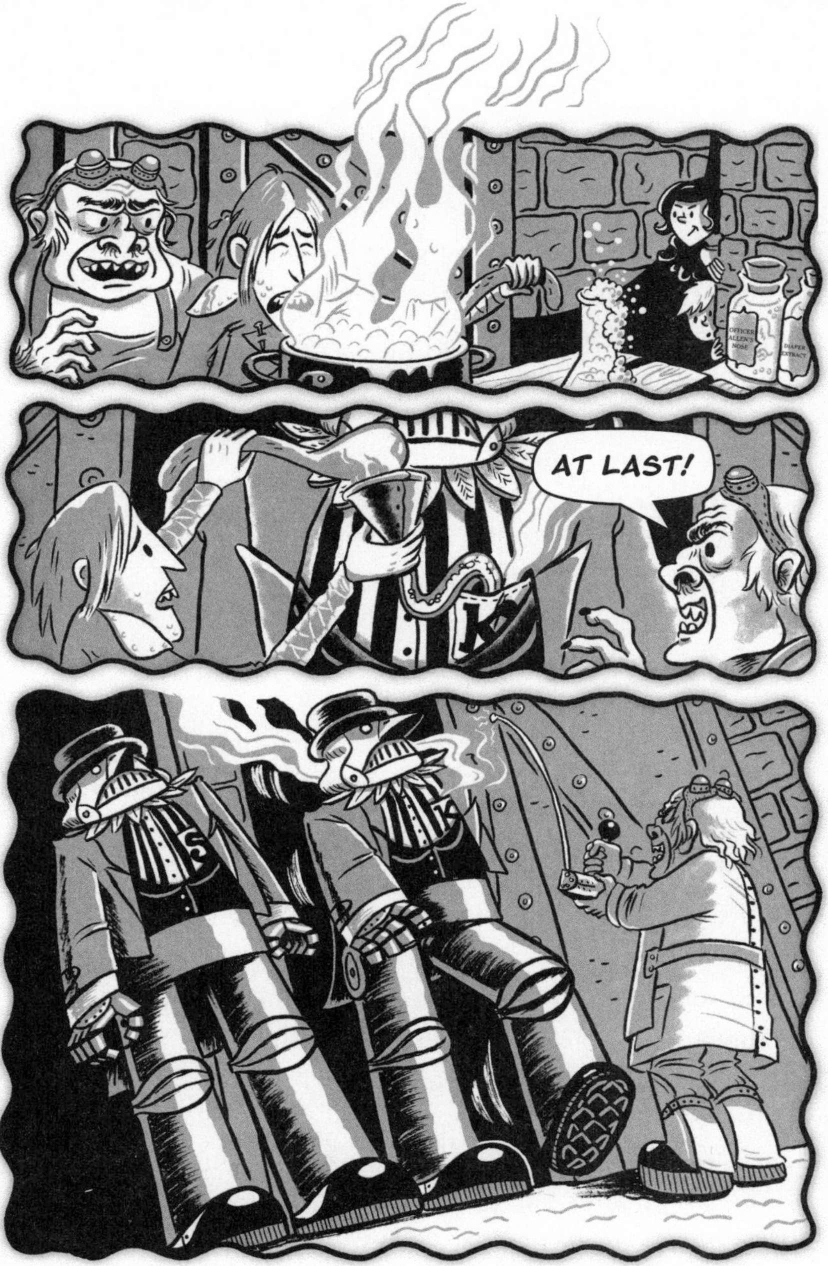
OFFICER ALLEN'S NOSE
DIAPER EXTRACT
AT LAST!

"This is amazing!" Wylder whispered.

The page coming to life in front of them was the most astounding thing Addy had ever seen. She couldn't help wondering what would happen later—what the robotic transformation at the climax of the comic would look like …

Krackle's log-like legs lifted and plunked back down with thundering precision. Its head swung from side to side, its eyes blinking red, its fuel pocket leaking a wisp of steam.

"You will fill the tanks while I make our arrangements for the train," said Professor Lickpenny.

"Yessuncle."

"What are the robots covered with?" whispered Wylder. "Looks like patchwork."

"Uh, human skin."

Some things were funnier when sitting at a kitchen table than they were in real life.

"Ewww!" Wylder did not whisper. "ARE YOU KID-DING ME?" He scrambled to his feet, knee-kicking Addy and upending his backpack on the way. A battered cardboard packet of leftover onion rings spilled across the stone floor like pennies into a fountain.

Lickpenny whipped around. "Nevins!" he cried. "We've been invaded!"

The nephew seized a red-nozzled canister from a hook on the wall. It was painted with a skull and cross-bones. At that very moment, Addy finally caught sight of Catnip. Horribly, the rat had jumped up to balance on the lip of the big glass pot with his pink nose sniffing—no, actually *dipping into*—a potion the color of hot dog mustard.

Lickpenny pointed the controller at the mechanizmos, pressing both his thumbs down together. This time the robot called Snap jolted to life and lurched steadily forward with its arms stretching toward Addy and Wylder, metal fingers flexing and groping.

Addy flew out of hiding to snatch Catnip from the brink of drowning.

"Wylder!" she screamed. "Turn the page!" Her fingers tucked under the rat's belly. "Get us out of here!"

THWIP!

The moment before Addy opened her eyes, she heard beautiful music. A violin and a flute. And a deeper note, played on a cello. Phew, safely out of that stinking laboratory! But where? One eye popped open, and then—*BOING!*—the other. Holy cannoli! She was sitting on a marble floor, leaning against a pillar and—*sludge!*—her hands were empty. She hadn't been able to hang on to Catnip as the sickening tumble of the page-turn happened.

"WYLDER!"

"I'm right here."

He was next to her, staring hard at the ceiling. Addy twisted her head around to see what he was looking at.

Incrediballoo!

The day Uncle Vim had drawn the final version of this page, he'd eaten about two pounds of M&M'S and drunk seven cups of peppermint green tea. He'd been too excited with his own masterpiece even to pause for supper.

"Where *are* we?" Wylder asked.

"At the hotel." She found her voice coming out in a whisper of awe. "In the lobby of the Banff Springs Hotel."

"Wow," said Wylder. "I've never seen anything like this!"

"It really exists, in Alberta—only not the same, of course. He made it kind of amazing, eh?"

Go, Uncle Vim!

Last summer he'd hitchhiked out west with his pal Mike to do some "research." Of course, Vim and Mike couldn't afford to stay in the luxurious hotel—they'd slept in a tent—but her uncle had spent his days in the Banff Springs lobby with his sketchpad. Taking visual notes in the real place helped, obviously, but Addy could see that the best parts were all his imagined details, like—

"Look at those amazing waiter guys!" Wylder seemed to be in a trance. "ServiDudes in tuxedos!"

"Where's the comic book? Give it to me."

"'Thank you for saving us, Wylder,'" said Wylder, using that squeaky voice again to imitate her.

Addy might have said thank you, might even have smiled, except …

"We're here without Catnip! We've got to flip the page and go back to Lickpenny's lab."

"Are you *nuts*?" Now he was paying attention. "Did you happen to notice the oncoming robot, covered in patches of human skin?"

"You turned the page too quickly! I didn't have time—"

"Of course I turned the page quickly! His hands were reaching out to twist our little necks!"

"But I didn't catch Ca-a-atnip!" Addy didn't mean to make that whimpery noise, but it happened, along with a hot prickle in her eyes. "He was drinking that disgusting—" She thought of all the things that she and her uncle had laughingly imagined were in the catalyzer. Hens' feet and snot and kale and …

She took a deep breath to steady herself.

"Look," she said. "I get that you're afraid. Wait for me here. I'll go alone and come back quick as anything. I can't just leave him there, you … you … worm sludge!"

She tried to snatch the comic from Wylder's hand, but he yanked it away.

"You shouldn't call me names all the time." He stuffed the comic under his shirt. "We'll talk about this when you've calmed down a little."

"Aaaaahhhhhh!" Addy spun around and stomped off toward the fountain in the center of the lobby.

Wylder watched her walk away. Maybe he should have been more understanding. Or at least handed over the comic—which was hers, after all. But no way was he going back to Lickpenny's lab! For a *rat*?

And if she went back there by herself, she and the comic might end up as robot chow, and then what would happen to him? Darn it, why did she have to get so upset? *Girls!* Always making a big deal about things. His mom was the same way. All Wylder wanted was to have fun. This was the coolest hotel in the non-history of the world. Hotel?! You could host the Olympics in here. Pillars the size of trees reached up to a sky-high roof of dazzling diamondy brilliance.

And what on earth was this? A rolling counter with stools to sit on, driven by a guy with an apron and a pointed beard. He pulled up with a smile and asked if Wylder wanted a milkshake, compliments of the hotel.

Wylder sat at the counter and sipped at cold, rich strawberry heaven while the contraption zigzagged through the lobby.

"This is a great idea!" he said. "How long have you been making milkshakes?"

"How long?" The driver looked puzzled. "It is simply what I do."

"Always?"

"My MilkshakeMobile and I have always been here. Sir," he added.

Wylder thought about this. Maybe if you existed on a page in a book, there *was* no sense of before or after. Your whole life was right there. Every time that page was opened, there you were. This milkshake guy had no childhood. He would never die. It was the same for anyone in any book: Winnie the Pooh or Superman or Hermione What's-her-name from Harry Potter. Every time you opened the story, there they were, eating, fighting, laughing—whatever. Every single time. Wylder didn't know if he should feel pity or envy. He finished the milkshake right down to the gurgly end. That helped. It was an amazing milkshake.

"Hey! HEY!" Addy's voice carried across the lobby.

Wylder jumped off. Who was she yelling at? Should he go and help? Not that he felt badly about her rat. But they were in this adventure together.

He was still hesitating when he heard his name called.

Isadora Fortuna swept through the lobby amid a blitz of flashing cameras. Wow, she must be really famous! A fleet of ServiDudes in black and white followed her, carrying parcels, her coat, an ice bucket with champagne and glasses, and probably toothpaste. Uniformed hotel doormen stood on either side of her, each trying to bow lower than the other. She ignored them both, because she was talking to *him*.

"Wylder Wallace! So pleasant to see you again, mysterious young man."

She looked even cooler than he remembered. Her pearly pistol and coiled whip hung from a belt, but now there was a knife in a leather sheath as well. Someone took a photograph as she reached to pat his shoulder. He was momentarily blinded by the bright light and had to blink several times. Was this what it was like for movie stars?

"Your friend Addy—the girl in pantaloons—is she here as well?" asked Isadora.

Wylder nodded.

"My niece has remained on the train," said Isadora. "I was going to lunch alone. But I prefer the company of young people. May I prevail on you both to join me?"

She smiled like the dawn. Why didn't Wylder's mom smile like that? If Isadora ever wanted him to tidy his room, he'd do it in a minute.

AND THAT'S WHEN THE HULLABALOO BEGAN.

Selfish, sludgy, comic-stealing Wylder Wallace! No fair, no fair, no fair! Did she have to physically tackle him to get back her own property? The comic book was *really* important to Uncle Vim. Plus, it was apparently their only way of moving around … and maybe their only way of getting home. Why did that smirking boy think it was okay to grab it? And then tell *her* to calm down? *Grrrr!*

Addy dodged the MilkshakeMobile (her idea, of course—"Quick, name your most wished for fast food," Uncle Vim had said) and paused by the fountain to let the spray sprinkle her face. This place was like the inside of one of Uncle Vim's wild dreams. It was a shimmering, clinking, crazy steampunk wonderland … so why couldn't she have fun for even a minute? Why was she so *worried* all the time? Because she'd promised to help Viminy Crowe launch his new Summer Special, and that did not include disappearing into some science-fictional dimension.

And of course because she had lost Catnip. Again.

Would she hear his voice in a room as big and busy as a circus? Catnip didn't exactly squeak. It was more of a rat meow with an underlying whistle, kind of like a chirp.

Her hands were soaking wet from holding them under the fountain's sprinkle, her shirt spattered and damp.

CHIRP!

What?

Addy's ears strained to listen above the hubbub of the hotel lobby. Had the violinist tweaked out a bad plink?

CHIRP! There it was again.

Addy's head whipped around.

Catnip! Alive and wriggling! *Not* perched on the rim of a bubbling cauldron in the villain's lair, but on the same page of the comic that she was on! Oh, but …

There was a big *but,* bringing a throb of rage to Addy's chest. Catnip was upside down. His tiny feet scrabbled against thin air as he swung slowly back and forth far above her. Professor Lickpenny's horrible nephew leered over the balustrade of the mezzanine. His grimy fingers gripped Catnip's tail, and his arm swayed casually above the crowd that clustered around the fountain.

Addy leapt onto the escalator, shouting, "Hey! HEY!"

If Nevins dropped Catnip, she'd drop *him*, the sludge-ball cockroach! Addy pushed past a lady's taffeta skirt and ducked under a gentleman's wool-clad arm, catching a whiff that she wished she'd missed.

What was going on here? In one hand, Nevins had Catnip. In the other, he grasped the mysterious parcel that he'd collected for his uncle. This was supposed to be the scene where the brat fell into the milkshake churn and Flynn had to save him. (Ironic, since Nevins's package contained the spare part for the lammergeyer, which would grab Flynn later in the comic.) That was what was *supposed* to be happening. But Nevins was nowhere near the milkshake churn. And where was Flynn?

The story was changing.

Addy stumbled up the escalator. "Don't you dare drop him, you measly dot!"

AND THAT'S WHEN THE HULLABALOO BEGAN.

The whole lobby seemed to gasp.

Some people were staring up at the mezzanine and others hurried in different directions, like they were trying to hide. Wylder saw one guy who gaped like a hungry fish.

But what were they looking at? Too many waving arms and fancy hats in the way. And where was Addy? Was all this fuss something to do with her?

Wylder tried jumping up and down, but it just made him dizzy. If only he could get a better view.

Duh! He took the comic from under his shirt. He smoothed it out and examined the pictures.

Now he could see the action perfectly ...

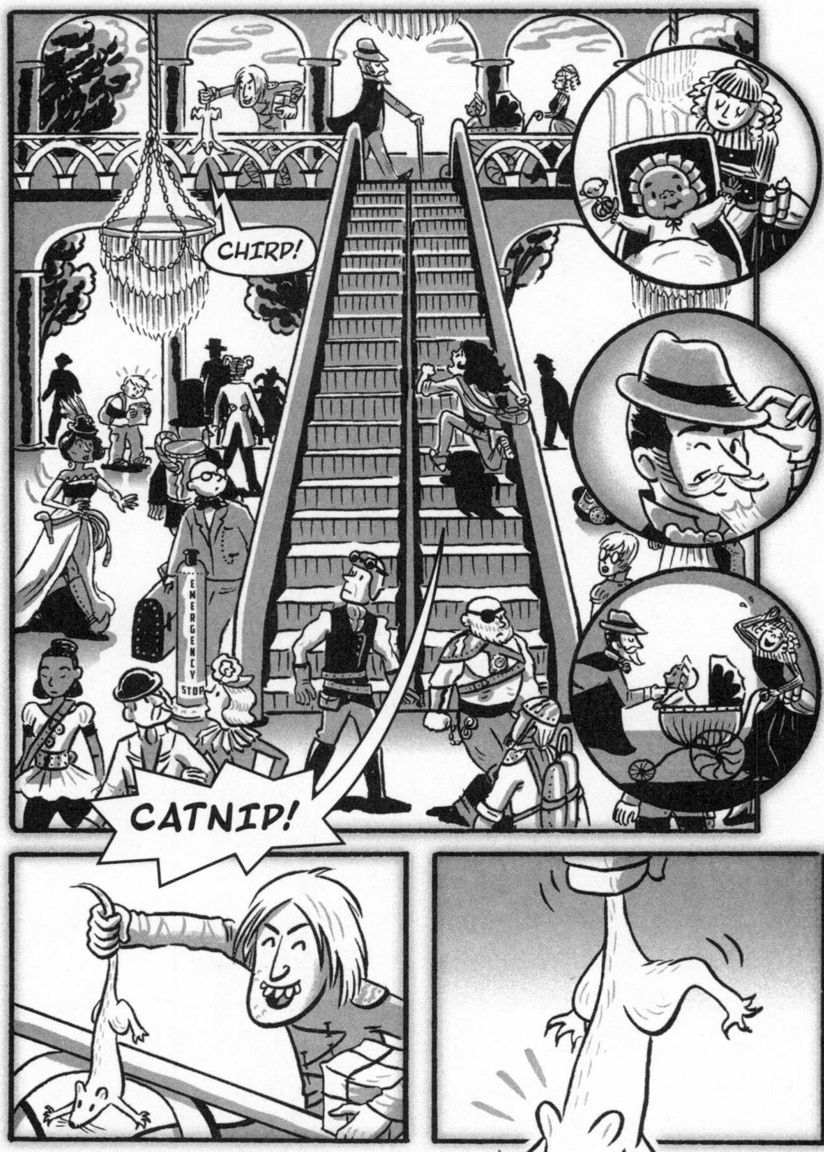
CHIRP!
EMERGENCY STOP
CATNIP!

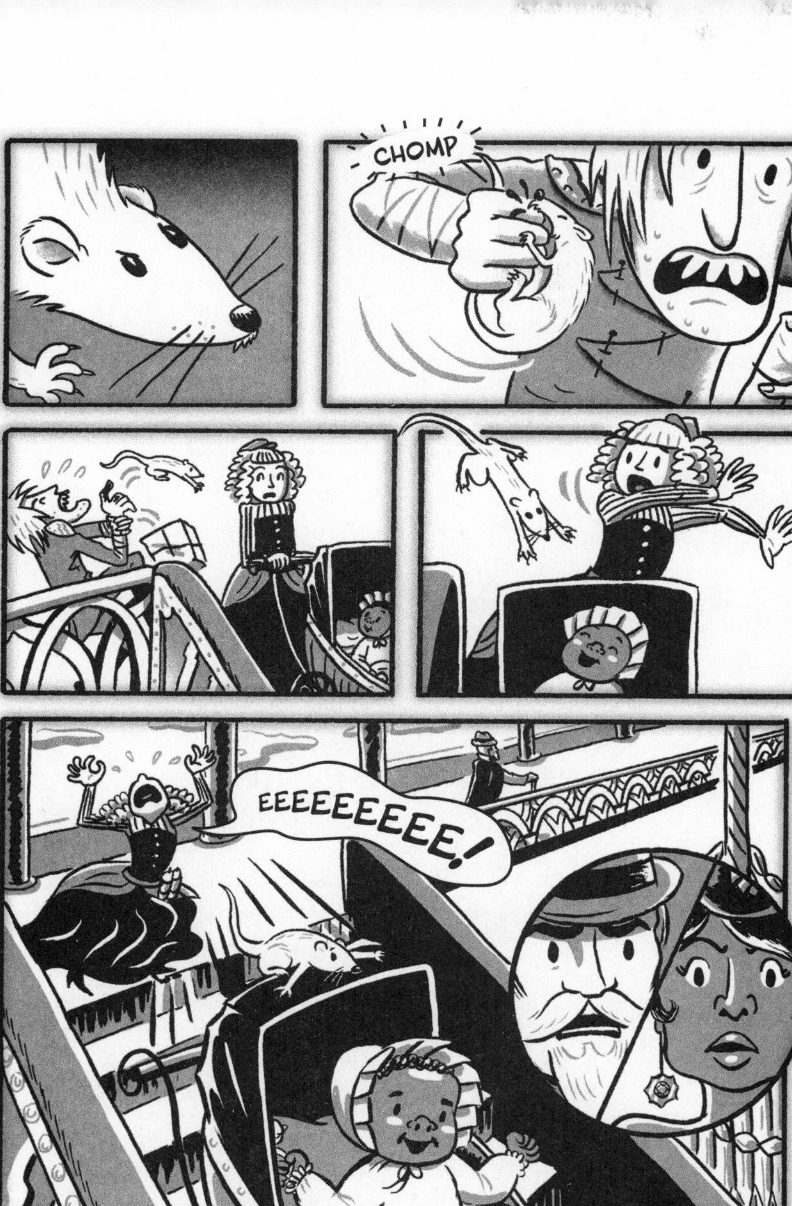
CHOMP
EEEEEEEEEE!

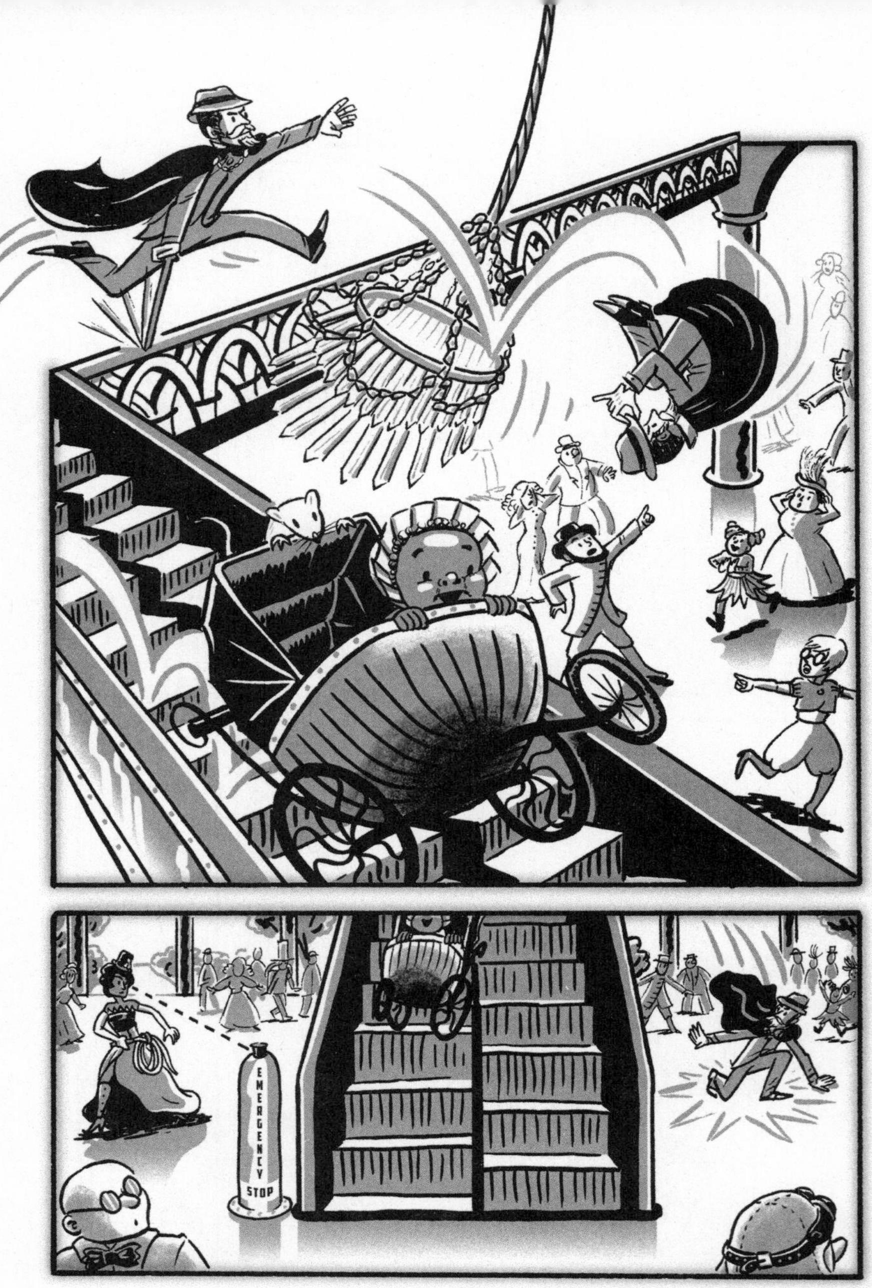
EMERGENCY STOP

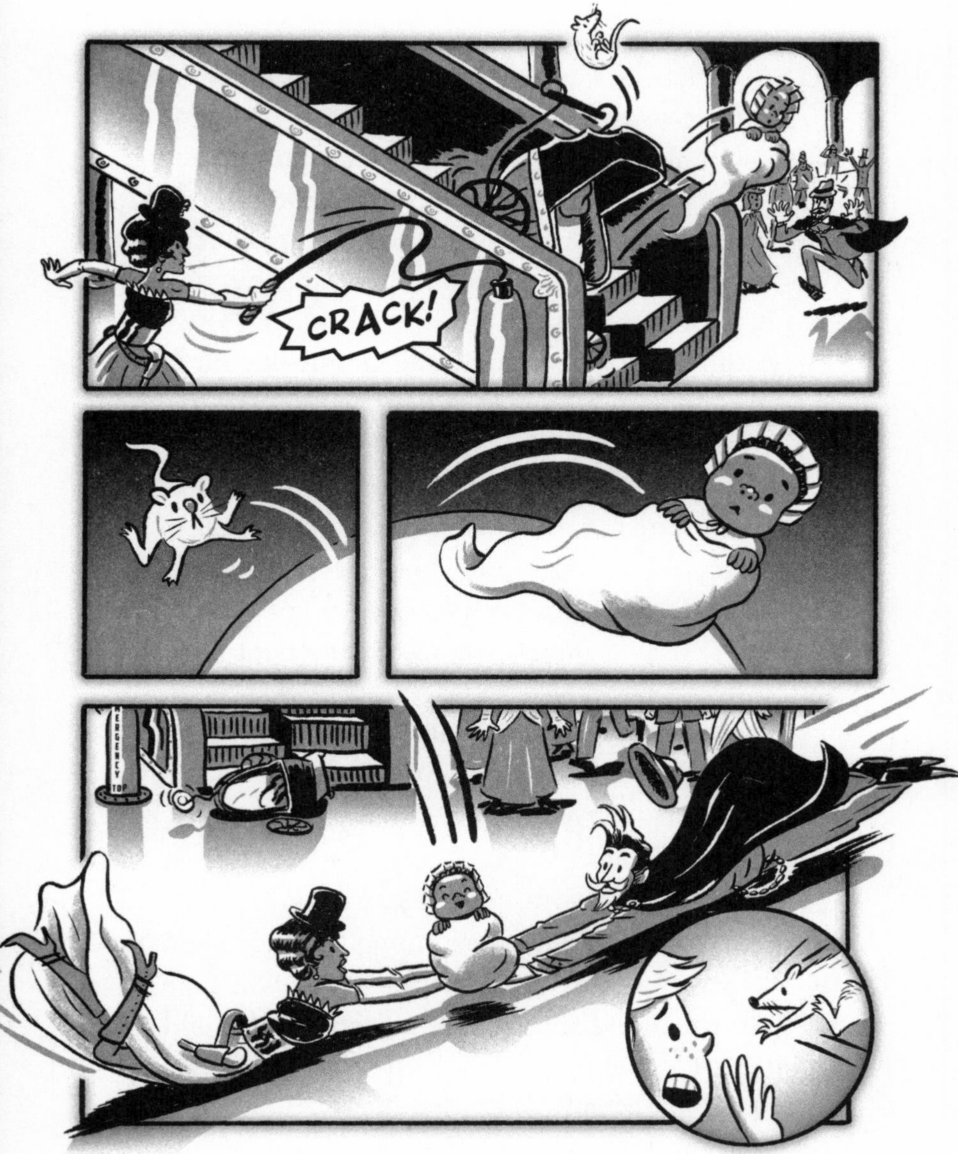
CRACK!

Wylder screamed.

The darned rat had landed on his face!

And *then*, using Wylder's nose as a launchpad for those skittery little claws, Catnip rocketed to the top of his head where he messed with Wylder's hair before burrowing down between his shirt and his backpack. Wylder frantically shrugged off the straps, but he still couldn't reach the rat.

You know that itchy spot in the middle of your back that you can't reach from over your shoulder or underneath your armpit? That was where Catnip clung, chirping away like a cricket. Wylder spun around and around until he got dizzy. When he stopped spinning, the rat scrambled up to his shoulder. Wylder turned his head and found two beady pink eyes staring calmly into his. Fast as a snake striking, Catnip bent forward and ... licked his cheek.

Ewww! Wylder shuddered all over.

"That's quite the trick, Cowboy."

Wylder froze. Ever so slowly, he turned around.

Flynn Goster was an acrobat and a trickster and a master of disguise—the coolest guy around. He could look like anyone, but his eyes shone with a trademark twinkle that was his alone. His mustache had a singular flair. He addressed women as "little lady" and he called men "cowboy."

And here he was.

The lobby was still in an uproar, everyone exclaiming

about the show-stopping rescue and applauding Isadora, who was trying to assist the baby's nanny as she tucked her charge back into the stroller. ServiDudes rolled here and there, picking up dropped items, mopping and tidying.

And in the midst of the chaos, Wylder was sharing a quiet moment with *Flynn*—it had to be him—who stroked his superb mustache.

"Is that your rat? Fine-looking animal. Mischievous. Reminds me of me."

Yes, his eyes were twinkling all right.

"*My* rat?"

Catnip gave him another lick. Wylder tried not to shudder. "Uh, yeah," he said. "Kind of. I mean, it's my friend's, really, but I'm looking after it for her. I mean, uh, yes, Mr. Goster. This is Catnip."

His heart was pounding. Wait until he told his friend Jerry! *Yeah, I was in this super-luxury hotel talking to Flynn Goster. Yeah, Flynn and me. Pals. Called me "Cowboy."* Jerry would pee his pants with envy.

Acting as though he did it every day, Wylder picked the rat off his shoulder and stroked him.

"Nice ratty."

Catnip cocked a little pink-lined ear. Almost as if he understood what was going on.

"I think you have me confused with someone else, Cowboy." Flynn touched his finger to Catnip's head with a smile. "My name is Mammon. Mr. Oliver Mammon, from Kalamazoo."

He said this in a loud voice, for the benefit of bystanders.

But then he looked straight at Wylder and winked.

It was lucky that Wylder shrieked, because Addy now knew exactly where Catnip had landed. Silly boy. What was so scary about a rat?

Addy raced down the escalator in a breathless whoosh! She snaked her way through the crowd that lingered around the baby carriage, pausing for a second to watch the nanny practically kiss Isadora's hand in gratitude. Talk about a plot twist, Addy thought. What if the baby had broken its neck halfway through the comic? She moved on, straight for her darling ratty-kins, who was—what the *heck*?!—being admired by Flynn Goster and *stroked* by *Wylder Wallace*?

And *whoa!*

Wasn't Catnip … bigger? Almost too big to fit comfortably on Wylder's trembling palm.

"Hi, Mr. Goster." Addy reached for her pet. "Way to save the baby!"

Catnip ran up her arm, tail zinging back and forth.

She couldn't help smiling at Wylder's look of relief when she reclaimed her rat. She wouldn't be so mean as to yell at him in front of his hero, but sure as sludge she'd get her comic back and then make him apologize, big time.

"I believe you've mistaken me for someone else," said Flynn Goster. "Both of you. Same mistake."

"Oh," said Addy. "Right."

She could feel Catnip snuggling under her chin, his tiny heart pattering beneath his soft pelt. She looked at Flynn's elegant gray gloves.

"You're the ... um, *billionaire* at the moment, right?"

Isadora swept up just then, her face shining with the glow of someone who's just won a race.

"Hello, my dears." The charm bracelet on her wrist clinked softly as she rested light fingers on Addy's shoulder and then shook Wylder's hand.

"Are you quite recovered from your flight?" she murmured to Catnip, stroking his head.

BUT HER EYES WERE ON FLYNN THE WHOLE TIME ...

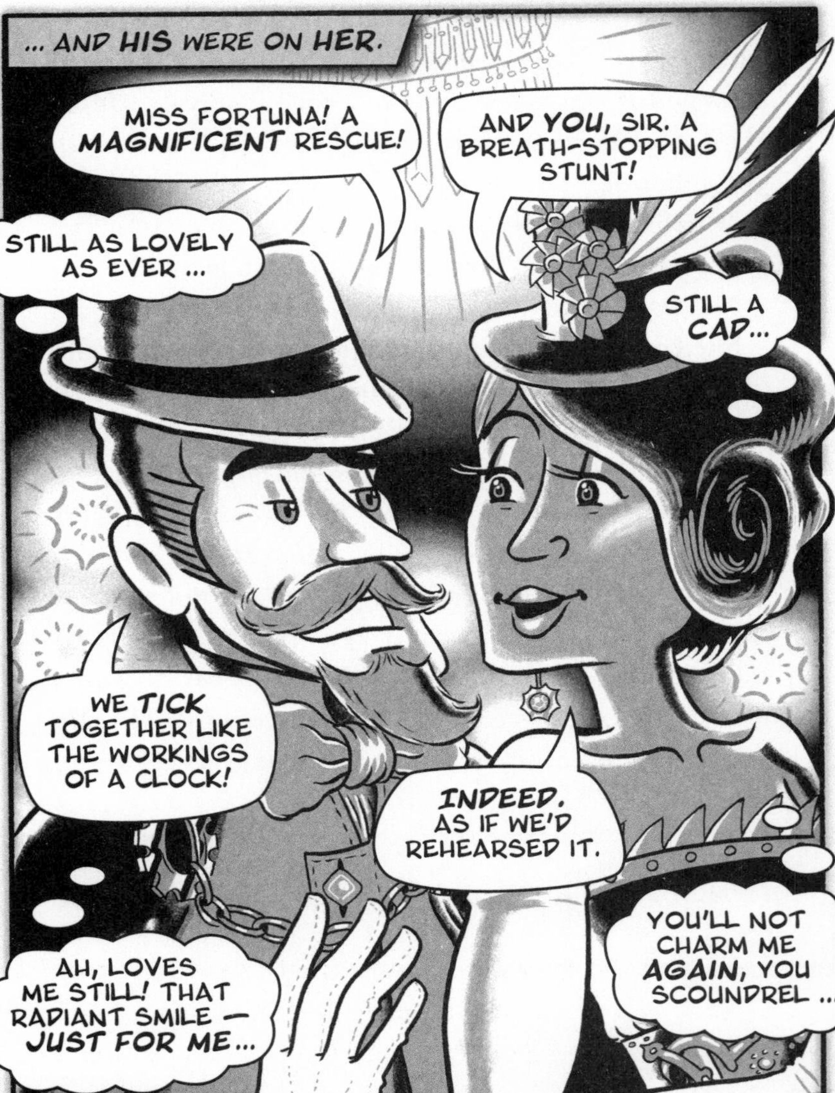
... AND HIS WERE ON HER.
MISS FORTUNA! A MAGNIFICENT RESCUE!
AND YOU, SIR. A BREATH-STOPPING STUNT!
STILL AS LOVELY AS EVER ...
STILL A CAD...
WE TICK TOGETHER LIKE THE WORKINGS OF A CLOCK!
INDEED. AS IF WE'D REHEARSED IT.
AH, LOVES ME STILL! THAT RADIANT SMILE — JUST FOR ME...
YOU'LL NOT CHARM ME AGAIN, YOU SCOUNDREL ...

Darting forward, Isadora planted a kiss on Flynn's cheek before turning to the photographers with a wink.

Laughter and cheers from the audience. Flynn stroked his mustache.

"Well, well, *well*," he said. "Aren't I the lucky fellow?"

"Kissing?!" Wylder frowned at Addy. "Is this what the 'FLYNN IN LOVE' teaser was about?"

"No comment," she said.

Catnip nosed his way into one of her pockets. Wylder turned his head away, as if he could cancel the kiss by not watching.

Flynn and Isadora continued to gaze at each other, eyes sparkling and cheeks aglow. The photographers edged closer, calling Isadora's name to make her turn her head. Addy didn't blame Wylder for thinking it was a bit sickening.

Funny how some of the comic story had changed, but other parts were working out exactly as Vim had written them.

Nevins scuttled across the marble floor, parcel in hand. Addy had a strong urge to kick him in the pants. Pay him back for torturing Catnip. Wouldn't that feel good?

Nevins deked around a ServiDude carrying a tray of lemonade. Addy charged after him, one hand cupped over the pocket where Catnip was getting a jouncing ride.

"Where are you going?" she heard Wylder call.

The revolving door spun around, taking Nevins with it. A lady holding a basket stepped in front of Addy, forcing her to wait for the next rotation. Wylder chugged up, puffing and red in the face.

"MISS ADDY CROWE!"

A silver colored ServiDude rolled across the lobby floor calling her name.

"PAGING MISS ADDY CROWE." It spoke in a slightly raspy voice. "VAPORLINK FOR MISS ADDY CROWE!"

11

"**F**or me?" A white corner of paper stuck out of a slot above the ServiDude's eye.

"What's a VaporLink?" Wylder peered over her shoulder. Or *around* her shoulder since she was taller than he was.

"It's Uncle Vim's version of a telegram."

"What's a telegram?"

Addy let Catnip run up her arm. "It's what they had in the olden days for fast communication, way before e-mail. They have telegrams in black-and-white movies, you know? Like special delivery letters."

"MISS ADDY CROWE?" said the ServiDude. "PLEASE PULL LEVER TO RELEASE VAPORLINK."

Addy's hand hovered in front of the robot's face.

Catnip, on her shoulder, sniffed excitedly. The lever was the nose.

Pull. Snap back. **Whirrr. CLICK.**

An envelope slid out from the right eyebrow and fell directly into her waiting hand.

"READ WELL. BE WELL," said the ServiDude.

"What does it say?" asked Wylder.

"Give me a chance!" said Addy. She ripped open the flap and stared at the paper in her hands. "It's from Uncle Vim!"

"Wow," said Wylder. "That's … *nuts!*"

Waaay beyond nuts. Addy's skin tingled up her neck and down her arms. She was holding proof that the whole world was skewy.

Addy held up the VaporLink to show him. In bold capital letters, the paper said: MESS-UP WITH DELIVERY! COMICS STUCK AT TRAIN STATION. HAVE TO GO SIGN DUMB DOCS. COME TO BOOTH IN ONE HOUR.

"Dumb what?" said Wylder.

"Documents," said Addy. "Dumb *docs*. He's not exactly Mr. Businessman. Anything official gets him riled."

"Wow," said Wylder. "It's like he's texting you across the barriers of time and space! How cool to get a VaporLink from the guy who invented them! That's like getting a drive home from Henry Ford or flying in the Wright brothers' airplane or … or getting a box of chocolates from Mr. Hershey!"

"Wylder, I know you think that I'm … that I'm …" What

did he think of her? "That I'm *sour* or something. But this is sludge-pit crazy. Uncle Vim needs me. And we really need to get out of his comic book."

"MISS ADDY CROWE," said the ServiDude. "WOULD YOU CARE TO SEND A REPLY?"

Addy's breath caught in her throat. "I can send a reply?"

"NO FEE FOR THE FIRST TWENTY WORDS. A PENNY A WORD OVER TWENTY."

"Cheaper than texting," said Wylder. "Unless you're on the Unlimited Plan, which of course I am, because my mother—" Addy raised her right eyebrow to shut him up, just the way Ms. Blaine did to silence the sixth-grade homeroom. She hadn't yet figured out how to raise the left one, but she practiced sometimes in the mirror.

"Where do I write my reply?" she asked.

"PRESS BUTTON TO RECORD REPLY."

The button turned out to be on the side of the ServiDude's head. You spoke into a little microphone and your message supposedly got transported into the vapor, somehow showing up in an envelope at the other end. Had Uncle Vim thought of every little detail in this whole world? How could his brain hold all this stuff?

Extremely unlikely that she could actually send a message, but she had to try.

"LADIES AND GENTLEMEN!" A Porter ServiDude across the lobby began to call out at a reverberating volume.

97

"ALL PASSENGERS FOR THE GOLD RUSH EXPRESS—THIS WAY, PLEASE. HUM-SHUTTLE TO TRAIN IS DEPARTING IN FIVE MINUTES. THIS WAY, PLEASE."

"What's the Hum-Shuttle?" said Wylder.

"A way to get on the train," said Addy. "It's like a moving tube, makes a humming sound. Uncle Vim got the idea from a midway ride."

Catnip nestled under her hair on the back of her neck. She scratched his ears with her fingertip while she considered what to say in the VaporLink. How long had it taken for her uncle's message to arrive? Was it instant, like a text? Or had he sent it a while ago and was now going bonkers looking for her?

"How long do you think we've been here?" she asked Wylder.

"Gee, I don't know. The train went through the mountains for a while. And then we got shot at and went to the laboratory."

"And now Banff," said Addy. "With stinking Nevins— who seems to have got clean away, in case you hadn't noticed!"

"And Flynn and the stunt and everything. It must be a couple of hours since we got here."

"MISS ADDY CROWE. WOULD YOU CARE TO SEND A REPLY? PRESS BUTTON TO RECORD REPLY."

Addy blinked away the prickle in her eyes. This was Uncle Vim's big day, and everything had gone wrong. She was supposed to be *helping* him, not screwing up his masterpiece! She cleared her throat and pushed the ServiDude's ear button.

"Look in your copy," she said, counting to four on her fingers, "of the Summer Special. I am trapped inside. SOS!" That was thirteen words. "I love you," she added.

That should do it. The whole explanation would take too many words, but he'd figure it out the second he looked in his comic book. *If* he actually received her message, that is. And *if* she and Wylder were in his copy too.

"THANK YOU," said the ServiDude. "YOUR MESSAGE IS SENT."

Addy looked at Wylder. Could it work? "What are the chances?"

Wylder shrugged.

"Imagine my uncle's face," said Addy. She thought of his eyes popping behind thick glasses, his long fingers dragging through messy hair, a dramatic moan of astonishment.

"Depends on whether we're in those pictures too," said Wylder. "In his copy as well as this one."

Impossible. But maybe. If Vim could see them, could he do something to help? He was goofy and unreliable at the best of times, which is why he made a good uncle. Not hero material. But who else could save them?

"Addy, look!" Wylder tugged on her arm. Flynn Goster was surrounded by admirers, causing a slight commotion. A diamond glinted from the tip of his cane as it swung with his stride across the lobby.

"Come on," said Addy. "We have to figure out how to get home."

"I'm not coming." Wylder folded his arms across his chest. "I've only just met Flynn. I want to hang out with him a little bit before we go."

"*Hang out?* You can't—"

But Wylder was already on his way toward Flynn.

"Wait!"

She scooted after him.

"THIS WAY FOR THE HUM-SHUTTLE!" The ServiDude made a sound like a sharp whistle blowing. "ALL ABOARD."

"See?" Addy nudged Wylder. "Your hero is going to be on the train. If you want to *hang out* with him, we'd better join the crowd."

"MR. OLIVER MAMMON," said the welcoming robot. "DELIGHTED TO HAVE YOU ABOARD."

"Mr. Gos—er, Mammon, sir?" Wylder stepped right up next to him. "Remember me? From back there in the lobby?"

"Sure thing, Cowboy," said Flynn. "Who could forget a boy with a rat on his head? No time to chat, though. I've got a train to catch."

"The Gold Rush Express, right? Big plans for the cargo, eh?"

"Wylder!" Addy poked him. Did he have *any* manners? "Sssh!"

Luckily Flynn did not hear. He was sailing toward the Hum-Shuttle passage through a rounded doorway.

"Children!" Isadora's voice rang out. "Wylder? Addy? Have your parents gone ahead? Come with me, won't you?"

"MISS ISADORA FORTUNA. DELIGHTED TO HAVE YOU ABOARD," said the ServiDude.

Wylder grinned like a boy with a dumb crush and scooted after her, but jerked back with a squinched face, as if he'd hit himself hard. Addy, right behind, crashed into him with a thunk.

"We bumped into the end of the page again," she mumbled. "Step out of the way. Let the rest of them go."

Isadora was already down the corridor. She looked back, but maybe she couldn't see them because of the cluster of waiting passengers.

"Why?" moaned Wylder. "Why do we get stuck every time we try to go anywhere?"

Addy pulled him to one side. "Where's the comic? Give it to me."

"Rolled up in the side pocket of my backpack," said Wylder. "And you can't have it. I don't want to end up in some creepy lab with metal monsters like the last time!"

"It's not *my* fault that some loony cop tried to shoot my rat and flipped over the pages!"

"IF YOU DIDN'T HAVE A RAT, NOBODY WOULD BE TRYING TO SHOOT HIM!"

"You really are a bowl of sludge."

Catnip had climbed on top of Addy's head, as if trying to squash the yelling. Addy took a deep breath. "Put. The. Comic. On. The. Floor," she said.

Wylder looked at her suspiciously but obeyed. Uncle Vim would be dismayed to see how bashed up his precious creation had become.

"Smooth it out a little," she instructed. "Good. Now, look."

"It's hard to concentrate while you have a rat on your head. Is that what I looked like when I met Flynn?"

Addy ignored him. "Like we figured out before," she said, "whatever is happening on the open page is stuff we can move around in. We had the whole drama in the lobby, and then … hmm …" Addy paused.

At least they hadn't hit a page bump in the middle of Flynn's acrobatics with the baby carriage. Thank goodliness, as Vim would say.

"If the action keeps going in the same place, the way it did in the lobby …" Wylder moved his finger over the panels in front of them.

"We can just keep moving?" finished Addy.

"Maybe," said Wylder. "Does that mean the next scene is somewhere else? Like back on the train?"

"Maybe," said Addy. "In the original they're loading extra gold here in Banff. That's why Flynn boards the train now. The gold stash is bigger."

"So if we turn the page," said Wylder, "we avoid the—" He jerked his head to the Hum-Shuttle entrance, where the final passengers were being hustled along. "And we keep going with Flynn and Isadora and all the action?"

"That's what I'm guessing."

Addy didn't have a chance to wonder if she was missing anything, because Wylder leaned forward and scooped up the comic book, turning the page in one determined motion.

THWIP!

Addy's scalp twinged with pain as Catnip's claws dug in deep. A dizzying moment of fog, a blurry somersault and then ...

They were outside looking at a glorious sunset, the kind you see in postcards. Sailboats scudded across a glimmering ocean. Splashes of scarlet and apricot and flamingo pink lit the heavens. Frogs croaked and cicadas whirred, accompanied by the gentle lapping of water against boat hulls. The air was balmy, with a faint scent of coconuts. And ... popcorn?

"We're not on the train," said Wylder.

"Rat-sludge!" said Addy. "No offense intended, Catnip." She reached up to bring her pet gently down from her head and hold him against her chest. "Another flashback I forgot about. Or has it moved? This is *not* where we need to be."

"Doesn't look much like Canada," said Wylder.

"You're right about that. It's Florida."

Although they had a clear view of a beach and the ocean beyond, they were sitting in the first row of a small stadium, a chattering crowd of sunburned tourists in the seats behind them and a glimmering pool of water in front, so close that Wylder reached out to trail his fingers across its surface.

"Warm," he said. "Nice."

Addy gazed up at the diving platform that towered above the pool.

"You don't have to feel bad about not being on the train with Isadora and Flynn," she said. "We're about to see them meet for the first time."

"Oh no! More mush?"

"Wait and see."

"So where are they?"

"Any second now."

"Do you think we could go swimming?" said Wylder.

"How about you read the sign and then ask me again." Addy pointed at a painted notice nailed to the struts of the diving tower.

I t seemed to Wylder that every time he turned around, he was inside a different scene, each more fantastic than the last. A steam train with robotic servants, a secret lab with an evil scientist, a hotel lobby with a MilkshakeMobile and Flynn Goster himself. And now alligator wrestling! It was like a video game with different levels. Each page of this comic book took you to a new level, only instead of slouching on the couch at home, you got to *be* one of the action figures racing around. Fun? Definitely. Addy wasn't as much fun to play with as Jerry, but the game—the comic—was fantastic. And when things got too scary, you could escape by turning the page. It was real and magical at the same time.

Wylder shrugged out of his backpack, settled in his

grandstand seat, sniffed the salty air and vowed not to let Addy bug him too much.

"Stop pulling at me," he said. "Gator wrestling sounds fantastic! And seats in the front row! Oops, sorry, sir."

He had bumped against a man with a pointed beard and a crisp white suit. The man looked down his nose at Wylder and said, "Quite so." Whatever that meant.

"Sure," said Wylder. "Quite so to you too."

The man shifted a fraction of an inch away from him.

"Come on!" Addy was on her feet, looking around. "Let's go."

"Go?"

"You know, *home*? Toronto. In the *real* world?" She tugged the VaporLink from her pocket and waved it in his face. "My uncle has a serious problem with missing comics, and I want to be there!"

"Okay, it's an emergency for your uncle," he said. "But why do *you* have to be there?"

Addy closed her mouth firmly and took in a deep breath.

"We're not supposed to be here," she said, clearly and slowly—not being mean, just being calm, working stuff out. "My uncle drew this comic, and he didn't put us in it. It's like—" She waved her hand. "It's like we wandered into a stranger's apartment. Sure, it's a great-looking apartment, and there's a party going on, but we can't stay here, eating snacks and watching the stranger's TV. It's wrong. We weren't invited. We have to leave."

"Where's the portal, the … the *door* to this party?"

"I don't know. That's what we have to find out."

"But I don't *want* to go."

His words hung in the air for a second. He wished he hadn't put it that way.

"You know what you sound like?"

"Yes," he said. A little kid whining about bedtime. "But I still don't want to go."

"Where's the comic?"

"In my back pocket."

She put out her hand, but he shook his head.

"Look, I know it's yours. And you can have it. But if you turn the page now, you might be missing the way back. Maybe the portal is here in this stadium. There has to be a bathroom, right? Maybe that's where the portal is. Or over there behind the striped tent. Why don't you go check the ladies' room?"

He could see her thinking about this.

A man in a top hat trotted out of the tent on the far side of the pool. He wore a tuxedo jacket over an old-timey bathing suit. He looked like the ringmaster at a circus, and the show was beginning! Wylder jiggled with excitement, knocking the guy beside him again. He apologized once more. The guy ignored him.

The ringmaster came close to where they were sitting and began to speak through a silvery funnel that made his words bounce around the small stadium.

"Ladies and gentlemen! Welcome to an evening you

will never forget! And a most *special* welcome to our distinguished guest, all the way from England—the Duke of Tooting."

Wylder laughed. He couldn't help himself.

"Tooting!" he said to Addy.

"Uncle Vim thought it was funny too."

"You know, *tooting*. Like—"

"Yes, I know."

With a flourish, the ringmaster gestured toward the man sitting next to them.

"*You're* the Duke of Tooting?" Just the name was enough to start Wylder giggling again.

"Quite so," said the duke.

Meanwhile, the ringmaster was walking up and down the pool deck in front of them, calling his carnival enticements through the horn. "Ladies and gentlemen, in just a moment you will behold the biggest alligator in captivity! Teeth like razors, tail like a thunderbolt—a deadly marvel to behold! Bring him out, boys!"

Four men rolled a cage from behind the tent. Inside was a gigantic alligator. Gigantic! As big as a dragon! Straining and sweating, the men pushed the cage up a ramp beside the pool. One of them leaned around with a long stick to flick open the barred door. The beast lumbered out of the cage and splashed into the pool to swim in angry circles, its tail frothing the water like a blender. Wylder happily noted that the walls of the pool were slick and vertical—the animal was not going to be able to climb out on its own.

"Isn't that amazing! Are you amazed, Duke?" The ringmaster's pacing brought him to stand next to the duke with an arm around his lordship's shoulders. Wylder caught a glimpse of the ringmaster's wrist—he wore a cool watch shaped like a key. The duke squirmed away. The crowd shouted and whistled and stomped.

"And *now*," the ringmaster rumbled over the ruckus, "as the sun's dying rays dapple the sea, we introduce our heroine—the first lady of adventure—as beautiful as she is dangerous: the one and only Isadora Fortuna!"

The tent flap parted and out she stepped. Wylder's heart almost stopped—Isadora was so young! Of course, this was a flashback. Years and years ago. But she looked like a girl. A strong girl, mind you. Her bathing suit was old-fashioned, almost like a dress, but you could see the muscles in her arms and legs. She ran lightly to the diving tower and began to climb. The alligator's tail churned the surface of the pool below her.

"I never liked this scene," said Addy.

"Does something go wrong?" said Wylder.

"Isadora has this bit in her act where the alligator seems about to snap her head off, and the audience is, like, 'Aaahhh!'"

"No kidding." Wylder watched the bubbling water.

"Usually she whups the gator, and everything is fine. But this time she's in trouble for real—as *if*, in my opinion—so Flynn jumps in to save her."

"Wow!" said Wylder.

"Except she's all, like, 'My hero!'—which is so dumb! They have this romantic scene with moonlight and ..." Addy glanced at the Duke of Tooting and then lowered her voice. "And they have a big smooch, and he gives her a present."

"What kind of present?"

"A big fat jewel. I know—dumb, right? I told Vim, but he insisted. I think he's kind of in love with Isadora himself. It's not like my uncle is super popular with the ladies in real life."

The cover said FLYNN IN LOVE? But this couldn't actually be a love story, could it?

"And *then* he dumps her! After about a page." Addy pounded her knees with her fists.

"Huh," said Wylder. "Just like our dads, eh?"

She blinked—so he knew she'd heard him—but she didn't say anything.

"Well, that's lucky," he said. "No happily-ever-after ending full of mush."

Halfway up the ladder, Isadora slipped and caught herself. The crowd gasped in unison. Hanging on by one hand, she pulled herself back onto the ladder and waved. It was all a stunt. The crowd cheered.

"See? As *if* she needs Flynn," said Addy. "When they meet in the hotel lobby, it's ten years later. Flynn really falls in love this time, and he figures he's still got it. But Isadora is all about revenge. And the gold."

"So wait! Is Flynn here already?"

"You don't recognize him?"

Isadora had reached the top of the ladder. She sidled to the end of the diving board and peered down at the turbulent water. The setting sun lit up her skin, making her look golden and mysterious.

"Don't do it!" someone shouted.

"Trounce the beast!" cried someone else.

The duke, next to Wylder, made a snorting noise. His suit jacket was open and he peered into the inside pocket.

"It's going to get mushy by the time the sun goes down," said Addy. "You won't like it. Let's check the washrooms." She held out his backpack.

The crowd was quiet, staring at the diving board. Water splashed up as the great gator swam in frenzied circles. Wylder did not want to leave and was considering how to say so when someone grabbed his arm.

"I've been robbed!" The duke's voice broke the held-breath silence. He could be Flynn, thought Wylder. Was this part of the trick? "This boy took my sapphire!"

"What? No! I—"

"You kept bumping into me, you pickpocket!" the duke accused him. "Your technique puzzles me, but the Tooting Sapphire is gone!"

The word "tooting" did not make Wylder laugh this time.

"The Florida Museum of Gems is buying the stone tomorrow. It has been locked in its case and hidden in my pocket every minute." He raised his voice again. "I shall have you arrested!"

Wylder wrenched free of the duke's grasp and staggered back toward the edge of the pool.

"Addy!"

She nodded vigorously. Time to go! But as Wylder reached for the comic, something hard and heavy whacked him across the back.

Water is much wetter when you have your clothes on. Wylder's shirt and pants, instantly soaked, ballooned around him, pulling him under. His feeble kicks didn't bring him to the surface. He gagged and thrashed, his shoes as heavy as boulders. He … he … he couldn't breathe …

He was drowning.

With every cell in his body, he pushed upward. His mouth met air just long enough to gurgle a scream and then fill with gator-flavored water. Down he went again, choking, flailing with his fists. Something crashed into the pool next to him, sending Wylder surging to the surface. A second later he found that his head was above water. He sucked at the air, chest fiery with relief. There was a hand under him, holding him so he could breathe. Twisting around, Wylder recognized the ringmaster …

The ground beneath Addy moved in a familiar way. She pushed damp hair out of her eyes, the smell of drenched wool carpet close to her nose. She knew where she was. She'd seen this room being drawn. She stared up at the wallpaper. Yep, she'd helped her uncle fill in the intricate pattern, a million interlocking wiggles that looked like something you'd find under a microscope.

"Help!" Wylder's voice croaked somewhere behind her.

She rolled over, water squishing out of her jeans. Oh no! There was a rip down the thigh, starting practically at her underwear! The alligator's claw must have—

"I'm drowning!" Wylder cried.

"Not anymore," said Addy. "You're on dry land." She tugged together the edges of the long tear, trying to sound as if she weren't sitting there practically pantless. "Not-so-dry land, actually. And not really *land* either." Who would have guessed it would be a relief to be back on the train?

Wylder lay on his back, hair plastered to his forehead. "I had a terrible, *terrible* nightmare!"

"It really happened," said Addy. "But—"

Sludge! Where was Catnip? She snatched at the strap of her shoulder bag and dragged it over. As she pulled, the bag began to move on its own, the best little quiver Addy had ever seen. She scooped Catnip out and blew on his wet fur.

"That's what I call a drowned rat," said Wylder.

"Very funny." Still holding together the rip in her jeans with one hand, Addy laid Catnip across her knees and gently rubbed him. Had he really grown today? Where had he found food? She felt like she hadn't eaten in about a week.

"Why is everything soaked? Where's my backpack? And where are *we*?" Wylder sat up.

"Stateroom 2. Isadora's. I grabbed the comic." Addy looked around. "Here, it's under me. That's lucky." She held the damp comic between her thumb and forefinger like something nasty. "I grabbed it from the gator pool. That must be why we're all wet. I flapped it around to dry while you were spitting up algae. And—*bam!*—here we are, back on the train."

"The gator pool." Wylder shuddered. "Don't remind me."

"You are *so* dumb and *so* lucky. That alligator was as big as this *room!*"

"Yeah, I noticed that." He banged the side of his head, trying to get the water out of his ear. "And Flynn was the ringmaster?"

"After you fell into the water like an oversized toad, I tried to grab you, but this claw came up and ..." Addy put her bag on top of the tear in her jeans. "And then Flynn did his hero thing, reaching in to save you. Only he tripped on your backpack and went flying."

"My backpack? It was *my* fault?" Wylder buried his face in his hands for a moment, but then lifted it again, eyes curious. "And what was the whole jewel deal? Flynn stole it, right?"

"For this issue, Vim gave Flynn a cool new gadget called a Zimmer. It's shaped like a key but worn like a watch."

"Oh, I saw that on his wrist!"

"It can open *anything*. So—*zim, zim!*—he unlocked the duke's case and 'Bye-bye, sapphire.'"

Then Wylder remembered. "But the gator ..."

"Yeah," said Addy. "The gator zoomed around, ready to snack on you, but he crashed into Flynn instead."

Wylder sank back onto the carpet.

"Isadora must have had a perfect view from the tower," Addy said. "Because she performed a majestic dive into the pool. Right next to the gator's head!"

"Just in time," breathed Wylder.

"Not quite."

Addy was at the truly horrible part of the story—the part where half the audience had fainted, where the sea-green water had been streaked a bloody scarlet, where the sinewy and astounding Isadora had whacked the gator's snout with her fist to get it to open one second after it had snapped shut around Flynn Goster's right hand.

"It all happened in less than a minute," Addy said. "She heaved Flynn's body over the rim of the pool and scooped you out like a tadpole. Tossed you onto the seats in the front row!"

Isadora was a seriously supreme character. Addy wished her uncle had given her face to Isadora instead of to that sneaky little Nelly.

"And *then*"—she'd saved the good bit for last—"while you were passed out cold, Isadora *stuck her arm down the alligator's throat!*"

"*What?!* Did she get Flynn's hand?"

"No, that was chewed up," said Addy. "But she saved the Zimmer. The gator must've decided it wasn't tasty enough."

Wylder looked a bit pale. "He lost his hand because of my stupid backpack. It's all so terrible. Will Flynn be okay?"

How could Addy possibly know? Nothing in the whole comic book was going the way it was supposed to. Vim's scenes weren't happening the way he wrote them. And she and Wylder were not just watching the story like a TV show or a movie—they were *inside* it. They'd become characters who did things to affect other characters and had an impact on the next panel, and all the panels after that.

Like real life.

"When we get out—which we *really* have to do—and aren't part of the cast of characters anymore, I'm hoping the comic will go back to the way my uncle wrote it. Flynn will still have his hand, Isadora will have her trick romance and Lickpenny will fail at everything."

"Flynn would be miserable without a hand," said Wylder. "It makes me feel kind of sick. Unless I'm just hungry."

Addy shivered. Every inch of her body was slightly clammy. She didn't really want to stand up with torn jeans and her underpants showing. She looked around the stateroom. Stacked under the window was a set of suitcases. Any chance Vim had put clothes inside?

"Wylder," she said, "wait for me in the corridor. I have to check something."

"What?"

"Just do it, would you?" She felt like a ninny, sitting there with her pet rat and her hands covering her lap. But no way was she standing up in front of him. Wylder gave her a look that shouted "You're weird!" as he left the room.

The clasps on the top suitcase sprang open at Addy's touch. Inside were clothes in her size! All through the comic, Nelly wore the same dress, vest and stockings. These must be her backups—identical, clean and only damp, not soggy.

Addy peeled out of her jeans and draped them over a chair beside the radiator. Maybe they'd dry out a little. Not that she could wear them again without a major patch job. She quickly yanked Nelly's dress and vest on over her T-shirt, fingers fumbling with all those buttons. Her sneakers were wet through, so she also pulled on the spare stockings and a pair of brown boots—just her size!

Addy peeked into the corridor.

"Wow!" said Wylder. "You look exactly like ... wow! You could be twins!"

Addy smoothed down her hair with her hands and adjusted the strap on her bag. Catnip had found a vest pocket big enough to hold him.

The BuzzBox mounted in the stateroom corridor crackled to life: "THE GOLD RUSH DINING CAR HAS NOW REOPENED, FOLLOWING FLOOD. ALL SERVICE IS NORMAL."

"Do you think they have burgers?" asked Wylder.

"I'm so hungry," said Addy, "I could eat an alligator."

"Ha-ha. Very funny."

"No, I'm starving too," said Addy. "But we are totally leaving as soon as we've eaten."

The dining car was damp but not sloshing wet. The booths, upholstered in fine gray leather, had been thoroughly wiped dry.

"This all happened because the comic book fell in

the pool?" said Wylder. "What if it had been a pile of dog poop?"

"Don't even say that out loud," said Addy.

A bubble-topped ServiDude rolled over to the table. Its sides were black and white, like a waiter's uniform.

"WAITER SERVIDUDE—HELP YOURSELF! HELP YOURSELF!"

"These ServiDudes are the best," said Addy. "See? Each spout or window offers up a different delicious thing to eat."

"Why is it crying?" said Wylder.

"Just leaking, I guess. From the flood."

But the stout little fellow seemed to be working just fine, serving up bowls of chicken soup with homemade egg noodles, warm crusty rolls slathered in melting butter, chocolate pudding, creamed spinach …

"Spinach?" Wylder nearly shouted. "What's wrong with you?"

"For Catnip!"

And two tall glasses of fizzing ginger ale.

"Gotta say," said Addy, "my uncle is a genius. And ServiDudes are one of his more awesome inventions."

The soup was delicious, the rolls flaky and buttery, and the spinach … well, Catnip certainly seemed happy enough. He made his way through the dish of green mush so quickly that he chomped on the serving spoon and left a perfectly formed dent of his two front teeth.

Addy held up the spoon to show Wylder. "Do you think Catnip looks bigger?"

"How would I know?" said Wylder. "Maybe. Something he ate?"

"Hmm. The last thing I actually saw him eating was"—Addy felt a swoosh of serious worry—"that boiling pot of muck in Lickpenny's lab!"

Wylder's hand, holding the last, best mouthful of chocolate pudding and whipped cream, stopped in midair. "Uh-oh," he said.

The food sat in Addy's stomach like a brick. Had Catnip eaten the catalyzer? Would it be poison to a rat? He did seem bigger, but he was jolly and energetic.

Probably fine, then.

A ServiDude rumbled over and efficiently cleared the table, loading dirty dishes onto a tray that folded into its own torso.

"We don't have a dishwasher," said Addy, "because my mom thinks it wastes energy. One of these guys would be incrediballoo."

"One hundred percent agree." Wylder tried to lick some chocolate from his lip, but only managed to smear it further.

The door of the dining car slid open, releasing a small torrent of water that splashed on the head of the VaporLink ServiDude who rolled in.

"PAGING MASTER WYLDER WALLACE," it said. "VAPOR-LINKS FOR MASTER WYLDER WALLACE."

"VaporLinks? For me?"

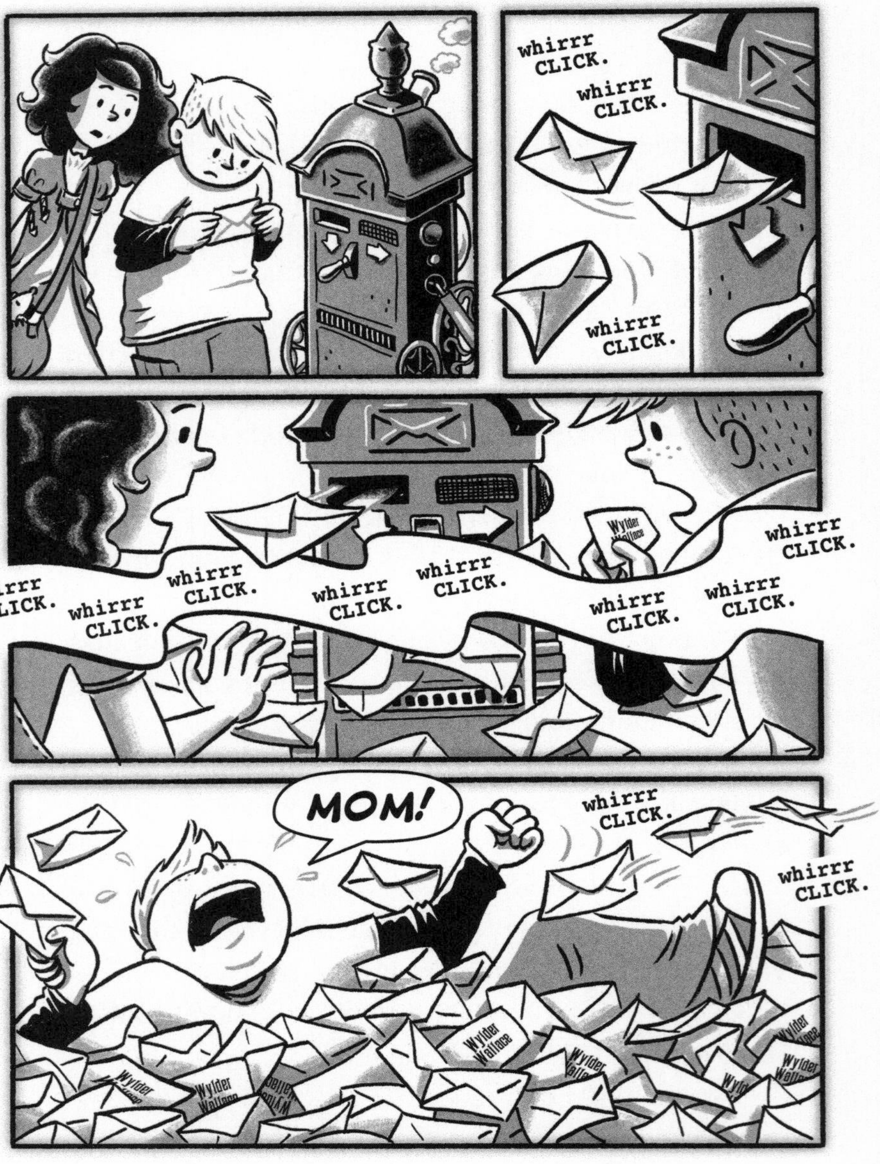
whirrr CLICK.
whirrr CLICK.
whirrr CLICK.
Wylder Wallace
whirrr CLICK.
whirrr CLICK.
whirrr CLICK.
whirrr CLICK.
whirrr CLICK.
whirrr CLICK.
whirrr CLICK.
whirrr CLICK.
MOM!
whirrr CLICK.
whirrr CLICK.
Wylder Wallace

"MASTER WYLDER WALLACE," said the ServiDude. "WOULD YOU CARE TO SEND A REPLY?"

"Would you care to shut up?" Wylder's face was red.

"It's not *his* fault!" Addy said.

"Fine. No reply," said Wylder. "You can throw these away. All of them."

"Don't you think you should at least tell her that you're alive?" asked Addy. Her own mom would want to hear that. If she ever had the time between two jobs to send one VaporLink, let alone—what? A *hundred*?

Wylder flushed. "Yeah, I guess so. Okay, how do I do this?"

"PRESS BUTTON TO RECORD REPLY," said the ServiDude.

Addy showed him the earhole.

"I'm fine," shouted Wylder. "No reception where I am." He made a "What else is there to say?" face. "Lots to tell you," he added.

Addy mimed blowing a kiss.

Wylder bugged his eyes at her, but then he said, "XX."

"No reception," said Addy. "That's a good way to put it."

"THANK YOU," said the ServiDude. "YOUR MESSAGE IS SENT."

"Let's go," said Addy. "We've wasted enough time."

"I kind of want another chocolate pudding," said Wylder.

"PAGING MISS ADDY CROWE," said the ServiDude. "VAPORLINK FOR MISS ADDY CROWE."

Addy didn't wait to be told what to do. She pulled the bot's nose. Had Uncle Vim answered her cry for help? Maybe he'd tell them exactly where to find the portal. Maybe he'd *drawn* the portal!

Snap back. **Whirrr. CLICK.**

She tore open the envelope and read the message in two seconds.

"No reply," she told the ServiDude.

"Is yours from your mom too?" asked Wylder.

Addy held it up so he could read: YOU KIDS ARE MESSING UP THE WHOLE COMIC! FUNNYBONES ON MY TAIL! GET OUT RIGHT NOW!

"Huh," said Wylder. "That's not much help."

No help at all.

14

"So nothing about *how* we should leave?" said Wylder.

"You read it. He just said to get out."

"So what are we doing?"

Addy was practically sprinting down the corridor while Wylder tried to keep up. His still-damp pants made that swishing sound as his thighs rubbed together. The train was through the mountains now. The view out the windows was flat, flat, flat. No more snowboarding for Flynn.

Thinking about Flynn gave Wylder a sick feeling. He pictured the gator's jaws closing. How could he stand to meet his hero again now? He wouldn't know how to apologize. What did you say to the guy whose life you had ruined? *Gee, sorry you tripped on my backpack and lost your hand. Good luck tying your shoes. In about seventy-five years they're going to invent Velcro, and that'll help.*

At least he and Addy were on the same side now: they both wanted to leave. He was feeling friendly toward her after the meal, and of course, she had totally saved the day by picking the comic out of the pool. He hadn't noticed before, but she looked kind of pretty in her Nelly getup.

"What are you thinking?"

"Nothing." He blushed. "Just, you know, time we went home."

"Yeah." She hurried ahead.

Time to let the story go back to normal, he thought. Give Flynn back his hand so he can save Isadora from the gator. Time to go home and explain to his mom where he's been and why he hasn't answered her hundreds of texts.

Addy plunged past a woman holding a baby.

"Mind where you're going, missy! You very nearly caused me to topple." She was still frowning as Wylder squeezed carefully past.

"Teach your friend better manners!" she told him.

"Me?" The idea of teaching Addy to behave made Wylder smile all the way to the bathroom.

Addy's theory was that the portal had to be somewhere in the bathroom, since that's where they came in. The door was locked. They waited outside. The train jiggled gently, and the food inside Wylder jiggled in sympathy.

"What's that?" He pointed to the metal sign beside the door. "WC—what does it stand for?"

"Water closet," she answered, with a hint of her old you-are-so-stupid manner. "It's another word for washroom. Uncle Vim tried out lots of new names for a washroom, but he couldn't decide which was the funniest. So he just went with the one they use in England."

"What other names did he try?"

"Silly stuff."

"Like what?"

"Ohhhh, like lavateer. I think that was one. Loo-loo lemon. Flush factory. Pipe room. What's so funny?"

Wylder was laughing so hard he leaned against the wall to stay up.

"Flush factory? Nice."

"You're as bad as Uncle Vim. By which I mean juvenile."

The door opened, and a green Janitor ServiDude came out.

"YER ROOM'S CLEAN," it announced. Wylder noticed that it had a squeegee mop circling underneath itself, so that it cleaned the floor as it rolled along.

The bathroom looked the way he remembered—a sink; a stack of towels; and the impressive toilet, a white marble throne with colored pipes twisting and branching behind it like tree roots. Flush factory, he thought.

Addy turned the handle of the closed door. "This is where we both came through from ComicFest," she said. "When I open it, we'll step together, okay?"

"And be home in Toronto."

"Yes."

"And everything will go back to normal in the comic?"

"I hope so."

"Should we ... uh, hold hands or something?" he asked.

"*Ew!*"

"Right. Course not. I don't want to either."

His cheeks felt hot.

"Ready? Set? Go!" She pushed open the door.

"Huh," said Wylder.

Addy took a deep breath. "Are you seeing what I'm seeing? The train corridor?"

"Yup." Wylder swallowed hard.

Addy closed the door. "Your turn."

CLICKETY-CLACKETY. CLICKETY-CLICKETY-CLACK.

She held out her hand. Wylder took it, warm and dry.

They said it together: "Ready, set, go!"

He opened the door for a second and slammed it shut.

"Sludge!" Addy tapped on the wall. "The portal has to be here somewhere."

"Right."

"Let's look. *Really* look."

There was no portal. They tapped on the walls, the floor, the pipes. They climbed on top of the sink to reach the ceiling. They opened everything that would open, looked inside and found nothing. They even checked the toilet tank.

"Now what?"

Addy shrugged. For once, she was out of ideas.

"So we're stuck here? We're ..." Should he say the word? "We're ... *trapped*?"

Playing inside a new world was great—as long as you could get out again. Being trapped there was a whole different thing. *Trapped*. Not a good word.

Wylder swallowed.

Addy was muttering to the rat, ducking her face into her shoulder bag.

CLICKETY-CLACK. CLICKETY-CLACK. CRUNCH-CLICK!

A new sound.

The bathroom door was opening. Addy perked right up. She put a finger to her lips, shifted the bag on her shoulder and brushed something off her cheek. She pressed her back to the wall next to the door, with Wylder opposite. There were tears on his cheek too, he realized, wiping them away.

The door opened enough for a head to peep through.

A head with stringy damp hair. Addy grabbed the hair with both hands.

"You sneak!"

"Owww!" whined Nevins. "How did you get out of jail?"

"What are you talking about?"

"Help!" he shouted.

Nevins squirmed and struggled. Addy pinned him down. She was skinny but strong.

"Helllp!"

"Shut up!" Addy covered his mouth with her hand but pulled it back in an instant. "Ew, gross! He slimed me!" She wiped her palm on her dress and stuck her elbow into Nevins's bawling mouth.

He made growling noises.

Addy glanced at Wylder. "Why did he think I was in jail?"

"Maybe he'd tell you if his mouth weren't full of elbow."

Addy grabbed the creep's wrists instead, digging in her nails. How did he know who she was?

"Lightbulb!" she said. "He thinks I'm Nelly."

"Yeah. That must be it."

"Meaning that Nelly is in jail. On the train, somewhere."

Nevins writhed around, trying to buck Addy off. The comic fell out of her pocket. Wylder jumped for it and helped her hold the bigger boy down. The train wheels were louder from floor level.

"What kind of trouble could Nelly get into?" he asked, panting a little bit.

"Who knows? She used to be a sneak and a pick-pocket, so maybe … ?"

"I thought she was supposed to be you."

"She's nothing like me."

Wylder knew better by now than to disagree.

"More plot mess," said Addy. "We just *have* to get out of here. You have the comic, right?"

15

Captain McGurk didn't seem to care that Addy's legs were not as long as his were as he yanked her along.

"Gold?" he barked. "Gold? What do you know about gold?"

"Ow!"

He had her skimpy little ear gripped between his meaty fingers, forcing her to skip and stumble along in front of him in the narrow, swaying aisle of the train. Wylder and Nevins were right behind, herded by another Red Rider named Officer McGuff. Addy squirmed, cheeks burning from the stares of tsking passengers.

And what exactly was she being accused of? The stupid captain thought she was Nelly—that much was clear. But what had Nelly done?

"How did you get from the lockup," growled McGurk, "to the second-class carriage, inside the ..."

"The flush factory?" came Wylder's voice from behind.

Not helpful, Wylder Wallace.

"Ouch!" His guard must have given him a poke.

McGurk had snatched the comic right out of Wylder's hand and stuffed it into the side pocket of his red jacket.

"Really, sir, it's just a kid's book! I swear!"

"That's what makes it suspicious. Children who *read* books are peculiar," the captain had said.

At the end of the passenger car was a smoked-glass door with gold letters that said BAGGAGE. Captain McGurk tapped on it with the toe of his huge polished boot, squishing Addy to one side.

He wrenched her ear again. Ow, that hurt! Addy vowed to tell Uncle Vim to draw this guy wandering through a meadow of poison ivy in the next issue. Make him fall into a sludge pit full of snakes. Maybe break a leg while chasing Flynn through an underground cavern full of bats ...

"Open up!" The captain's second toe-knock rattled the glass. This time the door swung open.

Stepping—or being shoved—from the bright, crowded passenger car into the long, dim space ahead was like entering a barn. Nearby shapes were easy to identify, but deepening shadows only vaguely suggested what might fill the gloom at the other end. Stacks of brassbound trunks sat along one wall, with suit-cases and mailbags and odd-shaped packages heaped in front of them. There were no windows. The main source of light came from feeble gas jets flickering up near the roof.

But one bright lamp shone in the nearby corner of the carriage. Here was a cage with iron bars from ceiling to floor. Next to it stood a Red Rider, now at full attention in the presence of his superior officer. Isadora Fortuna stood in front of him, eyes flashing and hat feathers a-tremble. Flynn Goster lurked next to her, hands behind his back, mustache drooping like wilted stalks of rhubarb.

And inside the small cell, behind a padlocked gate, Nelly Day perched on a stool, arms crossed over her chest and a scowl on her face. Her braid had come untied and her hair was a disheveled mess—just like Addy's own. Addy's heart hiccuped in her chest—wouldn't anyone's?—at the sight of herself behind prison bars.

"Huh," muttered Addy, her head twisted at an awkward angle. "Your prisoner is still in captivity. *I* am not the criminal here."

"Demon!" spat Nelly.

"Most perplexing," said the Red Rider captain. "Double the trouble."

"Captain McGurk!" cried Isadora. "The very man I wish to speak to. Your officer here"—she waved a dismissive hand—"is a slack-jawed, incompetent pinhead unable to make the simplest decision on his own. And *you*!" She stabbed the air with an angry forefinger. "Big bold leader of the Red Riders. Still bullying children, I see."

McGurk let go of Addy's ear and dismissed Officer McGuff and the other Rider. "Stand guard outside," he said.

Addy guessed that he didn't want his men to hear Isadora's scolding.

Captain McGurk cleared his throat.

Addy rubbed her ear and edged away from the policeman. Wylder's hand slid into hers and gave it a quick squeeze. She was so surprised that she squeezed back. And let go again, of course. She glanced over her shoulder to see Nevins picking at a scab on his cheek.

"Madam." McGurk tipped his hat.

Isadora cut him off with a *chhht*. "You and your men have disappointed me greatly." She was nearly as tall as the captain and looked him boldly in the eye. "Putting a small orphaned child behind lock and key!"

Nelly slumped her shoulders and put on a woebegone face.

"Unjustly accused and unceremoniously stripped of her liberty, without so much as a second voice in the matter. How dare you claim to represent *justice*?"

"Madam, you are overwrought." Captain McGurk passed a gloved hand across his sweating face, maybe trying to un-wrought himself. "Please measure your words. It is my responsibility to incarcerate all suspicious characters—for the safety of our passengers. And our cargo."

His eyes shifted. Addy followed his gaze.

Flynn.

Captain McGurk had chased Flynn Goster through two issues, and now here they were, face to face. Flynn, of course, had always triumphed, mocking the entire League of Best Western Red Riders as he made off with the jewels or treasure. But now ... Addy peered at the man who should be twirling his mustache, grinning at McGurk and saying, "Fancy meeting *me* here."

Flynn seemed shorter somehow and had no sparkle in his eyes. Addy didn't want to look, but she couldn't help it; the end of his right arm was a rounded knob of scarred skin. A stump.

"What's wrong with Flynn?" whispered Wylder. "Why is he staring at Isadora like that?"

"Staring" was an understatement. Flynn's gaze was *glued* to Isadora's face.

"Mush," said Wylder.

"Gag me," said Addy.

McGurk must have been considering the same abject character, not the hero he was used to chasing and cursing. Not the man he'd been guarding his train against. "The Gold Rush Express," he said, "is transporting—"

"Gold," said Isadora Fortuna.

"Gold," murmured Flynn. He sighed, massaging his stump with his other hand.

"A cargo of some value," said McGurk. "The girl under your protection was discovered in a previously locked stateroom—"

"A child's mistake," Isadora protested. "The room is next to our own."

"There was an eyewitness to her crime," said McGurk.

"That's me!" Nevins piped up. "I'm always looking out for my uncle."

The captain's voice swelled with authority as he ignored the brat and kept going. "I am now entirely convinced that something *very* suspicious is afoot." He pushed Addy forward into the light. "This person was apprehended in the act of taking her revenge on the witness!"

"But I trounced her!" shouted Nevins.

"You did *not*!" said Wylder.

"Silence!" barked Captain McGurk. "I see no reason other than skulduggery that two young scamps would be dressed identically—one of them prowling the fine professor's stateroom and the other one fisticuffing the professor's nephew."

Isadora examined Addy. "Call me flabbergasted," she said. "I hardly know the difference myself. Do you see her, Nelly?"

"I see her. Wearing my dress, is what I see." Nelly's eyes narrowed and her shoulders hunched.

"Uh, thanks for the loan of your clothes," said Addy. "Mine were soaked."

"Well, mine are wet too," said Nelly. "And now I don't have anything to change into! What makes you think you can paw my belongings?"

"They're *both* bad girls," said Nevins. "You can see by looking at them."

Captain McGurk jingled a key ring attached to his belt. He had trouble shifting the jacket out of the way because of a bulge in his pocket.

The comic book!

Addy bugged her eyes at Wylder, making sure he'd seen it. Oh, yeah, he was nodding hard. She mimed pulling the comic out of its spot. Wylder blinked. Would he have the nerve to steal from a policeman?

"You imprison innocent children," said Isadora, "proving that you are a chin-chuntering bullyboy. Captain McGurk, I will rouse such a protest, they'll hear it all the way to the prime minister's office."

"Madam, any further interference and I will put *you* in the lockup with your so-called innocent children!"

Addy expected Isadora to wrestle the man to the floor, but Flynn pulled her gently aside, allowing Captain McGurk to use his key to open the padlock. He pushed Addy through, closed the barred gate and locked it.

She was a prisoner.

Sludge. Double sludge. How would they ever get home?

Nelly hopped off her stool. The two girls faced each other—tousled dark hair, blue dresses and slightly grubby vests with big pockets.

"Pass me that fancy handbag you've got there," ordered McGurk.

Addy was about to object when she saw Wylder move into position behind the captain. Too bad Nelly couldn't pick the pocket for him. Wylder's eyes were glassy with concentration. What could Addy do—from behind bars—to help?

"Miss? Your handbag."

She would cause a distraction. Addy pretended to pass over her bag, but then snatched it back. Catnip was inside, along with her other stuff.

"Don't make trouble." Captain McGurk had his hand out, waiting.

"Oh, look!" Addy rummaged inside and found a Toronto subway token. She placed it on his open palm. "Not much use, since you don't have subways yet." She quickly pulled out the next thing. "Cinnaglom! My favorite chewing gum. Has gum been invented yet? This company advertises in my uncle's comic, so you could say that you owe your life to Cinnaglom!"

She knew she was blabbering, but come *on*, Wylder! Couldn't he see that she was providing cover? This was no time for second thoughts.

"How about *this*?" Addy yanked out her cell phone and waved it in the air.

"What the jiminy is *that*?" McGurk put his hand through the bars, trying to reach it.

Catnip scrambled out from the bag and up Addy's arm to her shoulder. He bared his teeth and made scary chirrup noises. McGurk pulled his fingers out of reach.

"*That* horrible thing again? I thought I'd put a bullet through its brain already. You deserve to be in jail for bringing vermin onto a public railway carriage. We'll lock you up and throw away the key."

Lightbulb!

"Hey, Flynn!" called Addy. "Where's your Zimmer? Will you get us out of here?"

She saw a tiny flash of vigor in Flynn's eyes. He looked to Isadora, lifting his stump to reveal the empty wrist that used to bear the nifty device.

Addy had watched the Zimmer being extracted from the alligator's throat, mixed up in a sludge of gnawed finger and bloody pulp.

"Isadora?" she said. "Have you still got—"

Wylder chose his moment. With a quick tug, he lifted the comic book right out of the captain's pocket. Success!

But not for long. As soon as Wylder had seized his prize, Nevins leapt in and clamped onto the comic with ten greedy fingers. He yanked it away with a shriek of triumph.

"Wylder!" Addy clenched the bars, trying to shake them loose.

Nevins darted into the shadows and scrambled up a stack of trunks on the other side of the train car, holding the precious comic book.

"Come back here!" Wylder raced after him.

Captain McGurk strode to the door to summon the guards from outside.

"Wylder!" Addy hollered. "Catch the stinking little monster!"

Nelly jumped up and down. "Hammer the squit!"

Isadora unlatched the whip from its clasp at her waist.

"Go, Wylder!" Addy yelled her throat raw. "Tackle him!"

Wylder lost his footing and bumped to the ground.

"Well, I'm jiggered!" Nevins was peering at the page in front of him. Addy could hear the scared surprise in his voice. "*I'm* in here," he said. "We all are. What *is* this thing?"

THWIP!
Too late.

16

The tumbling-in-a-dryer feeling of traveling through the comic book's pages seemed to last longer than usual. Wylder had time to wonder if it was because Nevins had turned the page instead of him or Addy. And then he was bouncing and jouncing at high speed, dense gray smoke whirling around him, making him cough. He was—it took him a minute to work this out—on the roof of the train. Good thing he was sitting down because the jouncing was pretty extreme, and he might easily have fallen off. Metal wheels squealed on metal rails. Being surprised was becoming second nature to Wylder. Forget turning the page—every time he turned *around*, something new was happening.

A gust of wind pushed the smoke away for a second, and he caught sight of Addy's face. She was near him, her eyes squinting against the smoke, the wind whipping her long dark hair. It seemed to be just the two of them up here.

"Hey," he said.

Her eyes shifted, and she nodded.

"That was crazy, huh?" He had to talk loudly over the noise of the train. Grit stung his eyes. "Do you know where we are?"

"On top of the train, wouldn't you say?"

He grinned. "Well, whatever happens next, I just want to say that we're in this together, Addy. We'll get home. I know we will."

"I'm not Addy," she said.

"What?"

"I'm not your girlfriend in the pantaloons. I'm Nelly. And I'm not going home with you. Can you stop chattering and help?"

"Hey!" Another voice, not too far away. "Who are you calling a girlfriend?"

Wylder considered jumping off the train in sheer embarrassment.

"And I'm *not* wearing pantaloons. I've got your dress on, remember?"

"Where are you?" said Nelly.

"Right here. I'm in some kind of trap."

She sounded close by. Also a little scared.

"It's around my waist," she went on.

"Me too," said Nelly. "It hurts."

The train swung into a turn. Wind carried the smoke away to the right, making everything clear for a moment. Yes, they were in a *devil* of a mess. The girls were trapped. A giant bird made entirely of metal was slumped asleep or dead in the middle of the roof. Addy and Nelly squirmed in its long talons as if gripped by oversized handcuffs.

Wait a minute. It wore a bowler hat. "Hey," said Wylder. "Doesn't this bird thing look like the robots?"

"Screaming sludge, Wylder! Help us!"

Addy was trying to wriggle free. Wylder stepped over Nelly and dropped to his knees, struggling to pry apart the talons that held Addy captive.

"Demons!" Nelly spluttered. "You're driving me mad! How did I come to be on the roof? In the grasp of a ... a ... what is this thing?"

"What *are* we doing here?" Wylder whispered.

"This thing," Addy said slowly, "is a lammergeyer."

"A what-er-geyer?"

"A kind of vulture. It's what the mechanizmos transform into. There's a scene near the end where Flynn and Krackle are fighting in the gold car. Krackle sprouts these awesome aluminum wings and carries Flynn off through the roof." Addy winced and slid a finger under the claw at her waist as if it was pinching her. "It's better on paper. Anyway, we have to get out.

Look around for a controller, Wylder. The lammergeyer needs one to make it— Oh, look! Over there!"

"Where?"

"By the trap door! It's Nevins! I bet he has a controller. Go after him and get it! And the comic!"

"Right. Of course. I'll go and ... er, *fight* him?" Wylder struggled to his feet. "Um, what is *supposed* to happen next?"

"I don't know! None of this is my uncle's story. There's no rooftop scene until we get to Toronto. Hurry, Wylder! What if Nevins comes back and wakes up this lammergeyer? It's up to you to save me."

"Me too," said Nelly.

"And Catnip," said Addy.

The rat poked his head out of her bag. His shiny pink eyes were impossible to read.

Wylder shuffled backward. "You know, I've never actually *been* in a fight before. I was always able to talk my way out of things. Oh no, wait—I'm wrong. There was this guy in my class in grade three. Smithers, his name was. He started pushing me on the playground. I took off my raincoat and—"

"Wylder!"

"Right! Sorry. I'm off now."

He took another step, and another. Turned back.

"Just to let you know, that fight didn't go very well. Smithers pushed me down, and his little dog peed on my raincoat. That's probably why I forgot about it."

Wylder heard shouts and bumping from the car below. He dropped to his hands and knees and scrambled along, his eyes peeled for the trap door.

Addy had never been on the roof of a moving train trapped in the talons of an oversized robotic bird of prey, so she couldn't compare the experience to anything else. What wacky plot twists had unfolded between where they'd been and where they were now?

Addy shifted. The steel prongs gripped tightly, causing fierce jabs of pain when she tried to ... um, breathe. The thumpity-thump of her heart was worse than the pain. Nelly's face—soot-smeared and bleary-eyed— mirrored Addy's feelings: furious frustration, cranky discomfort and flashes of lip-biting scaredness.

"I knew from the first minute that you were a demon," said Nelly. "I should have told the Red Riders and had you tossed from the train."

"Nobody wants us out of here more than I do," said Addy. Would Wylder catch up with Nevins? And would he have the guts to tackle him? If only *Wylder* was the one pinned to the roof and Addy was the one down there stomping on Nevins's face!

Something moved under her hand, and she jerked in surprise, sending a jingling shudder through the metal feathers on her captor's wings.

"Catnip!"

The rat poked his nose into Addy's free hand and then crawled up her arm to find a spot under her chin. His tail wrapped nearly the whole way around her neck.

"You hardly fit in there anymore." Addy tickled him between the ears. "Are you homesick, Catty? Like me?"

"Talking to animals is a certain sign of witchcraft," said Nelly.

Another blast of the gritty smoke enveloped them, making Addy's eyes water. Nelly began to cough, a wretched hacking that caused another metallic ripple. And then another.

Uh-oh, it wasn't the coughing that was making everything shake. Deep inside the lammergeyer's chest, Addy heard a *PRT-PRT-PRT*, like Uncle Vim's car motor turning over on a January morning. The wings trembled for a moment and then froze again.

Just then, Addy heard a croaking sigh from the side of the train—the kind of noise someone makes after hauling a heavy box up a flight of stairs ...

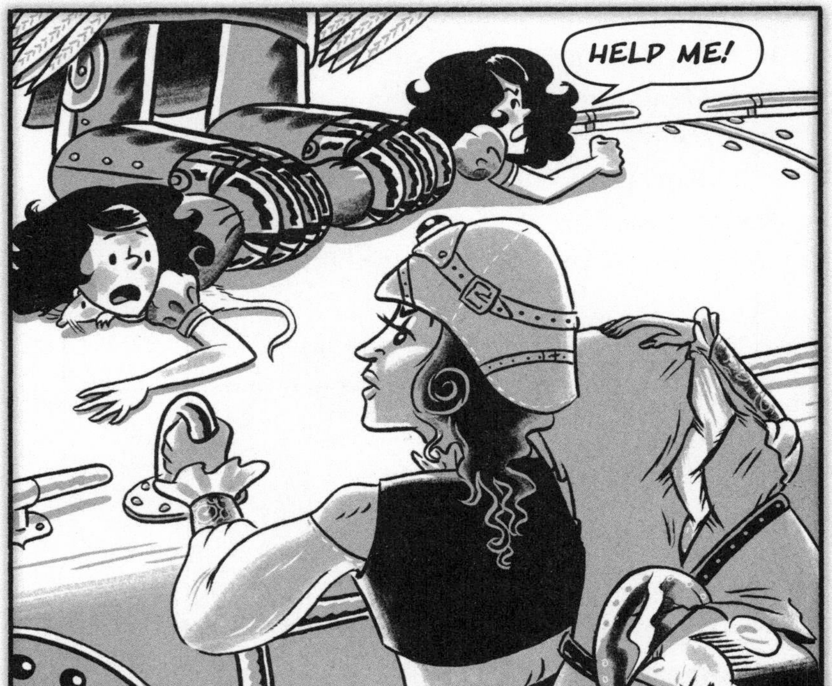
HELP ME!

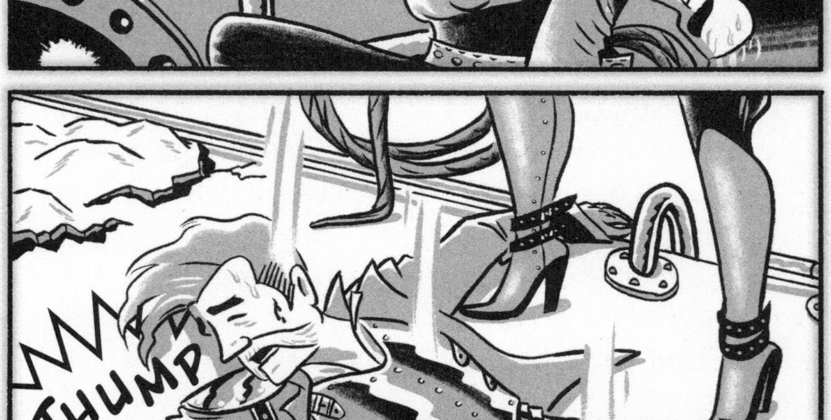
THUMP

Wylder found the trap door easily enough and climbed down a ladder. The inside of the carriage was a shambles. Upholstered seats had been ripped out of the floor and slashed. There were holes punched in the walls; windows were cracked or shattered. People were propped up in corners, bleeding and groaning and crying. It was like the aftermath of a gang fight, and this was the losing side. What had happened?

And where was Nevins?

Wylder made his way down the corridor, climbing over seats and dodging holes in the floor. He almost stepped on a Red Rider. It was Captain McGurk—red face, sideburns, pop eyes and all. He'd arrested them only minutes ago—minutes to Wylder, that is. How long had it really been? How many pages had Nevins turned?

Blood leaked from a gash on the captain's forehead, but Wylder didn't feel too sorry for him—after all, he had put Addy in jail.

"The gold!" he moaned. "They're going to get the gold!"

Before Wylder could ask any questions, he was bumped out of the way by an octopus-type ServiDude with a red cross on its domed top. Its arms ended in various tools like a thermometer, a bandage, a syringe and a saw.

"MEDICO SERVIDUDE AT YOUR SERVICE! TIME IS PRECIOUS! LIVES ARE AT STAKE!"

McGurk moaned some more. The ServiDude bent over and extended an arm with a flashlight at the end.

"SAY AHH!"

Wylder's doctor sounded friendly when she said that. This one sounded stressed and in a hurry. And a little bit crazy. The light shone into McGurk's mouth, ears and eyes, while dials and gauges on the extended arm lit up. A moment later a strip of paper emerged from a slot that looked like a mouth.

"DIAGNOSIS—CRUSHED LEFT LEG. READ RECEIPT AND CONFIRM."

Really? thought Wylder. McGurk's left leg looked okay.

"RECOMMENDED PROCEDURE—AMPUTATION! NO TIME TO WASTE! NURSE! NURSE!"

A new Medico ServiDude rolled up and snapped restraints around McGurk's wrists. The first ServiDude rotated its torso so the arm with the saw was in front.

Wylder backed away. He'd have to ask Addy if her uncle disliked doctors for some reason.

Something was happening at the end of the carriage. Wylder crouched behind a heap of broken seats. His heart was beating—well, of course it was, or he'd be dead. But right now it was beating fast and loudly.

CRASH! KER-POW!

"Snap, please stop!"

The voice was Professor Lickpenny's, but the words sounded all wrong. Wylder could not imagine the professor saying please to anyone. He shifted to get a better view.

"No more punching, Snap! You've done wonderful things this afternoon! All this lovely destruction is thanks to you. Now, be a good boy, and do what I say. Stop punching!"

"Uncle Aldous?"

"*Chht*, mosquito-brain. I'm busy!"

"But—"

"Did I or did I not tell you to close your dribbling mouth?"

That was more like the old Lickpenny—the nasty guy who yelled at his nasty nephew. The professor's hair was standing on end, showing the bald top of his head. Nevins was backed up against the window, out of reach of Snap and nearly out of Wylder's view.

The robot, standing almost as tall as the railway car, punched at the ceiling with heavy fists. **KER-POW!**

Lickpenny fiddled with the remote control. "Snap!" he shrieked. "Follow my command! When I hit the pause button, you pause, right? PAUSE! Yes! Yes, that's it!"

Snap paused, swaying slightly amid the wreckage. Lickpenny inched closer. He reached into the robot's chest pocket, then moved his nose in too. Was he sniffing? Wylder remembered Nevins attaching the siphon to Krackle's pocket back in the laboratory. The professor sniffed again.

"Nevins!" he barked. "You worm! Why does the catalyzer smell like … *onions*?"

"Uhh-uhh-nions?" Nevins sounded totally guilty. He knew something, but what? "Did you make a mistake in your formula, Uncle?"

Lickpenny turned on Nevins in a bristling fury. But as he waved his arms, he bopped Snap. Snap began to move, and the professor aimed the controller with renewed attention.

"Take a step!" he ordered, pushing one of the buttons. Snap lifted an immense leg and brought it down.

"Good boy!" the professor cried.

"Uncle," said Nevins, moving away from the wall, "when will you listen to *me*?" Nevins held a familiar roll of colored paper. Wylder felt a small pop of hope. The *comic*! Still in one piece and not too far away!

"What *about* you?" Lickpenny turned to his nephew. "Is Krackle in position?"

"Krackle won't follow orders either. Just like Snap."

"Useless maggot! Is he in lammergeyer mode?"

"The bird thing? Yes. He transformed just fine, and then stopped doing what I asked. He pinioned those girls—"

"*Girls?* Where did girls come from?"

"I thought it was only the one, but now there are two of them—both the same, like twins. Krackle has them in his claws, up on the roof. But he won't function, no matter which knobs or buttons I press."

"You crapulous cretin!"

Nevins made a choked whimper, like a bulldog with a mouthful of cake.

"It's not my fault, Uncle. I'm—"

"This is my moment, Nevins. Even Snap going berserk has worked wonders. The train is a ruin, the Red Riders are incapacitated and the gold car is *unguarded*. Go back to the roof and fly Krackle to the armored car. Go at once, you cack-handed cabbage!"

Wylder peered around the sheltering pile of wreckage. Snap was short-circuiting again, punching upward with fury. Left fist, right fist, left fist, right fist ...

KER-SMASH! KER-SMASH! CRRRRUNCH!

"No, Snap!" Lickpenny's voice rose to a shriek. "Bad boy! STOP!"

A hole in the ceiling of the carriage gaped open to the sky. Snap stamped its giant feet and swung its arms, bashing away at the ever-enlarging hole.

Wylder thought his head might pop. Addy was up there! He had to grab the comic *now*!

Nevins slunk away from his uncle. Wylder didn't stop to think. He leapt, bringing the other boy down with him, hurling his whole self at Nevins's right hand—the one holding the comic book. They tussled on the floor, Wylder trying awkwardly to punch Nevins but missing. He rolled him over, attempting to sit on him, but Nevins wriggled away. Wylder went for a headlock, but Nevins laughed and slipped out.

This fighting stuff was hard! Maybe he should have done more of it in school.

He focused on prying the comic book from between Nevins's fingers, but the other boy twisted around on the floor, kicked Wylder in the knee and scurried, like the rat he was, between the moaning passengers and away.

You blew it, Wylder Wallace! he thought. You'll never catch the little twerp. Addy will be killed by the lammer-whatsit.

But no way could he give up. Ignoring the pain knifing through his knee and the fear clutching at his heart, Wylder hobbled after Nevins. His breath came like a tennis player, in short, sweaty pants, but he kept going.

He heard a yelp of terror from the other end of the car. Seconds later, he stopped and choked back a laugh. Crazy to laugh with Addy still in trouble and his knee screaming in pain, but …

Nevins was the one yelping. He'd caught his foot in a hole where the seats had been pulled up. Medico ServiDudes were on the scene. Nevins's wrists and ankles were now in restraints. One ServiDude aimed a gigantic syringe at his backside. The thing was the size of a bicycle pump!

"THIS WON'T HURT A BIT," said the medico.

Nevins fainted.

Wylder snatched the comic out of his cuffed hand and hobbled over to the ladder that led to the roof. Wait a second! Addy had said to get the controller too.

He hobbled back and picked it right out of Nevins's front pocket.

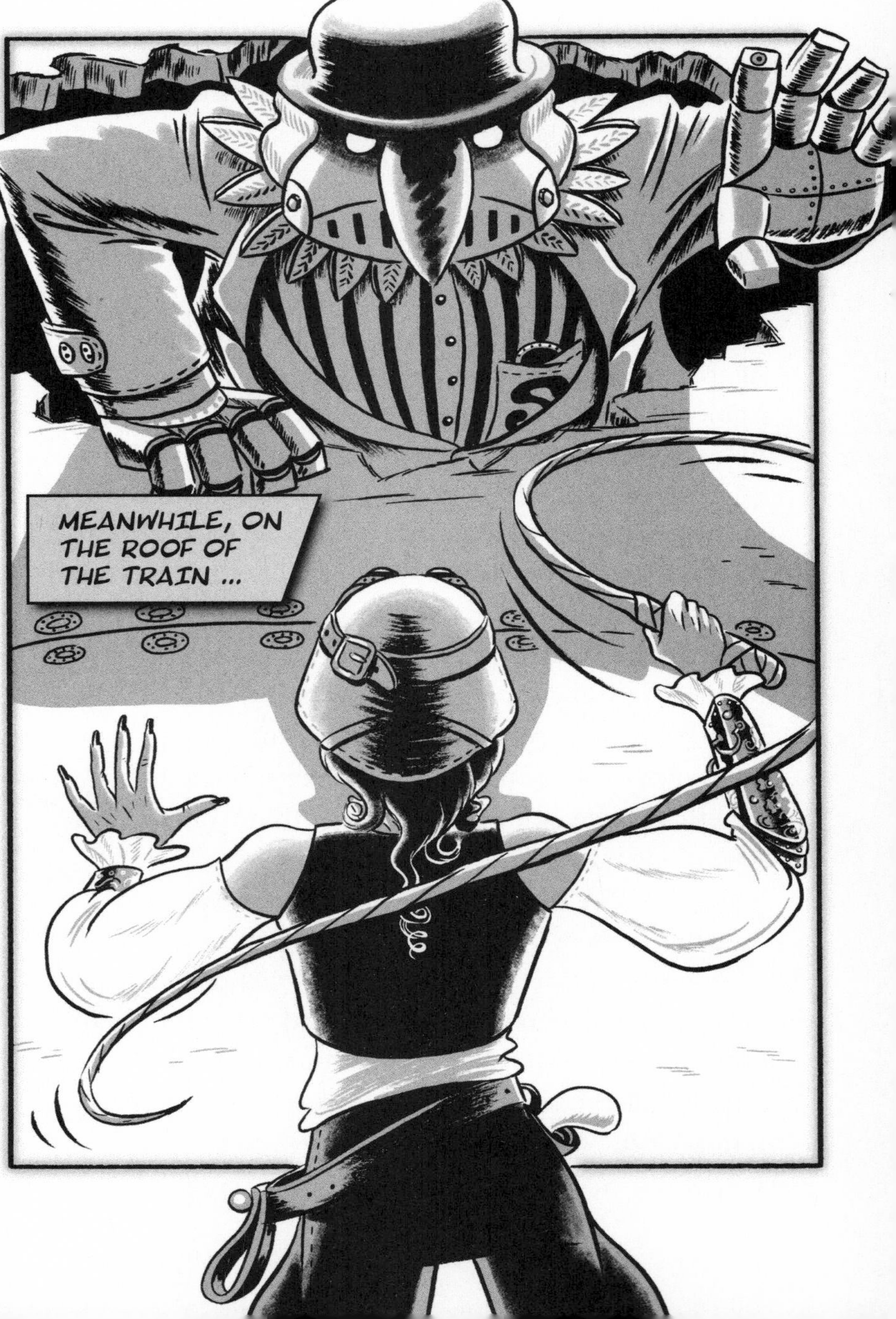
MEANWHILE, ON THE ROOF OF THE TRAIN ...

CRAAACK!

Wow, Isadora was seriously an expert with the whip.

CRAAACK!

Who knew that a robot could flinch? The crack of the whip next to Snap's jaw certainly seemed to have that effect. Or maybe the whip's whoosh was powerful enough to tip its head like that.

CRAAACK!

One of the flashing red eyes gave off a loud hiss— *PFFFT!*—and went out. The robot hauled itself all the way up, towering over Isadora. Addy would swear that its scowl turned into a smile.

How much worse could things get?

PRT–PRT–PRT, the motor inside the lammergeyer turned over again. Feathers rattled, the head clicked left to right and the talons clenched around Addy's chest.

"Ouch!" Quite a bit worse, she thought.

Where was Wylder? In trouble somewhere?

Did he get the comic book?

He wouldn't try turning the page without her, would he?

Could he?

Could Isadora win against a gigantic robot?

Was Flynn alive? Could comic book characters die if the creator didn't kill them?

How messed up was the comic book?

Where was Wylder?

"Look! Over there!" Nelly's finger jabbed toward the roof in front of them. Catnip's teeny toenails dug into Addy's neck as she peered through the shifting smoke, trying to see what had alarmed Nelly.

There was a hole in that roof too! Or ... no, a trapdoor had been flung open and a head popped out.

The very last head that Addy wished to see.

With greasy strings of hair flapping in the wind, Professor Aldous Lickpenny waved a controller. He shouted curse words at Snap and the Kracklelammergeyer, jamming his fingers on the buttons of the device with increasing fury. But neither one of the robots responded to anything its creator did.

CRACK! Isadora lashed at Snap's feet.

THUNKK. THUNKK. Snap's feet took two tremendous steps toward her, ignoring the cracking whip.

"Dispose of the enemy!" screeched Lickpenny. "Dispose of the enemy!"

PRT-PRT-PRT-PRT-PRT. Krackle-lammergeyer finally clicked into gear. **PRRRRT-PRRRRT-PRRRRT.** Its feathers shook and flexed, rattling like tin cans.

Addy's whole body felt the tug as tremendous wings stretched in readiness.

"Please, Auntie!" Nelly's voice wobbled with tears. "Don't let him—"

CRACK!

The bird tightened its grip around Addy as her brain began to spin again.

Where was Wylder?

Did he have the comic yet?

Any chance he might show up and ... help?

Isadora was too near the edge of the roof. Her whip might as well be a flyswatter for all it was doing to fend off Snap.

Lickpenny laughed like an evil owl hooting.

Snap advanced—**THUNKK, THUNKK**— denting the roof with each step.

Isadora dropped her whip and leapt to seize Flynn's sword from where it lay next to his broken body. Addy stretched her leg to poke him gently with her boot.

"Flynn!" she cried. "Wake up!"

He rolled over, eyes still closed, and flung out his handless arm at the exact right second to trip up Snap. The robot swayed, arms pinwheeling. Isadora darted forward and hurled her weight against it with a well-aimed shove. The mechanical monster fell over the side of the train in a crashing spectacle of sparks. Its powerful body must have severed the coupling, because the back half of the train jolted to a halt at once, accompanied by a deafening grinding and squealing.

"HELP!" Nelly bellowed. Addy tried to shout along with her, but not even a squeak came out.

In a sudden powerful gust, the lammergeyer flapped its wings, dispersing the smoke in a tornado of soot. Feeling a sharp wrench in her shoulder where the talon was now piercing her dress, Addy cupped protective hands around Catnip. The robotic bird lifted itself and its two identical prisoners a few inches into the air and then a few more.

"Addy!"

Wylder!

"You made it!" she cried. "Did you get the comic?"

"Got it!" He scrambled through the hole in the roof, blood spilling from his nose and Nevins's controller in his hand. He grinned and pulled the comic out of his pocket.

"So do something!"

He stuck the comic in his mouth and pointed the controller.

"The blue button! Try the blue button!"

He did.

Nothing happened.

Addy's toes dragged along the rooftop, bouncing over Flynn's body. She was practically flying!

Wylder hurled the controller away. He shrieked her name and leapt to the rescue.

Wylder concentrated on one thing: hanging on to Addy. He had the comic in his teeth and both hands on her booted ankle. His feet scraped along the roof. Man, that lammergeyer was powerful! Enough to lift all three of them? The girls were shrieking. Wylder planted his feet and braced himself. He gave a sharp jerk, and Addy came free!

She fell into his arms. He teetered, struggling for balance. Over Addy's shoulder he saw the lammergeyer sailing away, Nelly just a dot dangling from its claw. And then they were gone.

Out of sight.

He and Addy tumbled through the hole in the roof and into the car below. As he cried out, the comic fell from his mouth and fluttered to the floor.

18

Wylder knew where he was before he opened his eyes.

The air *smelled* familiar. Chemicals, air-conditioning, fast food. He made out pizza and barbecue sauce and even—could it be?—onion rings.

Wylder was lying on his back. He opened one eye to confirm what his nose had told him, and saw … Flynn's mustache. But it was a picture, not the real thing. He opened both eyes wide. Yup! He lay on the carpet in a corridor of the Toronto Convention Centre, next to the big cardboard train display for Viminy Crowe's comic book.

Wylder sat up feeling dizzy, the way you do after a long nap in the middle of the afternoon. But his trip to the world of the comic had not been a dream. No, not at all. His pants were still slightly damp. No backpack, of course. He'd left it back in Florida, pages and pages ago.

Addy lay beside him, still wearing Nelly's clothes— the puffy-sleeve dress, the vest with all the pockets and the lace-up boots.

Wylder let out a whoop of relief. He'd found the portal—or it had found them! They'd crossed over and made it home! Safe and sound.

"Addy! Hey, Addy!"

He shook her shoulder. She stirred, not quite waking up yet. Her hair fell away from her face, revealing a puzzled frown as she slept. Tuckered out from flying through the smoky sky and being rescued, eh? He and Salad Girl had come a long way.

Wylder rolled over to find the comic book on the floor beside them, open at the last page.

AND RIGHT THERE, ON THE INSIDE BACK COVER ...

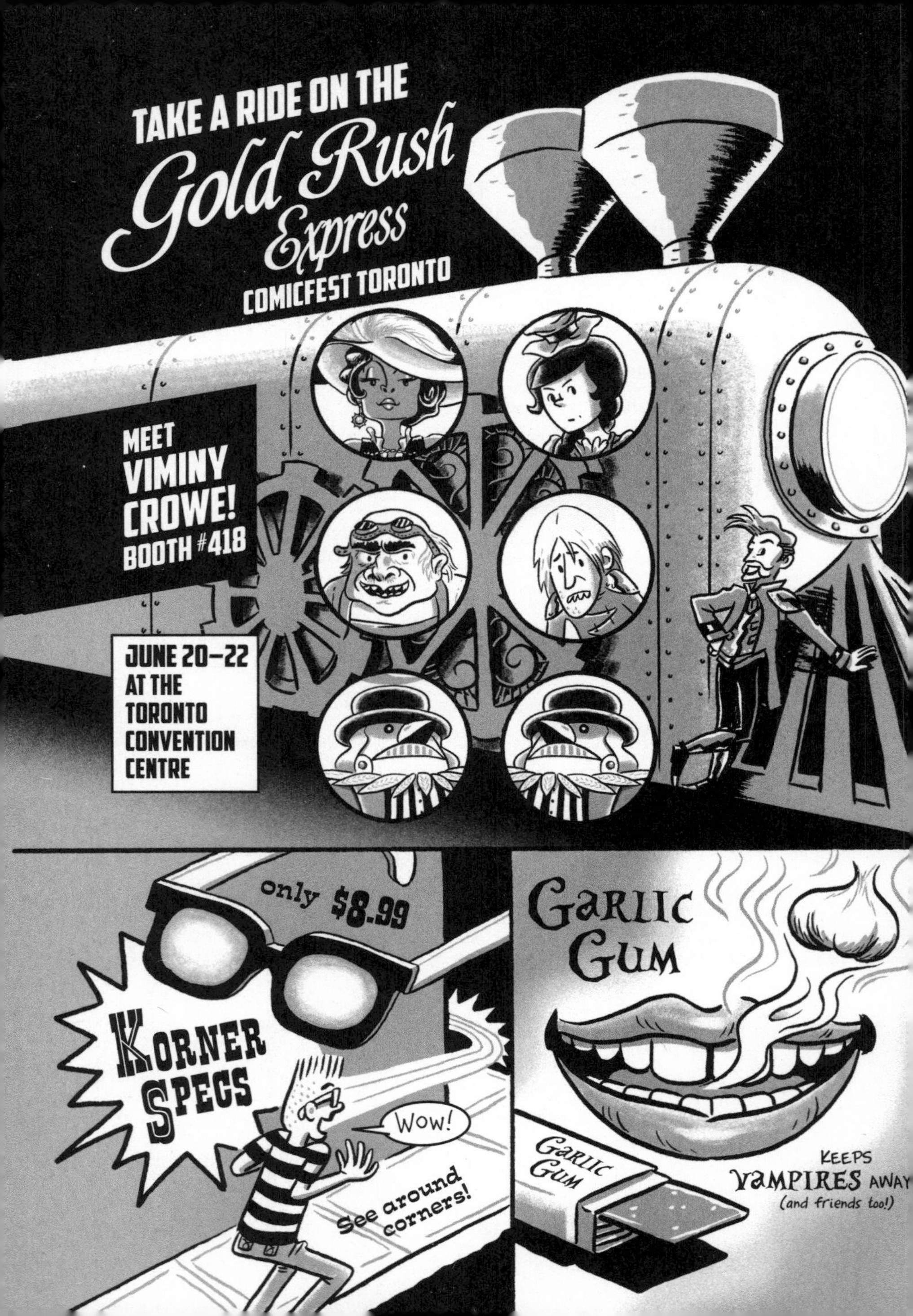
TAKE A RIDE ON THE
Gold Rush
Express
COMICFEST TORONTO
MEET
VIMINY
CROWE!
BOOTH #418
JUNE 20–22
AT THE
TORONTO
CONVENTION
CENTRE
only $8.99
KORNER
SPECS
WOW!
See around corners!
GARLIC
GUM
GARLIC
GUM
KEEPS
VAMPIRES AWAY
(and friends too!)

Take a ride? Yeah. Wylder remembered the swirling smoke, his determined leap into space, yanking on Addy's foot, feeling himself lifted into the air … that was a ride, all right.

The comic book had dropped out of his mouth when they fell. Did all the pages get turned to expose the inside back cover, where this ad was? Is that how they got home? Must be. Turning the pages had carried them *through* the comic, and it also got them *out* of the comic. The way back from the comic was different from the way in.

It didn't matter now. He was home. Today's adventure had been amazing, but it was over. He stood up and stuffed the comic in his back pocket.

How *normal* everything looked—as if he'd been here all day and never gone anywhere at all. The same booths, crowds and convention babble. People in their pretend capes and goggles and swords. What would they say if they knew that he had just *lived* this kind of adventure?

"Addy, come on! Get up!"

She groaned and rolled over onto her other side.

A security guard told them to move. "You can't sleep in the middle of ComicFest." The embroidered name badge on his uniform said ERNIE.

He helped Wylder to get Addy standing up.

"Oh, you're one of those actor people," Ernie said to her. "Who are you supposed to be? Wait a second!"

His eyes went to the cardboard train and then back to Addy.

"That's you! She's ..."

Beside the blown-up image of Flynn were smaller pictures of Isadora, Lickpenny, Nevins, the robots—and Nelly.

Wylder watched the guard's face. The man's eyebrows shot up. He was clearly having a lightbulb moment.

"You're that girl, aren't you?" he said. "Viminy Crowe's niece? Hey, he's looking for you. Making a big fuss. Did you know that?"

Addy blinked at Wylder. She didn't look like she knew anything.

"Come with me to the artists' lounge," said Ernie. "I saw your uncle there a while ago."

Wylder had planned to head straight home. His mom must be going a little cuckoo by now. But it seemed like Addy needed him. She leaned against him as they went up the escalator. He put his arm around her. It was embarrassing, but he didn't mind. And this was a chance to meet Viminy Crowe.

Addy's uncle Vim bounded across the lounge in three strides, dropped his big portfolio case and kneeled down to hug Addy, who had flopped onto a couch.

Vim was tall and thin, with arms and legs like a stick insect's. His eyes flashed behind thick, goggly glasses. He had a cloud of untidy dark hair, which followed him around like it was trying to catch up with him and never quite succeeding. His hands moved constantly, as if he were conducting his own life and the tempo was marked "As fast as you can play!"

He bounced up to shake Wylder's hand in both of his. "My boy, my boy!"

Wylder didn't even mind when the man let go of his hands and *hugged* him! A complete stranger and it felt *good*!

"Thank you, Ernie! An utterly heroical rescue!"

Viminy Crowe gently shooed the grinning security guard out of the room and closed the door. He bounded back over to where his niece lay with her eyes shut.

"She's a bit zonked," said Wylder. "She'll be okay in a minute, though, won't you, Addy? It takes a bit out of you, the page-turn." Listen to him, Wylder Wallace, the expert, telling Viminy Crowe how things were!

"Maybe some water?" he said.

"Yes! Get her something to drink, Wylder Wallace!" Viminy Crowe knelt beside the couch. "I jumped nearly out of my skin," he said, "when I got Addy's text and checked my own sample copy. There you both were on the train! Talking to Isadora Fortuna! It must have been magic, but what kind? How did you get in?"

"There was some kind of portal through the, uh, door to the, uh … ladies' room." Wylder gave him a bottle of water from the counter.

"Incrediballoo." Viminy unscrewed the cap and took a swig.

"But that worked only one way—*into* the comic. I think the way back must have something to do with the big display. That's where we came out."

He explained about landing next to the cardboard Gold Rush Express and seeing the advertisement on the back page of the comic.

"Consider me gobsmacked," said Addy's uncle. But he didn't stay gobsmacked for long. "That lammergeyer was Addy's idea—did she tell you that? We must have drawn eighty hundred versions till we got it just right. And not only the mechanizmos! Everything! The whole comic! And there you were, actually *inside*! Zipping around, fighting and eating and talking, teleporting from page to page. Living between two worlds. Words fail me—they absolutely fail me."

No, they don't, thought Wylder. He had never met anyone who talked so much or so quickly. Wylder was quite a talker himself, but getting a word in with Viminy Crowe was like interrupting a blizzard.

Vim tipped the water bottle and swallowed.

"Addy? Want some?" But she was dozing and not paying attention. He patted her arm and stood up.

"All afternoon I've been *riveted* by your adventure," he said. "Chewed up with worry, of course, but also ... chartreuse with envy! You have to tell me what it's like *inside*. I want to know *everything*. Do the ServiDudes make a noise when they move? Does the smoke from the engine smell like smoke? Is the sun warm? And Isadora ... is she beautiful? Did you try flushing the toilet? Was the alligator as big as it looks? Was it real? *Is the comic real?*"

He stopped talking and stared at Wylder. His eyes were intense and concentrated, full of longing.

"It's, uh, pretty real."

Wylder wasn't used to adults like Viminy Crowe. Mom wasn't enthusiastic about anything, except maybe worrying about how Wylder could fall in a hole or get lost. Dad hardly opened his mouth at all. The two weeks Wylder spent with him every summer were practically silent, except for the TV. Now Wylder wanted to say more about the Gold Rush Express, to give details, to somehow let Viminy Crowe know just how much he admired him and the world he had created. But the words were slow to come.

"Actually, it's so real you forget it's not real," he said at last. "It's ... *incrediballoo*."

A big guy with a beard and a portfolio case came into the room to get his jacket. He nodded at Vim. "Back tomorrow," he said. "Another day, another twenty thousand comic book crazies."

An announcement came over the loudspeaker. Ghost Kids Academy had giveaways galore. Hurry on over to booth number 781. Hurry, hurry. Last chance today.

Addy sat up.

Her uncle rushed over and took her hand. "You're awake, Addy-pie! Fantastico! You're here in the artists' lounge at ComicFest. You just missed Fred Ickenham, grumpy as ever. It is profundamentally great that you are sitting up. We were fretting about you, weren't we, Wylder Wallace? Do you want something to eat or drink?

Let me say that you look fantabuloso! The Nelly gear suits you! But how are you *feeling*?"

She looked him up and down and then slowly turned her body around, taking in the room. She frowned when she got to Wylder.

"You," she said.

"Yes me," he said. "Wylder. Remember?"

Come on, Addy—snap out of it!

Vim nudged her with the water bottle and she finally took a long drink. She coughed at first, took another big gulp and coughed some more before starting to swallow normally. It was like she was learning to drink for the first time.

Addy gazed up at the buzzing fluorescent lights while she finished the water. When she'd had enough, she handed the bottle back to her uncle and wiped her mouth with her hand. She got up and walked carefully to the old-fashioned gumball dispenser by the far wall. It was as if she was still asleep, thought Wylder. Groggy and slow. It reminded him of the time he went on the Whirligig at Wonderland. He'd had to lie down all the way home in the taxi. Mom had been convinced he was going to die.

"Should we take her to the doctor?" he said. "She's usually more ..." How could he put it? 'Lively' would be the polite thing to say.

Viminy Crowe turned his hands palm up in an I-don't-know gesture. "The doctor scenario has been playing in my brain," he said. "But I keep stuttering at the part where we'd have to tell what happened. A lie wouldn't be helpful, and the doctor wouldn't believe the truth. Even we don't know for sure what happened! At least she's on her feet now. Hang on a second."

His phone was ringing. He checked the caller's name. "I should take this. I've been dodging these fellows for hours." He swiped his thumb over the screen.

"Hello, Magnus!" said Vim. "How are you and all the other FunnyBones? I'm sorry I couldn't talk before. My niece was missing, but she's back now. Your timing is perfecto!"

Wylder went over to the gumball machine. You didn't need money to make it work—you just turned the handle. Addy was on her third or fourth gumball. Her jaw bulged.

"These are *delicious*!" she said, slurping.

He tried one. They were good, but they were just gumballs. Poor old Addy, he thought. She wasn't a candy girl before. It was all lettuce and stuff like that ...

Lettuce! Wylder took a quick gulp of air and scanned the room. Addy didn't have her bag. She must have left it on the train. The bag itself didn't matter—after all, he didn't have his backpack either—but how had she forgotten about *the rat inside*?

He took the comic out of his pocket. Would he be able to spot Addy's bag wherever she'd dropped it? Or had their stuff—and Catnip—disappeared when the comic went back to its original story? He had a moment of ... well, *something* at the idea of Catnip disappearing. A little shiver, for sure. He'd never liked the rat, but

Addy sure did. And it was a *living* thing, after all.

Wylder glanced at the cover of the comic and felt a ping behind his eyeballs. It was not a gulp moment or a shiver moment. It was a "Holy crap!" moment.

He gasped out loud.

"Addy!"

She didn't turn around. He thrust the comic at her.

"Look at *that*!"

Her uncle came over with a smile on his face.

"Relief is positively surging through my veins!" he said. "That was Magnus Snayle from FunnyBones Comics on the phone just now. The new issue of the comic—all ten thousand copies—is stuck at the train station, which means that Magnus hasn't seen it yet. Isn't that a wonderful piece of luck?"

Addy frowned down at the cover.

Wylder wondered why she wasn't jumping up and down in horror. Didn't she realize what was going on?

He knew. He opened his mouth to tell Viminy Crowe the bad news, but the man steamrolled right over him.

"All morning I've been yelling about those missing comics. Funny, isn't it? If they had arrived on schedule, it would have been catastrophonous! A 19th-century train story with two modern kids in it? Running around with blue jeans and cell phones? Ridiculoso! Fans would jeer! They'd never buy another Flynn Goster comic—the hero might as well be dead. Me too. The FunnyBones people would drop me like an old penny.

My career would be over, and I'd be back to selling soap for a living. Have you ever sold soap, Wylder Wallace?"

"Huh? No," said Wylder. "And I hope I never have to. But—"

"It's not easy. Trying to convince a grocery store manager that *your* lathery skin-softening product is beyond all others—the one that belongs on the shelf at eye level. Placement is key, you know."

"I'm sure you're right, sir. But listen, there's a big problem. The comic—"

"I've been dodging the FunnyBones' phone calls all morning. Now that you two have returned and everything in the comic is cleared up, I can finally face them. So I'm off to meet—"

"Mr. Crowe!" Wylder's shout caused Vim to rear back like a startled horse.

"Sorry, have I been talking a lot? I suppose I have. I do that when I get excited. My sister, Pippa—that's Addy's mother, a lovely lady, you must meet her—rolls her eyes, and—"

"Show him, Addy!"

She held up the comic, as if saying, "You mean this?"

Wylder grabbed it out of her hand. Viminy Crowe's glasses had slipped down his nose. He slid them back up.

"What's wrong, Wylder Wallace?"

Wylder held out his copy—Addy's copy—of the comic book.

"Everything."

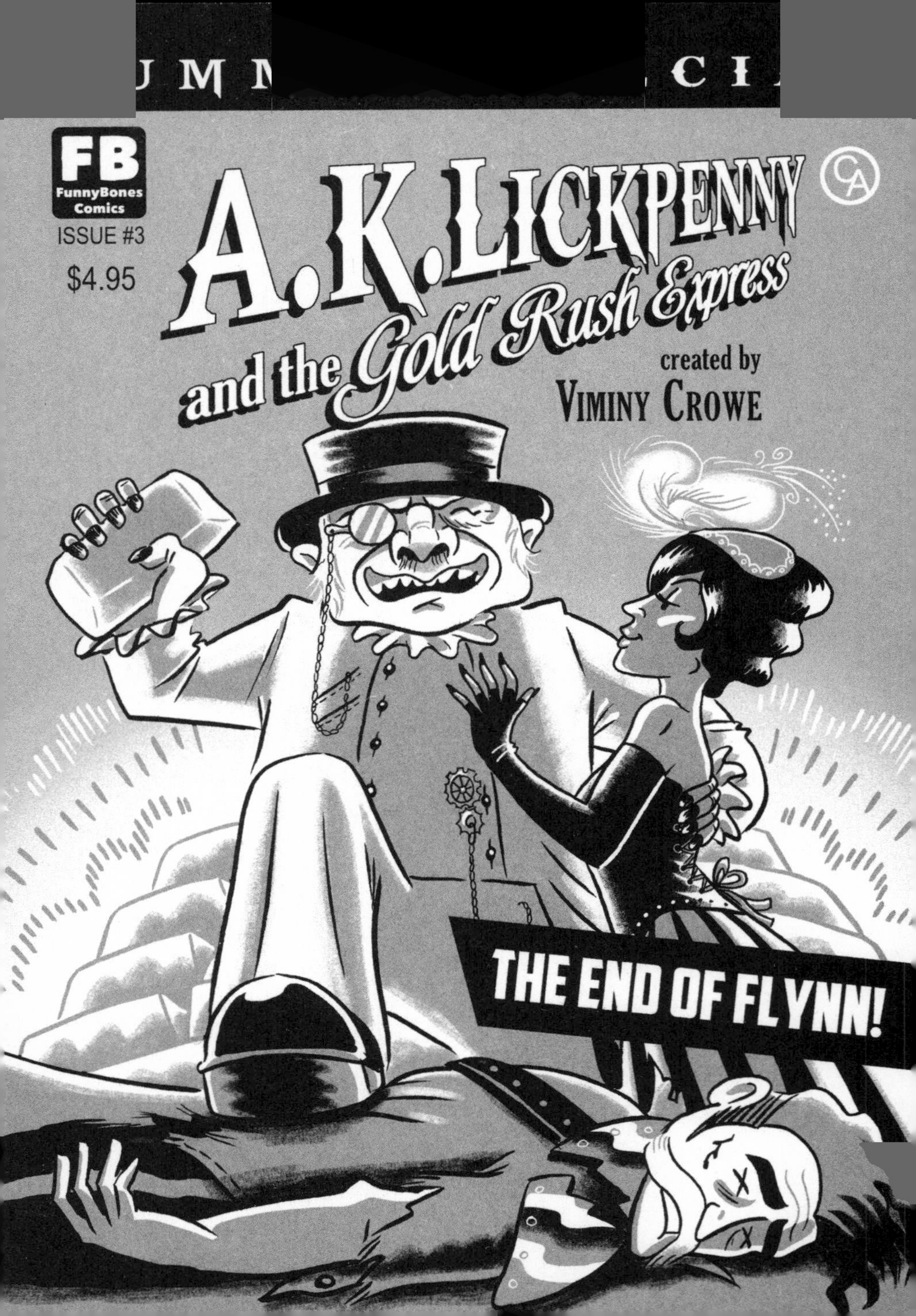
FB
FunnyBones Comics
ISSUE #3
$4.95
A.K. LICKPENNY
and the Gold Rush Express
created by
VIMINY CROWE
THE END OF FLYNN!

19

Viminy Crowe's mouth opened and closed with no sound coming out. For a few seconds, they stared, as if under a spell, at the comic in Wylder's outstretched hand. Vim compared his copy to Wylder's. They were the same. And both were wrong.

And then Vim started to hop.

Seriously. He nodded his head a few times, took a deep breath and began to hop from one foot to the other. Not very high, just an inch or so off the ground. More like skipping, really. He wore old-time running shoes, with black canvas tops and white rubber soles. His baggy cardigan flapped behind him as he skip-hopped his way around the room like a gray grasshopper.

Addy edged backward until she was next to the window. Probably dying of mortification, thought Wylder.

"Well, I am jiggered," said Vim. "Bottled, mottled and spun dry. This is a shocker, all right. But the key to surviving a shock is not to panic. Are you panicking, Addy? Are you panicking, Wylder Wallace?"

"Uh, no, sir," said Wylder.

"Good. Me neither. No panic here. I mistakenly presumed—when you two came out of the comic—that it would go back to normal. Ha! Lesson learned. Do not presume. Oh, and by the way, you don't have to call me sir. Makes me feel old. Uncle Vim will do just fine."

He joined Addy near the big window. The curtains in front were so thin you could see through them into the street.

Skip, skip, skip.

He was in great shape—not even breathing hard. His glasses slid up and down his nose, and his hair flopped around his head.

"Something alien entered the comic today. Something that shouldn't be there."

"Us."

"Right you are, Wylder Wallace. And you two affected the way the comic behaved."

He changed his pattern, hopping twice on the left foot, once on the right.

"Here's what I think is going on," he said. "When

Addy was a baby, she swallowed a button that looked like a chocolate caramel. The button gave Addy a tummy ache until she got rid of it—if you know what I mean. And then she was fine. I think *that*'s what's happening to the comic now."

Ew.

"You mean *we* were like Addy's button, making the comic sick?"

"Absolutissimo. Foreign bodies—viruses—messing up the story. *You*'re out, but some part of you is still inside, infecting the comic. What would that be?"

"My backpack," said Wylder.

"You had a backpack? Well, then, maybe that's it. The culprit, so to speak."

Addy stared through the thin curtains at the traffic going by.

Wylder wondered if he should mention Catnip. Had Addy forgotten him? Just then, Addy swallowed her gum. She bent over, coughing. When she finished, she took a hanky out of her vest pocket and wiped her mouth and eyes.

Uncle Vim skip-hopped to get her a drink of water, but he had to walk normally to carry it back so there'd be no sloshing.

"You are a cuckoo bird," Addy told her uncle.

"Have you been carrying a handkerchief all day?" Wylder asked.

"*You* are another one," she said to him.

"First things first," said Uncle Vim. "You must locate your impedimenta."

"Good plan," said Wylder. "What's *impedimenta*?"

"Stuff," said Uncle Vim. "Stuff you carry—stuff that gets in the way. You two should look through the comic and see where your stuff has ended up. We'll devise a plan when I get back. I have to see the FunnyBones people. It's ironic—I spent the morning yelling at Magnus Snayle to find the ten thousand copies of the comic so we could sell them. Now it would be positively cataclysmatical if they went on sale. What story will I tell him? The truth won't work."

His phone rang. He stopped hopping and shook himself all over like a dog. "Here's timing," he said. "Magnus Snayle himself."

Vim punched a button. "I want to speak to you, Magnus," he said. "I'm on my way to the booth. Don't leave or something horrible will happen."

He put away the phone. "The key to talking with presidents is confidence. Never let them know how much trouble you're in. I have to keep the FunnyBones people away from the train station. That's my job. Yours is to find your stuff."

He was practically fizzing with energy. Didn't he ever get tired? It made Wylder tired just to watch him.

"You thought of all this when you were skipping around?" asked Wylder.

"Skipping increases the heart rate and the flow of

blood to the brain. It's like instant IQ. I urge you to try it!"

Uncle Vim dashed over to give Addy a good-bye hug, saluted and swirled out the door, catching the tail of his sweater. He freed himself with difficulty.

"Until we meet again!" he said and finally disappeared.

Wylder sank onto the couch and closed his eyes, just for a second. The Crowes were an exhausting clan, he decided.

The loudspeaker announced that there was half an hour to closing. Doors would open again tomorrow morning at 8:30. Then Wylder heard his name.

He went rigid, as if he'd been electrocuted.

"Wylder Wallace, please report to the information booth. This is an emergency message for Wylder Wallace."

"What *is* that?" Addy looked up. "Who's calling you on the BuzzBox?"

BuzzBox. Ha-ha.

"My mother," he said. Only his mother would use a loudspeaker to track him down.

By now she would have sent about a thousand text messages to the cell phone in his backpack. Should he find a pay phone? Call her and try to explain? Would she understand? Not a chance. The moment she heard his voice, she would ground him for the rest of the millennium. Uncle Vim and Addy needed him. He couldn't go home now, especially when Uncle Vim expected him to help.

But ignoring his mom?

"Wylder Wallace! Please report to the information booth immediately."

He'd have to go. Addy was a friend, and Uncle Vim was super cool, but Mom was Mom. He opened the tattered comic book to the first page and called Addy over.

"You'll have to do this without me," he said. "I'm really sorry but I have to go, so it's up to you."

"Cut it out, now," she said. "The old mug is gone."

"The what?" He stared at her closely. "What mug? What are you talking about?"

"You know, the old geezer." She made a squinty face.

A horrible suspicion grew inside Wylder. No, it didn't *grow*—it had been there all along.

"Addy?" he whispered. "Where's Catnip?"

"Who?"

Her eyes were wrong. The tilt of her mouth was wrong. *She* was wrong.

"Your rat."

"Listen, you squit. I don't know what the game is, but I'm on to you. You're going to shake down this Uncle Vim fellow? That's fine by me, but don't be thinking you can pull the wool over *my* eyes. I'll be Addy if you want, but I get my cut. I'm fly, I am."

"You're ... *Nelly.*"

"And what if I am?"

Wylder felt as if his head was full of bells. He couldn't

hear himself think for the ringing. All the noise was screaming one dreadful fact.

He'd grabbed the wrong girl.

He remembered the dizzying smoke and the lammergeyer, with two girls in its talons. Krackle was a hideous mechanizmo—and so strong! It had been able to lift all three of them into the air—Nelly and Addy, plus Wylder clutching on to her.

Except it wasn't Addy. It was Nelly he'd dragged through the portal, and here she was, as sharp and scheming as ever. *And totally out of place!*

But if this was Nelly …

Oh no! No, no, *no!*

Wylder paged through the comic, looking for the scene on the train roof, afraid of what he might find. He didn't pause even when there was a clanking bump from the loudspeaker and another voice came over the air.

"Wylder Wesley Wallace, this is your mother speaking. You need to come here right this minute! Do you hear me? Do you hear me?"

His mother was in the building! But that wasn't the worst thing. Wylder stared in horror.

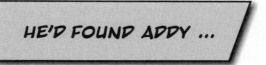

HE'D FOUND ADDY …

20

"WYLD*ERRRRrrr*!"

Addy screamed his name into the smoky wind, but it was no use. He had yanked free the wrong girl and—*POOF!*—disappeared into thick air while Addy was carried higher and higher into the sky.

The lammergeyer, being a mechanizmo, did not seem perturbed that half its load had suddenly evaporated. But Addy, being human, was choking on her own desperate screaming—*and* the sooty train smoke. And she was way higher up than a person should be without a helmet and a safety net.

VVVRRRKKK! The bird dropped suddenly, taking Addy's stomach with it. ***FWAP-CLANK-FWAP!*** It

zigzagged upward and then sideways, and then—
VVVRRRKKK!—executed another crazy drop.

Even if Addy closed her eyes to pretend this wasn't happening, one dismal thing was true: stupid sludge-face Wylder had grabbed Nelly instead of her.

And she was now alone.

Oh, except for Catnip, whose claws were digging in so deeply that Addy was certain she had blood trickling down her neck. The **FWAP-CLANK-FWAP** of wings was background noise to the string of sludge-related curse words in Addy's head. Why had Uncle Vim created a place where things went wrong on every page, and there was *no way out*? What page was Wylder on? What wrong thing was happening where he was? If the story had kids warping it in two different directions, how would they ever fix it for Uncle Vim?

Worse, Wylder had the comic book! So what would happen to Addy? It was like sitting in a car with someone who is driving the wrong way. Or watching TV when someone else has the clicker.

Sludge.

Think on your feet, Addy told herself. But what if your feet weren't touching the ground?

What if your dad had a girlfriend, and your mom worked too much, and your uncle needed more care than a little kid, and this person who you'd just met held your life between his teeth but had disappeared and ... *whoa!*

They flew above the smoke, the bird circling back over the scene below. Addy's heart kicked her ribs. It was like looking out the window of an airplane. Oh! So this is what people meant by a bird's-eye view!

From up here, Addy saw why the back part of the train had lurched to a halt on the track just before she'd been scooped into the air. Isadora and Flynn had toppled Snap from the roof. His fall had smashed the coupling between the cars, releasing the front carriages to continue the journey. The engine, the coal car, the flatbed with Isadora's folded balloon, the armored car holding the gold and the row of fancy staterooms were all steaming away, onward into the late afternoon.

Professor Lickpenny jumped up and down on the roof of the moving train, waving his arms with the controller held high. Addy's captor kept swooping in lazy circles, ignoring its master.

Snap's crushed and broken body lay under the gleaming wheels of the stalled passenger car. A leg stuck out in one direction, and a hand sat by itself in the grass, palm open to the sky. Addy watched Isadora climb to the ground to inspect the damage. Nasty Nevins was hopping perilously on the roof, hollering as his uncle got carried away on the front half of the train.

Uh-oh.

Like a flickering light with a bad connection that suddenly clicks on, the lammergeyer began to fly in a

straight line toward Lickpenny. The wings beat faster—
FWAP-FWAP-FWAP. The talons tightened, pinching her stomach. With a few strong wingstrokes and a downward plunge, the lammergeyer hit the shaking roof of the moving train. Addy felt like an offering, a tasty morsel brought to Lickpenny's feet.

"Finally!" snapped the professor. "What's *wrong* with you? First Snap goes awry and now you!" Lickpenny reached over Addy's head to smack the lammergeyer's beak with the controller. As if hitting a metal robot would have any effect. It's not like training a dog. Or a rat.

Catnip was smart enough to slip down Addy's arm into her big vest pocket before Lickpenny noticed him. If Addy was scared, imagine how poor little ratkins must feel! Well, fatty ratkins, actually. Addy put her hand gently over his quivering back. My only friend is a rat, she thought. But I'm lucky to have him. Better to face a crisis with a rat than with no one.

"And *you!*" Lickpenny's face came *waaay* too close. "You break into my laboratory, you break into my stateroom and you destroy my magnificent Snap. But now! I have you in my clutches, you ... you sneaky, smutty-faced spy!"

"None of the above," said Addy. She couldn't quite breathe. Not surprising, considering the grip of metal talons around her middle. And the fact that Lickpenny's mouth had never met a toothbrush.

"You don't scare me one bit!" said Addy. If only saying it out loud would make it true. She was more scared than she'd ever been.

"Ha!" Full blast of nasty breath. Lickpenny's eyebrows pointed down in a dark *V* over his nose. Addy remembered Uncle Vim's drawing lessons: "Look what you can do by changing the angle of a line. Up for a smile! Down for a frown!"

Lickpenny reached out and poked her cheek with a gnarly finger.

"Bug off!" Addy whacked his hand away. "Don't touch me, you slud—"

"You are a brazen chit. But your skin ... your s-s-skin ..." He chuckled, a rank wheeze. "Yes, your skin will be a splendid addition to my next lovely mechanizmo. Krackle and Snap have a sister in the making. Poppy needs only a few more patches on her neck and cheeks. Yours will do very nicely indeed."

Addy's hands went up to protect her face, so he pinched her arm instead.

"Stop it!" She tried to kick him, but that made the lammergeyer's claws dig deeper into her stomach. Her lungs were being squeezed, and her heart was bruised from banging so hard.

"Ha-ha!" Lickpenny shuffled his feet in a little dance and jabbed her, grinning with yellow teeth. "I will complete my splendid Poppy and torment Isadora Fortuna with the same slice of the knife! What will that stroppy show-off do when her ward disappears, eh? *Eh?*"

Of course! He thought Addy was Nelly.

"But before all that, I will possess the GOLD!" He jabbed her again. "I suppose Isadora and Flynn Goster are working together to steal the riches on this train? Ha! Romantic fools!"

Addy's panic that he might actually be able to peel her skin from her face was weirdly accompanied by a quiver of pride that he was a truly terrible—and therefore excellent—villain. Uncle Vim, with Addy as consultant, had created this creep!

He leaned in close again, blowing foul puffs with every word. "Only *I*, Aldous K. Lickpenny, am brilliant enough to have conceived of a plan to foil the Red Rider guards and the Majesty Bank! I may have lost my beautiful Snap, but his final sacrifice of stopping the train was an ingenious one. Flynn Goster and that brazen woman are trapped on a useless vehicle, while I sail away with the gold! You may wonder how I can carry off a half-ton of gold bricks, but I—"

Addy rolled her eyes. "Yeah, yeah," she said. "You have an almighty lammergeyer and a net of filigreed tungsten strong enough to carry the weight of the whole stash of gold. I know the plan."

Since she'd helped Uncle Vim devise it.

Lickpenny's face slowly turned violet as his eyes crossed and spittle foamed along his lips. "How can you know this? Did Nevins tell you? I shall cut out his tongue!"

Lickpenny moved the lever on his controller back and forth. Nothing happened. Not so much as a *PRT-PRT* from inside the lammergeyer. The train rattled along while the robot bird sat like a bag of old auto parts. Lickpenny ground his teeth together in fury.

"First, Snap!" he barked. "And now Krackle too!" He glared at Addy. "I smell sabotage! This must be *your* doing!"

"You're blaming *me* because Tweety Bird doesn't do what you want?"

"Perhaps when you sneaked into my laboratory you fiddled with the wires? Or tainted the catalyzer? No doubt hoping to diminish my powers by corrupting my magnificent mechanizmos."

Uh, *no*. Addy hadn't done any of those things. She had a memory flash of Catnip perched on the rim of the pot of bubbling gloop. Had the rat peed in there, by some lucky chance?

"I. Shall. Not. Be. Thwarted!" railed Lickpenny. "Krackle may be having a moody morning, but he has brought me a fine specimen of youthful skin."

"Too bad for you," said Addy. "Your plan was a pretty good one, but it's going to fail."

"How dare you! Be silent!"

Lickpenny cracked her on the head with the controller, which actually hurt. A *lot*. She couldn't help the tears prickling her eyes. She chomped on her lip to stop them from leaking out.

Lickpenny thumped on the controller again. Nothing. He teetered on the jiggling rooftop, making his way to the backside of the lammergeyer, kicking at its wings and tail feathers.

Think, Addy told herself. Think! Don't waste time being rude to a cartoon character. *Do* something. *Two* things. No, *three*!

One, escape from the lammergeyer.

Next, escape from Professor Lickpenny.

And finally, escape from this world!

Her head throbbed. Her ribs ached. Her legs were twisted awkwardly, in a not-quite-sitting position.

Think, Addy! Think!

She'd come into the comic world without the comic book, right? So there *had* to be a way to get *out* as well. She was missing something, right at her fingertips …

She felt in her pocket for Catnip, stroking his silky fur. He stirred under her hand and darted out to say hello.

"What was *what*?" said Addy. "Achoo!" she added.

The professor shook his head and retreated.

"Achoo!" Louder. "I must be allergic to something."
She held her arms over her chest. Could she possibly
keep the rat a secret? The chewing buzz continued, low
and urgent.

"Achoo!"

In moments—*POP!*—the second claw was gone.

"Go, Catnip! You're amazing—a rodent mechanizmo! It must be the catalyzer you snarfed up." Addy faked another sneeze. "You'll have arugula for the rest of your life," she promised. "With kale for dessert."

"What devilment is this?" Lickpenny was right in front of her, bending over to pick up a mangled claw. His eyes bugged and his mouth gaped. "How is this possible?"

Then he caught sight of Catnip, still in a chewing frenzy. He grabbed Addy's arm, scrabbling to catch the rat's tail.

"Get off!" Addy kicked Lickpenny's shin—hard.

Another *POP!* Just in time. The third claw gave way, making the final prong lose its hold. Addy's insides were jumbled from being held captive so long. She slumped to her knees, wrenching her arm from Lickpenny's grasp. Catnip bounded to her shoulder and hissed like a cat. The professor tried to snatch him, but Catnip hissed again ... and bit off his fingertip!

Lickpenny howled, holding his hand up high, blood spurting like a fountain, showering them both with red droplets.

"Not sorry for you," said Addy. She scrambled away across the shaking roof, clutching Catnip to her chest. Imagine the poor rat's digestive system! Having to swallow all that metal, plus Lickpenny's nasty fingernail!

A loud crack and a cry made her spin back around. The lammergeyer's remaining claw had snapped shut— this time around the left leg of Aldous K. Lickpenny.

S econds ticked by like soldiers on parade. Wylder could hear them at the back of his mind—*tick-tock, tick-tock*—while he lined up all the things he had to do. He'd grabbed the wrong girl, which meant that Addy—the right girl—was still inside the comic. He had to go and find her and bring her back. And he had to do it fast.

Tick-tock.

Forget about Mom. She'd be going crazy, and he'd be in deep trouble when he got back, but he could not—simply *would not*—walk away from Addy. He had no choice, especially since it was his fault that she was still there. Nothing brave about it—just a thing he had to do, like breathing or swallowing.

Tick-tock.

He couldn't wait for Uncle Vim. Who knew how long he might be talking to this Magnus Snayle guy? Wylder had to find Addy *now* and trade her for Nelly.

Nelly stood by the window of the artists' lounge, peering down at Front Street, hands and forehead pressed against the glass. "Horseless carriages by the hundred!" she said. "*Voosh! Voosh!* But where are the ServiDudes? I haven't seen a one."

"We don't have ServiDudes." Wylder bent over the table, paging through the comic.

"Most of the girls are wearing pantaloons," said Nelly. "Like your Addy."

"She's not *my* Addy."

What if that stupid bird dropped her and she crashed to the ground? Could a real person die inside a comic book?

Stop it.

He riffled the pages, scanning quickly.

There was Isadora hauling Flynn down a ladder on the outside of the train. There was Professor Lickpenny on the roof of a different train car, one that chugged on ahead. He shook his fists, lab coat flapping, and his comb-over wasn't *over* anymore.

There, weirdly, was Nevins pausing in the train corridor to pick his nose.

And then *whoa!*

Wylder was pretty sure that none of this was in Uncle Vim's original comic. The characters were acting on their own. Saving Flynn was what *Isadora* wanted to do—not what Uncle Vim made her do. Which was amazingly cool, but scary to think where it could lead. If Vim wasn't in charge, wouldn't things get way out of control? What if Lickpenny succeeded? What if Flynn died? What if Addy ...

Stop it!

Wylder had a lightbulb moment of his own. Addy didn't have a copy of the comic, so she couldn't move too far away from where he'd left her. Right? He skipped ahead a bit, pausing to see her mouthing off to Lickpenny even while she was trapped.

That Addy!

What next?

He jumped ahead another couple of pages.

Would Wylder Wallace please come to the information booth for an important message?

"That's you he's calling, isn't it?" Nelly stood next to him. "Someone wants you something frantic. Is that part of your game?"

"What?"

"You have some game going on," said Nelly. "I can tell. I won't give you away. I'll even come in with you. But there has to be something in it for me too. I want half."

"Half of what?"

"I worked on my own until Aunt Isadora took me in. Mostly I've been a proper lady since then. But fair's fair. You want my help, we share the winnings."

Wylder tried to imagine what Nelly thought the winnings might be. The prize *he* was after was named Addy. And there she was again, on the page in front of him.

Yikes!

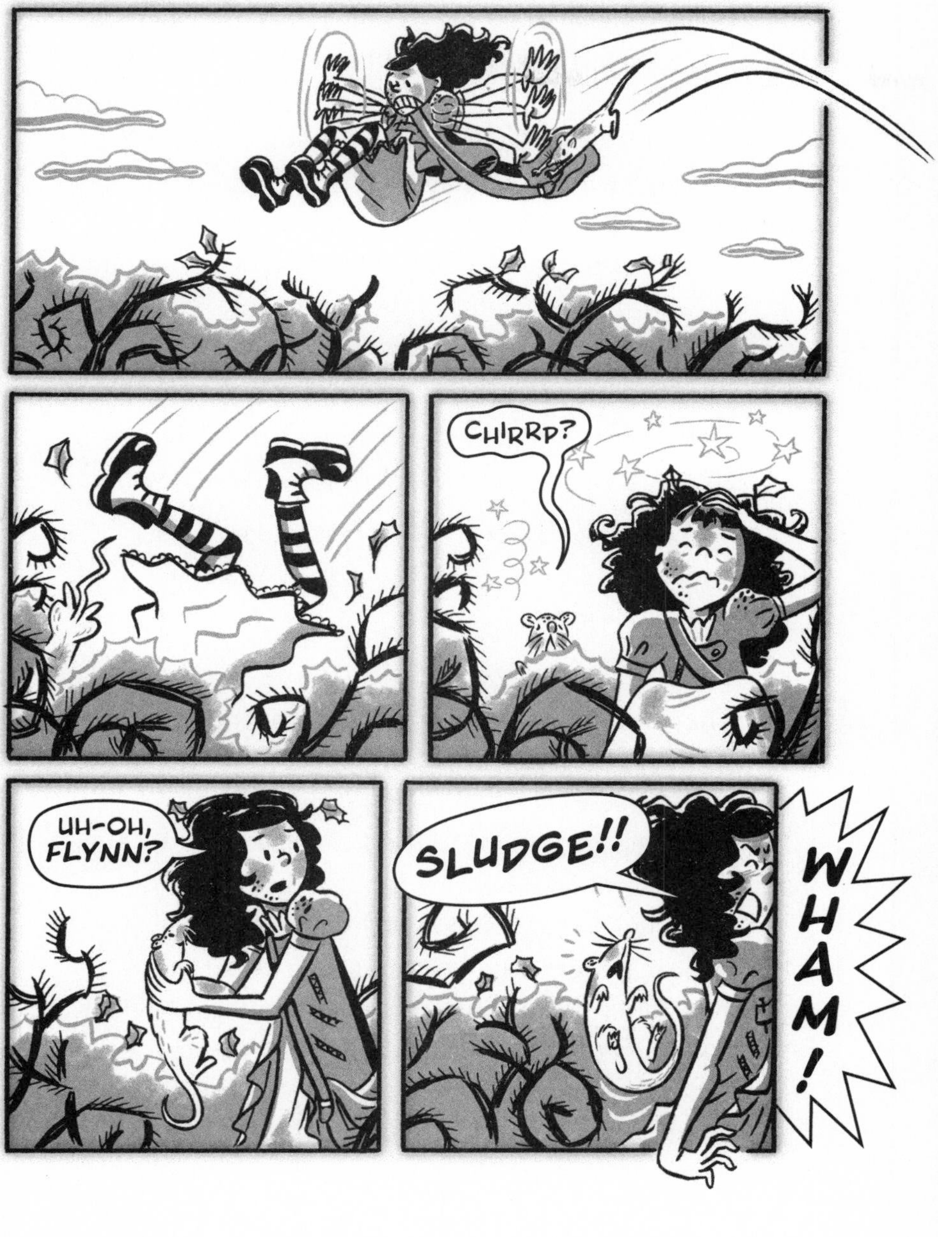
CHIRRP?
UH-OH, FLYNN?
SLUDGE!!
WHAM!

Wylder heaved a sigh of relief. He knew where to look—or close to it, anyway—if he could find the dang portal.

He began to sweat as his feet went into action.

"You can have half of what I make," he told Nelly. "I'm going to write Uncle Vim a note, and then we're *outta here!*"

He found a pen on the table and thought for a second.

Dear ~~Mr.~~ Uncle Vim,

Got the wrong girl. Addy still trapped in comic. I'm going back to get her. Please find my mom at the information booth and tell her I'm okay.

Wylder Wallace

Hurrying along the wide hall of the convention center, Wylder swiveled his head, on the lookout for his mom. Nelly struggled to keep up, huffing and puffing.

"This place is strange!" she said. "I haven't been feeling myself since I got here."

"No kidding," said Wylder.

"Why are people waving at me?" she asked.

"They think you're part of the show," said Wylder. "One of the actors. Wave back." He was looking for the dimly lit hall with the ladies' bathroom where he'd found Addy and gone into the comic.

"Sorry, mister!"

Nelly had bumped into an older man in a navy blue suit. She giggled like a silly girl—not like herself at all—and scampered after Wylder. "Hurry," she whispered.

"What?" But Wylder quickened his pace.

"Hey!" the man called after them. "The brat stole my wallet! Security! Thief! That girl picked my pocket!"

Wylder gasped. "Nelly!"

But she had zoomed ahead. He looked back to see the man pointing at him. A security guard in a turban was steaming through the crowd.

"That boy in the orange shirt is part of the gang!"

Wylder flat-out ran, catching up to Nelly around the corner, where she was leaning against a wall, gasping for breath.

"You stole that man's wallet!" He tugged her arm.

"It should have been easy pickings," she said. "His coat was hanging open. But I bungled it. It's this place. I'm not myself."

"They think I'm guilty too!"

They were at the LARPing arena. The hall with the ladies' bathroom portal must be up ahead on his left. *Had* to be, right?

"Give me the wallet, Nelly."

"No."

"I get half, remember? That was the deal." He looked back, saw the top of a turban and dragged Nelly around the next turn. The corridor opened up to the main exhibition hall. Many of the convention vendors were closing for the night, but a few booths and displays were still open.

Time ticked by. Addy was stuck at the bottom of the page, with no future unless Wylder saved her. And now he had to worry about security guards as well as trying to find the portal. Drat, Nelly! What if he didn't get there? What if—

Wylder Wallace! Please come to the lobby right away.

The lobby? Wait a minute! Wasn't the lobby right there, five steps away? Uh-oh. Wylder steered Nelly into an about-turn, but too late. He heard a familiar voice.

"Wylder? *Wylder*!"

Mom! Wylder's heart jumped into his throat. He almost choked on it. Part of him wanted to run over and hug her. But there wasn't enough time—not in the entire future of the world—for him to explain what he was doing and why he had to do it *now*. He *had* to save Addy. Funny how a girl you met at lunch—and didn't even like right away—could be the most important person in your life by dinnertime.

With his mother's voice echoing after them, Wylder nudged Nelly past a booth of pink-haired trolls lined up around a troll castle.

"Who's the dame?" she panted.

He didn't answer. Now they were headed straight back toward the security guy. They were trapped! He saw himself and Nelly in handcuffs in a police station, going into juvenile detention for petty theft, getting visited by his weeping mother. And meanwhile, Addy would be ...

"Twain!"

A high-pitched voice.

A little kid was pulling at his dad's hand. "Me wanna go on twain!"

He meant "train."

"Not now, Roger," said the dad.

"Pweeeease!" The kid pointed with a plastic light-saber. His face crumpled as his dad picked him up and carried him away.

Wylder dragged Nelly onward. Sure enough, standing beside a pair of double doors marked WIGMORE was the Flynn Goster display—the big cardboard engine with portraits of the characters decorating the side. The repair guy must have fixed it and moved it here. TAKE A RIDE ON THE GOLD RUSH EXPRESS! A sign next to it announced tomorrow's lineup of convention speakers in the Wigmore Room. First on the list was "Viminy Crowe 9:00 a.m."

"Ow!" Nelly put up her hand to shield her eyes. "Too bright!" A light had suddenly beamed from the train engine. It shone directly at her before blinking off a second later.

Wylder stood completely still, the pieces clicking in his mind—nearly, but not quite, fitting together. The big cardboard engine had been right outside the bathroom this morning. The maintenance guy had been fixing the light. And here next to it is where they'd landed an hour ago. Maybe the portal *always* had something to do with the train display.

Take a ride, he thought.

"Aunt Isadora!" said Nelly. "However did her photograph find its way to this place? And the yellow-toothed professor? Who would want his likeness?" She ran her finger over the pictures on the side of the engine. "Whatever next?" she said. "That's *me*!"

Wylder grasped Nelly's arm. No way was he going into the comic without her. He tapped the silvery cardboard as if he were knocking on a door. Nothing. He stepped inside to turn the steering wheel. Still nothing.

"Why do I look so silly in the picture? My hair isn't like that. Is it?" Nelly patted her hair and then seemed to remember the wallet in her other hand. She began to riffle through it.

"Give me that." Wylder took it from her a bit roughly. He turned his back to check inside and read the name on the gas company credit card. Nelly danced around him, trying to snatch the wallet back, but he easily held it away from her. She wasn't as strong as Addy.

The security guard would be coming soon. Maybe Mom too. He had to buy some time.

"Hey, Norris Bowden!" Wylder yelled. "We found your wallet!"

He flung it down the hall, keeping a firm hand on Nelly's wrist so she couldn't lunge after it. The light on the train display flashed on again, illuminating the entrance to the Wigmore Room.

"What demon light is chasing us?" cried Nelly. She backed away, bumping Wylder against the double doors. He heard the click, felt the doors swing open and tumbled through them, still holding Nelly's arm.

An eerie blast of the train whistle seemed to con-gratulate Addy on her escape. She crouched on all fours, trying to keep her balance on the shaking roof-top, with Catnip perched on her shoulders as if he were the rider in a game of horsey. The afternoon sun cast a glow of pink and gold on the leaves and bark of the sil-ver birch trees that flanked the rail line.

The whistle blew again, drowning out Lickpenny's barrage of bad words. Since the controller didn't seem to be working the way it was meant to, he was using it as a hammer, bashing away at the talon that held his leg.

The train lurched to an unexpected stop in a series of shuddering hiccups, metal wheels screeching against the iron rails. Addy slipped across the roof like butter on a pancake, just catching hold of the guardrail before the final jolt. Krackle slid toward her, metallic feathers clattering like crazy, dragging the squawking professor behind.

Addy didn't waste a second. She knew she'd better get to the ground right now, before the train began to move again.

"Now or never, Catnip." She crawled to the ladder that dropped over the side. The rat was snuggled against the back of her neck, heavier than ever with all that talon supper inside him.

"Don't sneak away!"

Addy had her feet on the rungs.

"Don't leave me trapped, girl," wheedled Professor Lickpenny from his snare on the roof. "I can pay you handsomely. A gold brick for the loan of that ... creature of yours."

"Fix your controller," called Addy. "Since you're such a genius."

She scurried down the ladder, ducking as he flung curses like clots of mud. Finally on firm ground, she looked toward the other half of the train. No sight of anyone headed this way. No Red Riders coming to the rescue, and no Wylder either. Where was he?

And why had the train squealed to a stop out here in the middle of a forest? What if it was because of some dire new catastrophe? Instead of starting the long hike back to the stalled cars, Addy crept forward—past the armored car with its cargo of gold, past Isadora's hot-air balloon under its striped tarpaulin, past the coal car and along the side of the engine—to peek at whatever awaited in front.

Holy cannoli! A humongous pine tree lay across the railroad tracks, its spiky branches poking in all directions.

"Blast my buttons!" An exasperated voice startled Addy from above. The train engineer was climbing down from her seat to inspect the damage. "It'll take hours to haul that out of the way."

Her co-driver scratched his head. "Yes, ma'am, it will. And the ServiDudes are useless outdoors because of their rollers." He kicked at the uneven ground. "I wonder, was it that same flash flood that caught us a while back?"

The tree had been uprooted by a *flood*? Holy cannoli! Dropping the comic book into a pool in Florida had toppled a tree in Ontario! It was one of those "Where does something really begin?" examples that Addy's social studies teacher was always making them think about.

Addy retreated quietly. She did not want to get stuck helping to move a giant Christmas tree.

Way down the tracks in the other direction stood the waiting carriages. Catnip's tail coiled around her neck, and his nose sniffed her ear. Addy's feet scrabbled over the pebbles by the rails as she hurried along in the shadow of the train cars.

"You impertinent snippet! I shall have your skin yet!"

Addy looked up to see Professor Lickpenny shaking his controller over the guardrail above. Why had she given him a thing about skin? She shuddered and began to leap, rail tie to rail tie, Catnip riding her shoulder.

Where the stinking sludge was Wylder? Why hadn't he come looking for her? He had the comic book, so he knew where she was, right? He must have realized by now that he'd grabbed the wrong girl. So where was he?

A boulder freckled with orange lichen shone in the sun, a jewel amid a patch of waving sweetgrass. Silver birch trees swayed slightly in the breeze, like a cluster of giraffes. Addy paused on the track. When would she next sit with Uncle Vim while his colored pencils deftly turned a green scribble into a lakeside woodland?

And what about her mother? What if Addy was stuck here and never went home again? What if— Her eyes blurred for a second before she rubbed them really hard. No crying.

What if Wylder hadn't come to find her because he wasn't *here* anymore? Because he'd found a way home? Would he have left her alone and just gone back to the real world? Addy stubbed her toe on a stone and pin-wheeled her arms to keep her balance, heart banging in her chest.

Would she go home without Wylder if she had the chance? She didn't think so ... but how could a person know what she'd do in a crisis until a crisis came along?

Maybe somewhere in the chaos of the train ahead, Wylder was in trouble too. Maybe *he* was waiting for *her* to rescue *him*, right at this very same moment!

Her trot speeded up to a gallop.

Hang on a second! She nearly skidded to a halt.

There was that stone again, crowned with orange lichen. And the grove of birch trees. Addy turned to look at where she'd come from. Boulder, low bushes, tamaracks—Uncle Vim had reused the same background for several panels, like an endless wallpaper as the train zipped through the landscape. Somehow it altered the size of the world, so that what had looked like a long walk to the stalled half of the train was reduced to only a few more steps. Straight ahead, a minute away, was the beautiful, marvelous, wonderful string of cars, stretched out and waiting.

And—holy cannoli!—the carriage that had been stalled by Snap's huge body was *moving*! Toward *her*! Addy scrambled off the tracks out of its path. What was making it go without a locomotive? The cars slowly click-clacked past her. Something must be pushing from behind. She caught sight of a child waving from a window and waved cheerily back. But what if it had been a wave for help? Last thing she knew, the passengers on the Gold Rush Express were in grave peril from Lickpenny's rampaging robot. Were people hurt inside the train? Was Wylder somewhere with them?

"Hold it here!"

A cry came from the roof of the shiny red caboose. Addy looked up to see Isadora signaling to someone behind the final car of the train. The whole parade groaned to a stop.

"Nelly!" called Isadora.

Before Addy could say a word, Flynn Goster stepped around the corner of the caboose, looking tall and strong and perfectly fit.

WELL, FANCY MEETING ME HERE! AREN'T I A SIGHT FOR SORE EYES!

How was he even conscious, let alone pushing a train? What else had changed in the story? His bright eyes danced beneath a lock of dark hair that fell over his forehead. He was impossibly handsome, even Addy could see that. He'd unbuttoned his jacket and his pleated white shirt was disheveled, the neck open to show a gleam of sweat on his chest.

"Good to see you too," Flynn went on. "The little lady up top will be more than delighted to have you back under her watch."

"What about *you*?" said Addy. "Wasn't so long ago you were in a dead faint, without your—" She stopped herself. It was pretty rude to discuss missing body parts, even with a fictional character. "I mean, I've only been gone for … um, what *is* that?"

The end of Flynn's right arm was not a stump. Instead, he flexed the fingers of a remarkable—and large—robotic hand.

"Fair Isadora performed a miracle, did she not?"

"Isadora?" Well, why not? She could do pretty much anything. "Oh sure, Uncle Vim. No unicycle? No harp?"

"Aiming for perfection," Uncle Vim had said.

"I am becoming acquainted with my new appendage," said Flynn. "Watch this!" He held his thumb to the side of the train car and burned a hole straight through it.

That would be the blowtorch, thought Addy.

"Very useful," she said.

But then the hand began to tremble, and Flynn's eyes widened in surprise as the jiggling fist reached up and shattered a train window with a single punch. Flynn quickly calmed the quiver with his regular hand, looking mortified.

"Still learning," he said.

Just then, Isadora, carrying Flynn's sword, leapt from the top of the train and landed beside Addy on the trackside scruff, as neatly as if she were a cat. She laid down the weapon to hold Addy's face in her hands and look tenderly into her eyes.

"My poor dear child. Filthy! And bedraggled. Very nearly as woebegone as the day I first met you."

She thinks I'm Nelly, thought Addy. She's being kind to someone else.

Addy's tears welled up and spilled over, trickling down her cheeks. Isadora pushed tangled strands of hair from Addy's forehead and began to daub at her face with the corner of a handkerchief. Having her face gently cleaned of smoke grime with a lace-edged square of silk was enough to make Addy long for her mother.

"Is this *blood*?" said Isadora.

"Yes," said Addy. "But not mine. Lickpenny spattered me with his."

Flynn had recovered his cool after breaking the glass. Using the diamond-edged saw in his pointer finger, he efficiently zipped away jagged shards from the window frame.

"Is the wicked villain dead?" he said.

"Uh, no." Addy turned to show them where the professor was pinned to the distant roof.

And nearly gagged.

A dark shape, like an enormous vampire bat, was approaching across the sky with a faint whirr. Sitting astride its shoulders was a stout and cheering pilot. Krackle and its master were on the move, and speeding right toward them!

23

"**Q**uick," said Addy. "Just so you know, I'm Addy— not Nelly."

"My goodness," said Isadora. "The likeness is startling! But where *is* Nelly?" Her fingers strayed to her pistol holster as she eyed the approaching lammergeyer.

"I thought … I was hoping she'd be here with you."

Addy's thoughts fuzzed for a second. And then one came through loud and clear.

What if Wylder *and* Nelly had left the comic altogether?

Maybe they weren't on a different page. Maybe they were in Toronto.

Addy looked around. Was she alone?

She heard beating wings and shuddered. No time to waste thinking "poor little me." She did not intend to meet that bird again up close. She glanced around for a place to hide. Could she get *under* the train?

"But where could Nelly be?" Isadora's voice turned shrill. "This is no time to wander off!"

Flynn patted Isadora's arm and pulled her under the shade of the caboose. "Do not distress yourself," he murmured. "Your plucky lassie has the heart of a lion. She'll turn up! Perhaps she's only canoodling with a new beau?"

Blech! thought Addy. No way!

Flynn's arm slipped around Isadora's shoulder. Her head rested for a moment on his chest.

Double blech. Good thing Wylder couldn't see. Isadora was never supposed to be in love—Addy had made sure her uncle avoided anything mushy. Isadora only used Flynn to get the gold, setting up the next issue, where the hero would be chasing *her*.

FWAP-CLANK-FWAP!

Flynn and Isadora raised their eyes in alarm. Addy felt a chill as a great shadow engulfed them.

FWAP-FWAP!

"Ha-ha!" cried Lickpenny from the air. "All in one spot, awaiting your doom!" He waved his controller, which seemed—horribly—to be working again. Krackle swooped low enough for Addy to see the zigzag pattern on the soles of the professor's boots. **WHOOSH!** A breeze from the metal wings ruffled her hair as the mechanical bird flapped and turned in midair.

"It's smiting time!" Flynn winked at Isadora and flexed the knuckles of his robotic hand.

FWAAP! WHOOSH!

Krackle, flying on a tilt, dipped so low that— **POW!**—the professor's foot struck Isadora's shoulder and knocked her to the ground.

"Ha-ha! Contact!" shouted Lickpenny.

"My dear?" said Flynn to his sweetheart.

Isadora flashed him a sparkling smile, proving that she was not hurt. She grasped the hilt of Flynn's sword and whirled the double blade with a flourish.

Flynn scooped up Addy and dropped her like a kitten on the platform of the caboose.

"Stay put," he said.

The comic book heroes were ready for battle, and Addy had a front-row seat. But—sludge!—did they stand a chance against the robotic monster? Catnip crept out from her bag, hissing.

"That's the best you can do, Professor?" Flynn taunted. "Kicking a woman?"

"Arrogant wretch!" called Lickpenny. "Your minutes are numbered!"

"I think not." Isadora assumed a fighting stance. "You are up against a sharp blade and a sharp wit," she said, winking at Addy.

"The blade moves like light through a dark room," said Isadora.

"Quick and bright, impossible to follow."

Isadora's feet danced, and her arms swung so quickly that the air hummed. The lammergeyer dove and retreated, dove again, but its moves were no match for the lightning swordplay.

"Ha!" cried Isadora. "And my wit not even called upon!"

Lickpenny's voice was hoarse from shouting. "Up! Back! No, *no*!"

As Krackle hovered, awaiting another chance, Flynn stepped forward. From under the middle fingernail of his mechanical hand shot a startling length of titanium wire as fine as dental floss. The wire entwined itself tightly around the bird's metallic feathers and bound shut the giant beak.

FWAAAAAPPP!

The whole mechanical mess crashed to the ground, skidding slightly as it hit the railroad track, dumping Lickpenny from his perch. The professor scrambled out of sight, cowering behind the hulk of the bird's body with only tufts of his thin, greasy hair showing.

Flynn winked at Isadora. Isadora lowered the sword and smiled back.

"Holy cannoli," whispered Addy, finally breathing again. She suspected that the hiccuping noise was Lickpenny, crying as he faced defeat.

Flynn swept Isadora into his arms.

Ew, blech! They were going to kiss! Addy closed her eyes.

But when she opened the left one, just to peek, Flynn had pulled out of the embrace and was staring in alarm at his trembling robotic hand. Addy had the feeling that he'd forgotten how he came to have such a peculiar thing attached to him. His face turned slightly gray. He shifted sideways, as if someone were yanking on his sleeve, and then slowly bent double, his mighty hand dragging him into a puppety dance.

"Whatever is the matter?" Isadora leapt toward him.

Flynn straightened up, sweat gleaming under the perfect lock of hair on his forehead. His regular hand held tight to Snap's wrist, shaking it gently, and then not gently at all. Was the robotic hand *fighting* its new master?!

"Flynn!" cried Isadora. "What ails you?"

Lickpenny's laughter filled the air like a sucking drain. He waved a pair of scissors in triumph. The hiccup sound had been his quiet snipping of the wire ensnaring the lammergeyer! He now pointed his controller directly at Flynn and twisted a dial.

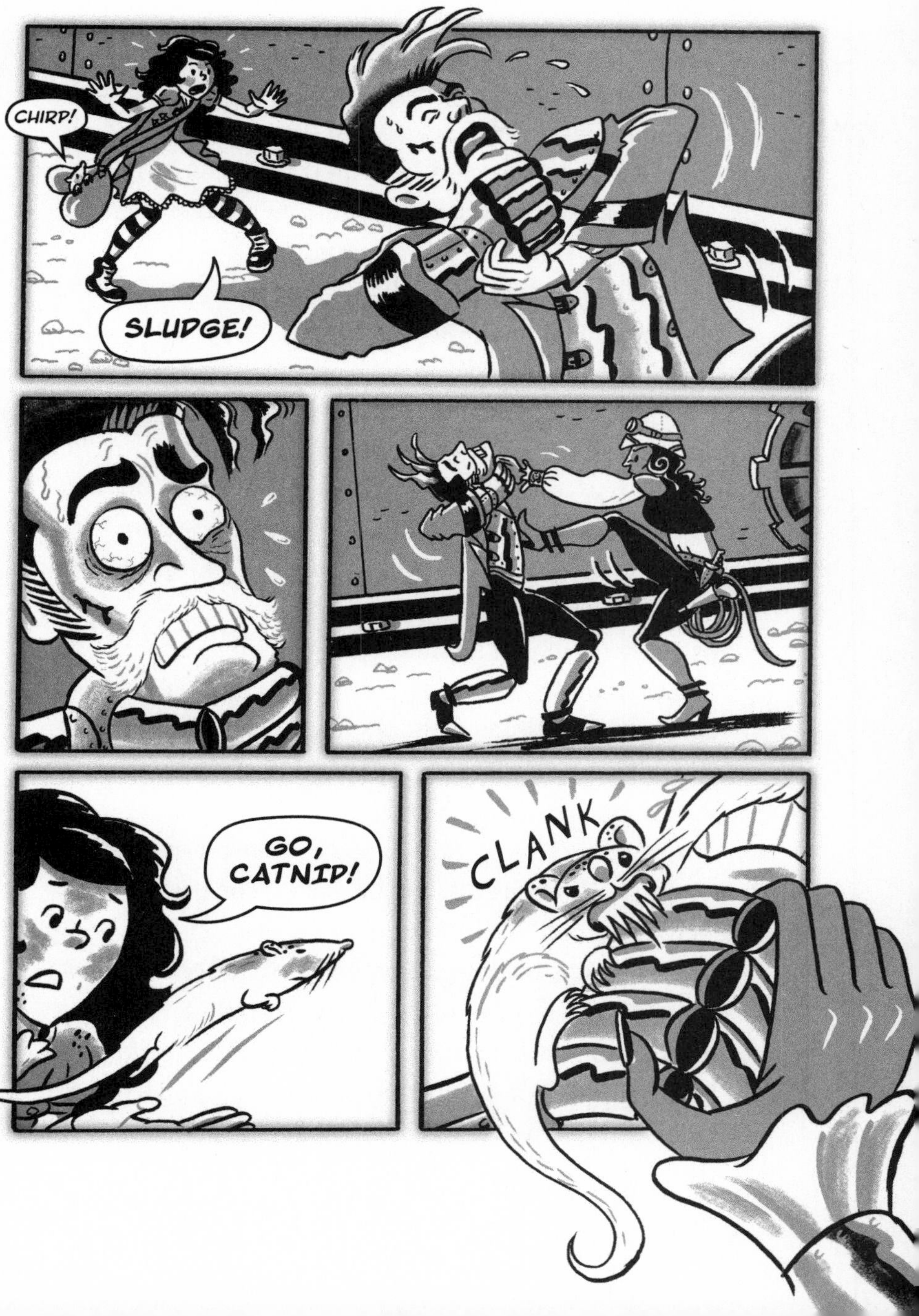
CHIRP!
SLUDGE!
GO, CATNIP!
CLANK

Were Catnip's teeth duller after their work on the lammergeyer's talons? Were his jaws tired? He just didn't have the oomph and barely dented the evil fingers.

"Ha-ha!" Lickpenny and his steed were again in the air. They floated just out of reach. "You'll have to cut it off to pry it loose!"

Isadora glanced at the villain; her mouth set in a determined line. She undid the sheath at her waist and withdrew a hunting knife with a blade so sharp it looked transparent. Addy gasped. Would she really cut off the hand that she had so carefully sewn on?

Flynn's real hand tore at the robotic grip on his throat. He spluttered sounds that made no sense. Did he want the hand to come off? Or was he telling Isadora not to do it?

His body twitched; he blinked and tried to speak.

"ZZZzzzmmmm ..."

"Don't cut!" Addy nearly flew down the steps of the caboose.

Isadora paused, knife hovering.

"You've. Got. The ..." Addy's voice came out in breathless bleats. "ZIM-mer!" She finally said. "The gadget from the gator's throat!"

Isadora's face lit up. She fumbled for the cord around her neck. "I am not familiar—" she stumbled.

Addy broke the cord with one swift tug. Could she make it work? The brilliant device that opened *anything*! Could she use it to save him?

Lickpenny kept his controller pointed at Flynn.

"Revenge is *mine!*" he screeched. "*You* belong to *me!*"

Isadora raised her knife again. "Addy, dear, use your tool, or I'll use mine!"

Addy pushed the button on the Zimmer.

POP! The first finger loosened.

POP, POP, POP! The metal hand fell away from Flynn's throat, vibrating slightly. He staggered and fell forward onto his knees, coughing and gasping for air.

Yesss! Addy laughed out loud. She'd done it!

Isadora tucked her knife away and twirled Addy with a whooping cheer. Flynn managed a wan smile and wiped his mouth with his own hand. His cheeks were livid, his eyes glassy and not very hero-like. Isadora and Addy together reached to hug him, but Addy noticed a moment too late that Lickpenny had swooped in close, his controller once more aimed at Flynn.

Flynn's robotic hand shot up, socking Isadora on the side of her head. Isadora toppled over, and Flynn moaned, "Noooo! Forgive me!" He leaned toward his sweetheart just as Krackle whooshed by with a rattle of feathers, knocking him off balance.

"Hey!" shouted Addy. "Stop! Stop all this right now!" She'd won the battle already! This was no fair!

But Flynn's hand didn't care about fairness. It seemed to have a brain of its own. It darted out and snatched Addy's ankle with bone-pinching strength, sweeping her off her feet and into the air to hang upside down like a dead duck in the window of a Chinese restaurant. She couldn't have screamed if she'd tried.

"This isn't me, lassie!" cried Flynn. "I'd never harm you. Never!" With a mighty heave, he hurled Addy as easily as a baseball. Catnip chirped from her flying shoulder bag as they sailed together through the air.

Nelly landed on top of Wylder, knocking the wind out of him. The floor was moving, and he couldn't see anything until she rolled to one side. Where were they? What was with the smoke? Had the room caught on fire? He sat up, gasping. The comic book was in his hand.

Definitely not the Wigmore Room!

Not any part of the convention center. Not even the real world.

CLICKETY-CLACK, CLICKETY-CLACK.

He had found the portal—or the portal had found him—but where in the comic book were they? Not the bathroom. On the roof of the train.

Wylder's breathing came almost normally now, but he didn't have his balance yet. He stayed sitting down.

The smoke swirled around him, and the floor kept swaying.

Addy, he thought. Rescue Addy.

He had been on the train roof before. So was he back at the moment when Nevins had flipped all those pages and everyone had ended up here? Or maybe— since Wylder had left the comic for a while and come back—maybe *this* plot would *not* be an exact replay of the old one. Maybe Addy was somewhere under these clouds of smoke, and maybe she wasn't.

"Addy!" he shouted. "Addy, are you there? It's me, Wylder!"

Nothing.

The girl next to him lifted her head. "Nelly," she mumbled. "I'm *Nelly*." She struggled to sit up. "My stars!" she said.

The train veered gently around a curve, and the smoke streamed away to the left. Wylder used the moment to peer at the comic book, and there he was!

The comic book was open at the page he'd marked, the one with Addy in the bramble bush at the bottom right-hand side. Wylder and Nelly were now in the panel at the top left.

Wylder concentrated so hard on making the right deductions that his brain felt like one of those speeded-up traffic movies: *stop-start-zoom.* The big train display and the beam of light were connected to the portal— *that* was for sure. He'd seen it outside the Wigmore

Room just now and outside the bathroom this morning. And it seemed as though when you went through the portal, you landed on whatever page of the comic was open! When he saw Addy in the bathroom that first time, the portal opened right there. This time, he was on the same page as Addy, the one he had been looking at, *but in a different scene from her.* He was at the top of the left hand page, and Addy was stuck at the bottom of the facing page. The question was, how to get there? He didn't want to go through the story, fighting Lickpenny and the lammergeyer. That might take forever, and he might not escape!

He peered at the next panel to see what might be in store.

Oh no.

Wylder turned slowly.

Captain McGurk held Nevins by the scruff of the neck. "It is forbidden to climb onto the roof of a moving train. Especially now, in an emergency situation."

Wylder hardly heard this. He couldn't take his eyes off the metal spike that was now the captain's leg. That Medico ServiDude really had cut it off.

"Ho-ho!" called the captain. "Come back, girl!"

But Nelly had scrambled away, vanishing into the smoke.

"Let me *gooooo!*" whined Nevins.

"Hello, Captain McGurk," said Wylder. "Nice leg."

"Don't get cheeky," said the captain. "You're coming with me."

"I'll come quietly," said Wylder. "I'm just going to bring my hands down long enough to turn this page."

"This *what?*"

"This page."

THWIP!

Wylder smelled something sharp and piney, like air freshener or deodorant. Or pine trees. He was on the next page, and things were going badly!

He leapt to his feet. It was exhausting, bouncing around the story like this! You had to be alert every second. Something always seemed to be going wrong. The disaster on this page could be called Bad Day on the Railroad Tracks. Lickpenny flew his robotic lammer-geyer at Isadora, who slashed with her whip to keep it at bay. Flynn—poor old Flynn Goster—lurched toward Wylder, waving his new robotic hand. Or was the hand waving him? Here it came now! Wylder ducked under a wild swing.

"Sorry, Cowboy!" Flynn staggered down the train track as if the hand was pulling him along.

Wylder didn't stop to think how cool it was to get an apology from his hero. He was not here to help Flynn. He had come a long way to find someone else.

"Addy!" he called. "Addy, where are you?"

She had flown into a bramble bush, but which one? Wylder was on the right page, but there were dozens of bramble bushes. The darn things were everywhere.

"Yoo-hoo, Addy?"

"Wylder!"

There she was, down the track!

"Addy!" He ran toward her and then stopped. He couldn't exactly hug her, even if that's what he felt like doing. She bashed her way out of the bush, rubbing her arm, her face lit up in the biggest grin. Her hair was a crazy mess, with twigs and stuff all through it. She waved and ran toward him, and then she stopped too, the grin sort of fading to an awkward smile.

"Hey!"

Wylder could tell she had a lot more to say, just like he did. "Hey back," he said.

She was still in Nelly's clothes, but Wylder had spent the last hour with Nelly. He could see the difference between the two girls now. Addy's face was sharper, smarter, with no pout. And she had the rat slung around her shoulders like a scarf. Definitely Addy.

"You found me," she said. "Finally. Not bad for a … I mean, not bad."

He ducked his head. He'd set out to do something big and he'd succeeded. Not bad at all.

"Yeah," he said.

"I got stuck. I wondered if it was a page bump."

"Looked like it," said Wylder.

"Did you see me take Lickpenny? And zimmer Flynn out of choking himself? I saved his life! Holy cannoli, I am so *pumped*!"

She was fizzing with energy.

"Yeah, that's great. Uh, listen, Addy. We should—"

"Hey, look out!"

The lammergeyer swooped low. The children flung themselves to the ground. Wylder heard the metallic claws clash together, and then the bird was past, leaving behind a smell of burnt onion.

"That was close, eh, Addy?" he said. "Addy? Addy?"

The mechanical bird turned around and headed after Flynn, who was staggering down the track. Isadora, in pursuit, high-stepped down the tracks, and Addy chased her.

"Come on, Wylder!"

He scrambled to his feet. The wind was in his face, and his hair blew up off his forehead.

"Wait up!" he shouted to Addy, who did not.

Flynn's robotic hand changed direction every second—pointing here, there and everywhere—firing some kind of laser beam. Flynn frantically tried to control it with his real hand, but not a chance. The laser finger pointed at a pine tree and—*ZZZZZTT!*—the needles crackled into flames. It pointed at one of the railroad ties and—*ZZZZTT!*—another burst of fire. Now the hand forced Flynn to aim straight at Isadora and at Addy right behind her. And at Wylder! Flynn howled and tried to throw his arm away from its target, but the hand was too strong. The finger remained steady, ready to shoot. All Flynn could do was shout a warning:

"It's ducking time!"

Addy and Wylder fell to their knees, faces down. Catnip was thrown from his perch on Addy's shoulder. He bounced on the ground and skittered into her bag. Isadora executed a sideways somersault and landed in a crouch, whip at the ready.

ZZZZTT! The beam passed over their heads, burning a hole through the trunk of a tree.

"Take cover!" Isadora ordered them. "Behind the rock!"

Wylder crawled after Addy to a spot behind a boulder. The stony ground hurt his knees. Isadora leapt in front of them as Flynn shot sparks at the railroad ties.

"This is dangerous!" said Wylder.

"No kidding!" Addy brushed her tangled mass of hair back from her face. She didn't look upset at all. She looked kind of excited.

"So let's get out of here!" Wylder held the rolled-up comic like an ice cream cone.

Above their heads came a fwapping sound. Isadora called out. Wylder followed her gaze to see the lammergeyer rising from the ground, its talons tightly gripping Flynn's mechanical hand, lifting the kicking hero slowly into the air. Lickpenny, on the bird's shoulders, waved his device with a look of glowing triumph.

Isadora uncoiled her whip as she ran toward them. Addy stared after the mechanical monster. "I'll bet you a hundred dollars that Lickpenny is going to use Flynn to break into the armored car. Give me the comic book."

"I've been trying to tell you!" pleaded Wylder. "We can leave now. The ad for ComicFest on the back page will take us home!"

"These people need us!" she screamed. "We can't just leave them to *die*!"

She lunged for the comic in his hand. He yanked.

THWIP!

25

Whoa! Where on earth … ?

Addy was dead sure she had never been in or even seen this place before. Not in real life, and not in the comic book either.

Uncle Vim had definitely not drawn this place.

Not the beach, spotted with palm trees that clicked in the gentle breeze like train wheels. Not the pale pink sand where she and Wylder had landed in a bumping muddle. Sand so fine that it clung to Addy's clothes like icing sugar. Not the turquoise ocean with the perfect arc of a rainbow on the horizon and white-tipped waves rolling toward shore. Not the merry group of laughing kids, tossing a beach ball and doing cartwheels. And what was that sweet, spicy smell? So strong it was like inhaling a flavor. The smell of cinnamon.

Catnip scrabbled his way out of Addy's bag, whiskers quivering. Addy picked him up, nose to nose, grateful for this small, loyal creature in the middle of such strangeness. Was his brain big enough to grasp the hugely weird day he was having?

She cuddled him while she scanned the beach, looking for clues.

"Did we end up in Florida again?" said Wylder.

"I'm still mad at you." Addy held up the comic book. "This is *mine*! Keep your paws off."

He opened his mouth, but she hadn't finished.

"*Not* Florida. And definitely not 1899." She paused for a second. "It doesn't look like *anywhere*."

Just when she was getting used to being one of the characters in the comic book, fighting battles and sassing nasty villains, *now* they get zapped to another crazy world? How unfair was *that*?

"There's practically a war going on in here." Addy shook the comic with a clenched fist. "And suddenly we're ... wherever this is!"

Wylder raised his palms as if to say "Stop, okay?"

Addy stopped, but mostly because she'd breathed in another huge waft of cinnamon, and it was the most calming, comforting thing she'd ever smelled. She closed her eyes and thought for a second about one of Uncle Vim's specialties: banana-cinnamon pancakes. Mmmmm.

"I need to tell you some stuff," said Wylder. "I've been ... well, it was an accident, but I got out. Out of the comic. I was in Toronto—"

"Yeah, actually? You got *out*? I wondered where you were."

"With Nelly," he said, not quite looking at her.

Addy let it sink in. "So how did it work with her? She's just paper and ink. Did she ... get, like, *dimensional*?"

"Uh—"

"Seriously, how did you get out? And didn't you notice it was her *and not me*?"

"Total luck," said Wylder. "We went through the back page of the comic. I figured that out later, but—"

"We ..." said Addy. *"We."*

"I thought it was you."

"It wasn't me. It was Nelly. I got left behind."

"I know that! That's why I came back—to get you. But I met your uncle and everything! And the main thing is, I can get us home now. I'll show you. We should just go. Right now."

Addy knew from Wylder's earnest, pleading face that he had not meant to be selfish when he'd left her to possibly *die* and have her skin sliced off to decorate a robot named Poppy. As much as she wanted to, she couldn't blame him for any of this.

But—and it was a big *but*—even if he *could* actually get them home, there was still a whole lot wrong. And she had a pretty firm suspicion that the wrong stuff could be made right only by staying in the comic. If they were still even *in* the comic, that was. Addy glanced over at a giggling circle of children who were tossing a beach ball back and forth. Where *were* they? It was creepy how *nice* everything was after the scary bird and Lickpenny's moldy teeth and the smoke and the severed hand …

"Okay," she said at last, "tell me how you think the portal works."

Wylder yelped and pointed at the ocean. "Look!"

Addy spun around to stare.

"It's *Cinny*!" said Wylder.

Cinny?

"Holy cannoli! You're right."

The golden animal in a striped bathing suit rode a surfboard, flashing his famous cheeky grin. As his wave rolled onto the beach, gum fell down like rain. *Real* gum! A couple of pieces hit Addy on the head. The boys and girls—all swaying happily in a moment of cinnamon worship—unwrapped what they caught and popped the gum into their mouths. Cinna-Monkey, nicknamed Cinny by children everywhere, was the beloved mascot for Cinnaglom gum. He'd been tossing gum since Addy was born.

Lightbulb!

Addy pulled out the comic. "Look. Right-hand page. *This* is where we are."

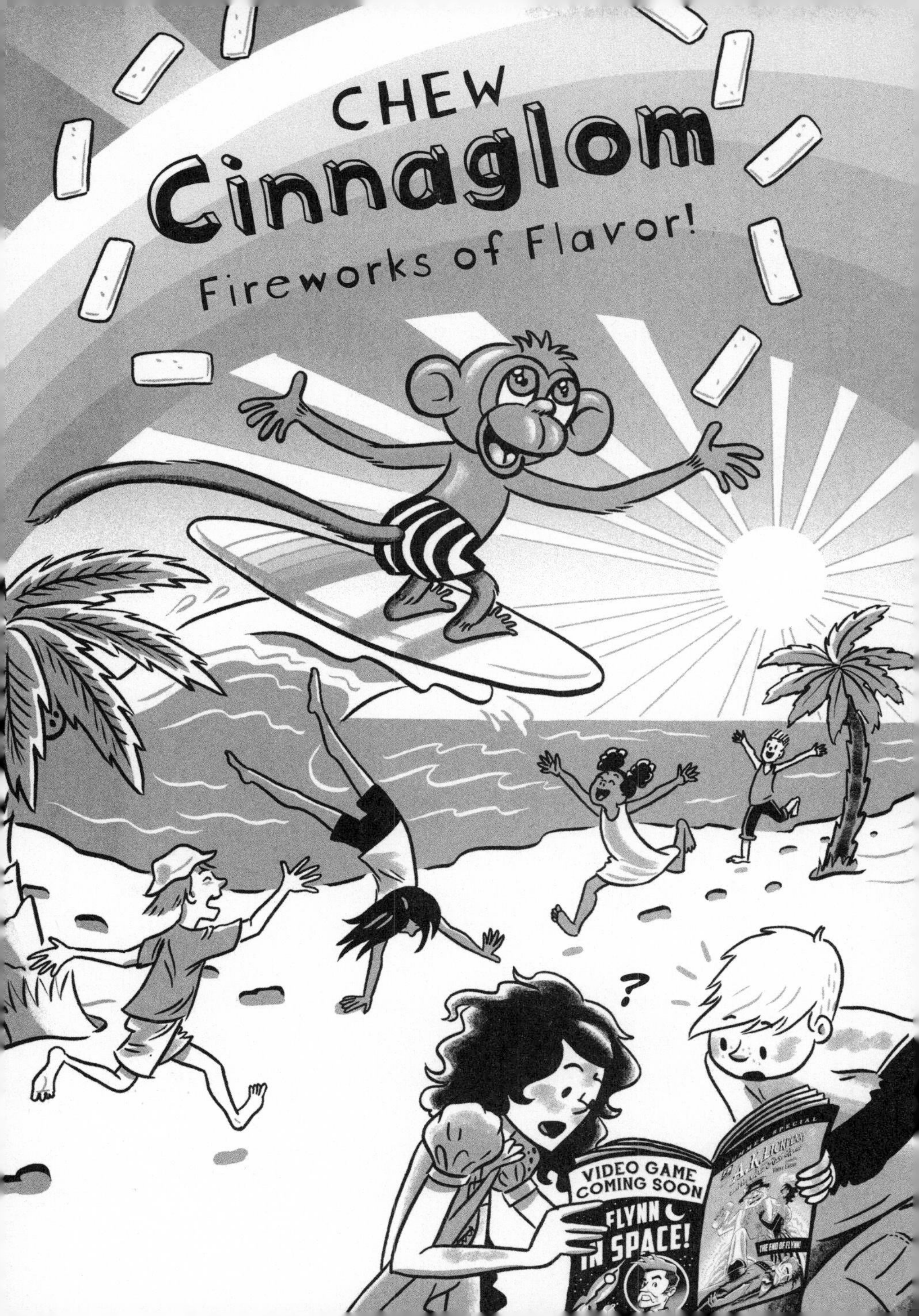
CHEW
Cinnaglom
Fireworks of Flavor!
?
VIDEO GAME COMING SOON
FLYNN IN SPACE!
SUMMER SPECIAL
A. K. LICKPERS
THE END OF FLYNN!

A blue-headed macaw with vibrant yellow plumage swooped over their heads, laughing the way parrots do—as if they know your secrets.

"We're in an *ad*?" said Wylder. "That's *crazy*!"

Addy never paid attention to ads. They were basically invisible, as far as she was concerned. She skipped over them and kept reading the story.

But she'd recognize Cinny anywhere.

"The Cinnaglom people are pretty good sponsors, my uncle says. They really like the comic. They once sent us a whole carton of free gum—a hundred and forty-four packs. I chew it all the time."

"But how did we get here?" Wylder sounded as if his head might pop off from trying to figure it out. "I don't mean whose fault—I just mean *how*?"

"I guess when we were ... you know, *fighting* ..." Not Addy's proudest moment. "The page got turned. And here we are."

"That might be the craziest thing that has happened this whole day." Wylder unwrapped a stick of gum and offered it to her. She folded it over and put it into her mouth.

"Hey!" Wylder looked around on the sand. "Where'd the wrapper go?"

He unwrapped another stick, watching carefully. The shiny colored paper vanished as it left his hands. *Poof!* Just gone.

"Holy cannoli," said Addy. "I guess there's no such

thing as litter in the world of advertising. Too bad we can't do that trick at home." Catnip turned over in her lap and she scratched his ears.

"And speaking of home," said Wylder, "are you ready to go? Because I totally know what I'm doing now and your uncle is waiting. All we have to do—"

"Wait a sec," said Addy. "No sudden moves, okay? Can you explain why you think we should go when everything is still a big fat mess? And it's all our fault?"

"Your uncle said we're like a computer virus, that we're infecting the story."

Addy's gum was losing its flavor already. She spat it out and watched the blob disappear before it hit the sand.

"It's too late for us to fix stuff," Wylder said. "Viminy Crowe for sure would want us to go."

"He would?" How did Wylder Wallace know what Addy's uncle thought about anything?

She slid the sleeping rat onto her shoulder and laid the comic across her knees so they could look together at the whole double-page spread.

"Uh-oh," she said.

THINGS IN THE STORY WERE GOING TERRIBLY WRONG ...

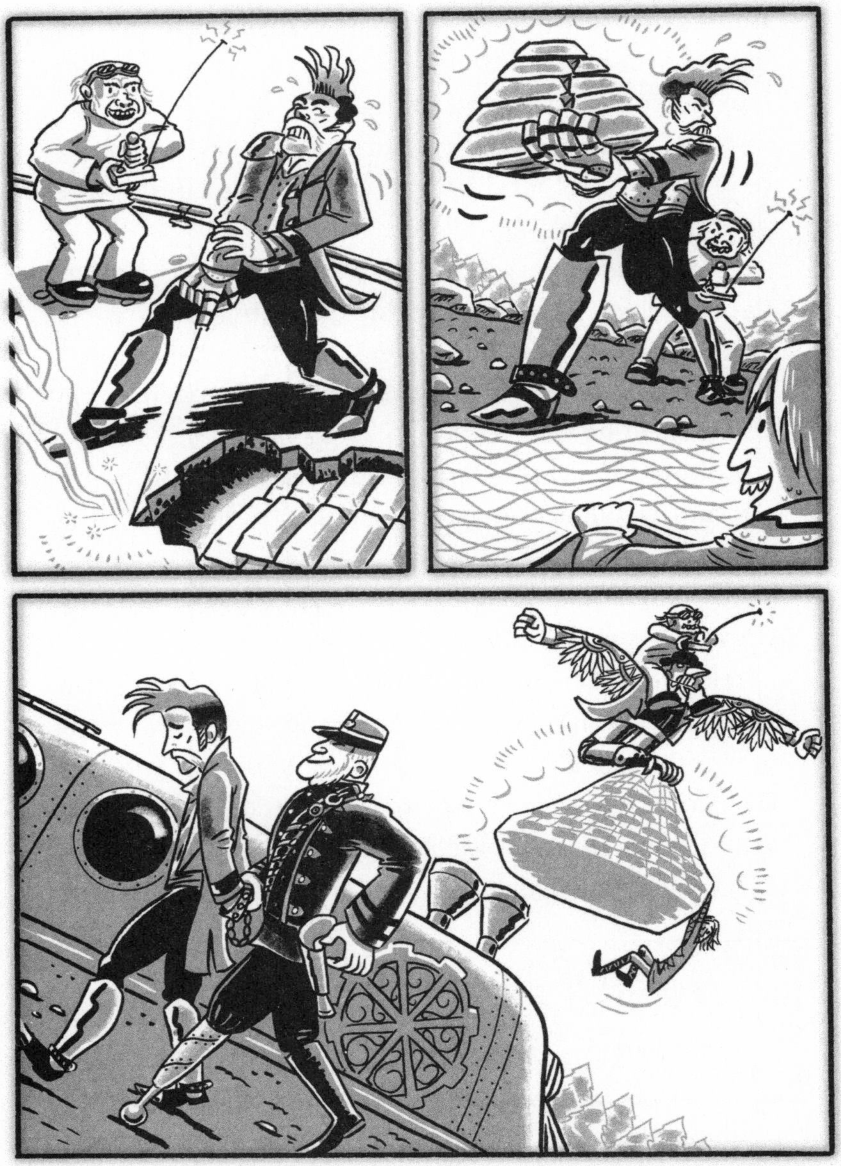

Wylder peered over Addy's shoulder. "*Lickpenny* uses Flynn to get the gold?" he said.

"The way it was supposed to be, Lickpenny used Snap to open the roof of the armored car, and then Isadora and Flynn hijacked the gold at the last minute. Now Lickpenny is forcing Flynn to use Snap's hand." Addy was quiet for a moment. "Shreds of the old plot keep showing up. But the characters are twisting them into a new story."

"Acting on their own," said Wylder.

"Lickpenny is a creep," said Addy. "But Uncle Vim made him so smart that when the story breaks down and he gets to think for himself, he is actually capable of taking over the world. McGurk is just a dough-brain. And Lickpenny is kicking Flynn's butt."

"It's not Flynn's fault!" Wylder had to defend his hero. "He was trying to save me when he fell in the pool. Isadora did a great job of sewing on the robot hand, but her idea totally backfired."

"Yup. Everything is coming up Lickpenny. The only one who has got the better of him so far is *me*." Addy looked pleased with herself for a second. "Which is why we have to stick around and fix the story."

"No!"

"Yes."

"But your uncle—"

"Please stop telling me what Uncle Vim thinks. He's *my* uncle, not yours. We have a couple minutes of peace here in paradise. No flying robots or evil chemists—just a surfing monkey and gum falling from the sky. So why shouldn't we figure out a way to fix the story? And don't say, 'But'!"

"But—"

"I told you not to say that! And I know what you're going to say next. Us being safe is more important than the comic. Our moms are worried, blah-blah-blah. But everything I care for most is about to disappear. *Pffffft!* If Uncle Vim moves away, I'll *die*. This issue of the comic *has* to get fixed, and it *has* to have a great ending."

"Do Flynn and Isadora get together? Is kissing in the balloon your uncle's idea of a great ending? Because I do not think—"

"No one will buy the comic if Lickpenny gets the gold and Flynn gets beaten and Isadora's balloon crashes. Ten thousand copies will go into the garbage—or the recycling—because of us. FunnyBones will drop Uncle Vim, and he'll never be able to pay back the money he borrowed from my mom—because of us. My uncle will have to go back to selling soap in Saskatchewan and won't live with me anymore—because of us. We can*not* let this happen!"

"Your uncle was on his way to meet with Magnus Snayle when I left."

Addy's face turned from determined to panicky. "Does Snayle know what's going on?"

"Not yet. Vim was hoping to keep him away from the comic as long as he could."

"How much time do we have?" said Addy.

"Maybe not much. That's why we should leave." Wylder shivered. A cloud had appeared out of nowhere to block the sun. The earth shook a bit, the way it does when a subway train runs under where you're walking.

"Are you saying—is my uncle saying—that if we leave, the comic will go back to normal? As if we were never in it?"

"I hope so," said Wylder.

"Because—think about it—the first worst thing that happened wasn't so much about *us* as our *stuff*. It was Flynn tripping over your backpack and losing his hand. You going to Toronto didn't bring his hand back."

Wylder felt his face heat up.

"Oh," said Addy. "That's it, isn't it? Our stuff."

Impedimenta, thought Wylder.

"Your backpack?" She looked down at her dress. "My jeans? What happens if they stick around?"

"I don't know."

"My jeans are in still in Nelly's room. Your backpack is in Florida. Even if we go home, our stuff stays and keeps messing up the comic."

"Your jeans haven't messed up anything," said Wylder quietly. "But anyway, we're only guessing that those things matter. I don't want to be the person who tells your uncle that you got smashed on the rocks by a lammergeyer. Your uncle loves you. Whole. And my mom loves me."

"Enough mush." Addy rubbed Catnip's head. "You've made your point. But you know you'll feel like a loser if you go back without *trying*. Think about that, Mr. I Don't Want to Tell Your Uncle. And anyway, you're not in charge of me! I want us both to stay and fix things. Come on, Wylder!"

All Wylder had wanted was to find Addy. Now that he had, he saw that maybe there was more involved. You couldn't rescue someone who did not want to be rescued.

"Your uncle might've said something about stuff,"

he mumbled. He *would* feel like a loser if he didn't even try to fix the story he had wrecked.

Addy seemed to realize that his resolve was melting. She brushed the sand off her hands with a couple of brisk claps. "If one of us is about to get captured or amputated, we'll just turn the page and escape, okay?"

"I don't— *Amputated?*"

"Okay?"

Wylder sighed, suspecting he had just agreed.

A girl in a dazzling pink bathing suit landed a triple backflip right at their feet, sending up a fine spray of sand. Her skin was as smooth as a plastic doll. Her tight curls bounced, and her teeth glittered as she sang out: "Cinnaglom is like fireworks of flavor!" she said.

"Uh, yeah," said Addy. "Like that's important."

The girl's sunny smile wavered for a moment. "Is that a ... *rat?*" she whispered.

Catnip sat up on Addy's shoulder and sniffed.

There was that subway rumble again. The girl bit her lip and hurried back to her friends. The water sparkled, the palm fronds clicked, the breeze smelled sweet. It was all kind of perfect.

"Let's make a plan," said Addy. "Step by step, let's take out the traces that we were ever in the comic."

"But every move we made changed something. People talked to us, bumped into us. We affected them in every panel."

"True. But we didn't leave our *stuff* behind in every panel. Let's go collect what we dropped."

"Starting with my backpack."

"Right. And my jeans. Anything else?"

Cell phone? No, that was still in his backpack. But there was something—

A merry tinkle of music interrupted his thoughts. The beach kids had joined hands in a circle and were singing, faces lifted to the sky.

"It's the jingle," said Addy. *"Put sparkles in your mouth with fireworks of flavor!"*

She let Catnip run down her arm and stood up.

"I say we start at the beginning, with the Red Riders and the gold. We'll zip through to where we are now to make sure we haven't left anything behind."

"But what about here in Cinnaglom?" said Wylder. "That bouncy little girl could be telling her friends about the rat right now. Messing stuff up all over again."

"Cinnaglom isn't part of the story—it's an ad. As far as the comic is concerned, you and I have disappeared. When we turn the page, we'll go back to being part of the story, visible again." She held up the comic book. "Ready for page one?"

Her eyes were dark and fierce. How had he ever confused her with Nelly?

"Okay," said Wylder. "But here's the deal. You can lead the way and make the rules because you're such a ... I mean, because this is your idea. But *I* get to hold the comic. And don't say, 'It's my comic.'"

"Well," she said, "it's not *your* comic."

But she was smiling when she gave it to him.

Another rumble, longer and deeper than before, like the note on a church organ that makes the floor vibrate. The singers had stopped in the middle of their jingle. They huddled together in scared silence, the beach *trembling*.

Addy and Wylder stared at the panel where Lickpenny was forcing Flynn to laser-drill a hole in the train car roof. *What was happening to the picture?* The lines, the figures, the whole panel shook.

The next rumble was the strongest yet. Sand swirled around them as Wylder grabbed Addy to keep himself up and she clung back. Was it an earthquake? The sky was blue overhead but ominous clouds gathered on the horizon.

And then they heard the voice. A deep, resonant voice that came from the very air around them.

"ADDY ..."

The comic in Wylder's hand seemed alive for a moment, shaking violently. The Cinnaglom ad was still there.

> **BUT EVERY PANEL ON THE FACING PAGE WENT GRAY. AND THEN ...**

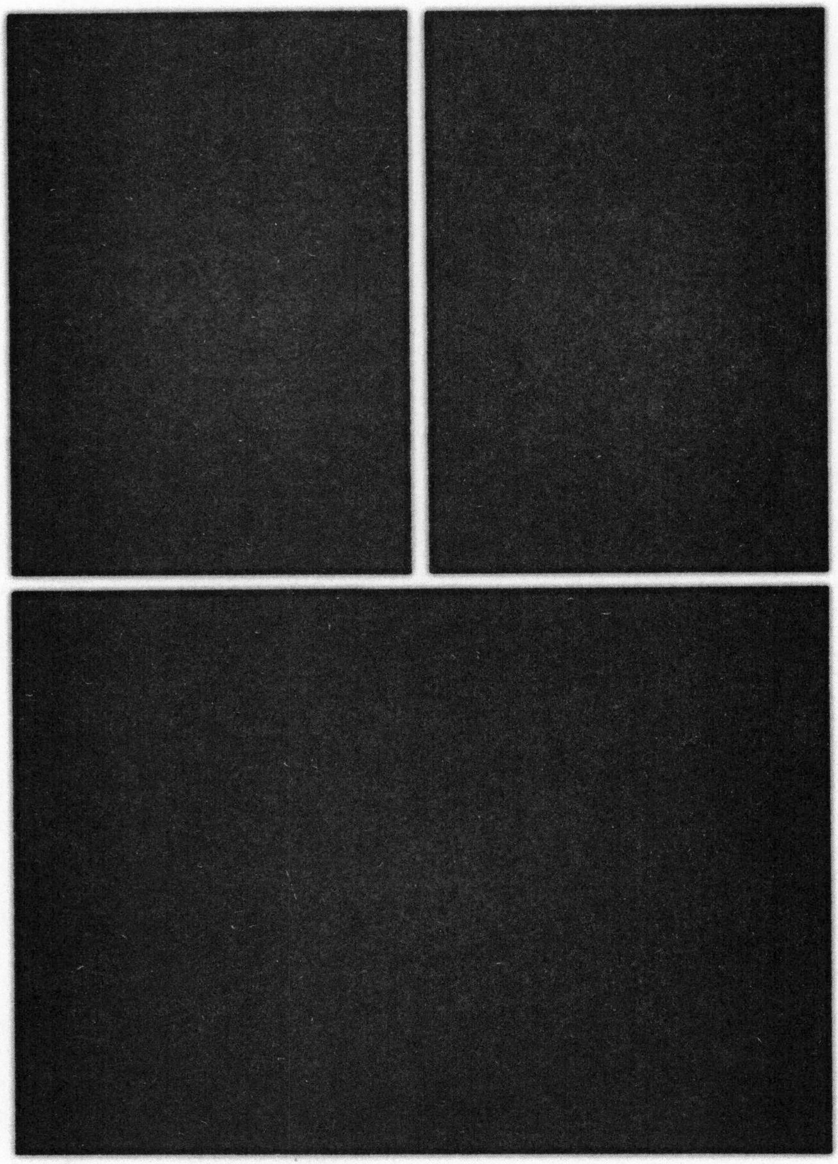

ADDY!"

There it was again.

Wylder didn't know anyone who spoke that low or that loud—whose voice was so powerful that it came from all points of the compass in the same breath.

And yet the voice was strangely familiar.

"ADDY, WHERE ARE YOU?"

"Who is that?" he said. "He knows your name!"

"Could it be ... ?" Addy looked around in confusion. Cinny was still surfing, but the waves were swollen, and his balance seemed precarious. On the shore, the kids stared at each other in confusion, the beach ball abandoned.

Addy pointed. "Look," she whispered.

The comic changed as they watched. The black page lightened, first to gray and then to white. The panels were blank, as if waiting for someone to draw the story.

You read in books about someone's heart sinking, and it sounds so unlikely. And then it happens to you. Wylder's heart went straight down like an express elevator, from his chest to his stomach.

He couldn't help wondering what would have happened if they'd been in the comic world when it went blank.

He didn't like this feeling of helplessness. This was worse than being trapped in the car wash last spring with his dad. Worse than watching a skateboarder collide with a lamppost.

He discovered that he and Addy were holding hands. He wasn't the only one who needed a friend.

"Wait!" Wylder had hardly blinked and the panels were filled in again. How had that happened?

"It was just some cosmic hiccup," said Addy. "See? The pictures are the way they were before."

Flynn doing Lickpenny's bidding. Nevins dangling, the lammergeyer hauling gold, McGurk and his new peg leg.

The blackout was a passing phenomenon, an eclipse. The story was back to the way it had been.

Or was it?

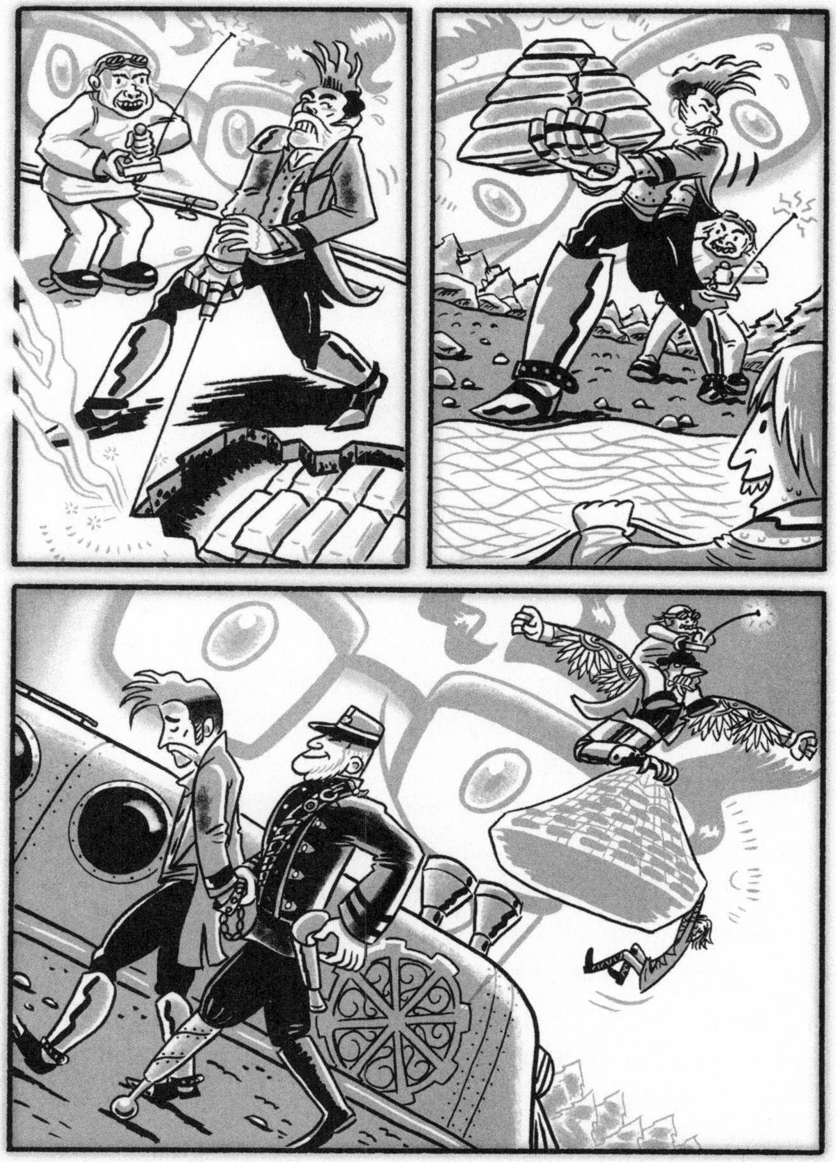

"Uh-oh," said Wylder. "Is that who I think it is?"

"ADDY! WYLDER WALLACE! ARE YOU THERE?"

"Sludge deluxe," said Addy. "*He's* here!"

"I don't get it," whispered Wylder.

"He must have found the portal. Uncle Vim is inside the comic."

Talk about massive muddy mess-ups! Addy's brain skipped around in one-word hops: *What? Why? No!*

"This is bad," said Wylder.

A dense gray fog rolled in over the ocean, devouring Cinna-Monkey and his gliding surfboard. The smiley beach kids began to whimper. Maybe they'd never seen bad weather before.

Addy nudged Catnip inside her vest and buttoned up. She tapped the comic in Wylder's hand. "You agree?"

He nodded, firm and certain. "Prepare for takeoff," he said. "Tell me when you're ready."

Addy closed her eyes, anticipating the yucky, spinny motion. Truth was, she'd nearly been convinced that Wylder was right, that they should just go home. In maybe ten more seconds, she would have let him flip to the back page, where the flashy ad for the

Gold Rush Express at ComicFest would have transported them to Toronto.

But now!

Uncle Vim had come looking for *her*. Addy tingled with certainty. What Wylder had said was true, and here was proof. Uncle Vim loved her more than he loved his own comic, and he was risking everything to find her when he thought she was lost. She was trying to save the comic, and Uncle Vim was trying to save her. But really, they were doing the same thing. Telling each other how much they cared.

"Are you ready or not?" Wylder nudged her.

She blinked sneaky tears out of the way. Deep breath.

"Yes," she said. "Go."

He slid his thumb between the cover and the first page. Addy watched so closely that she could practically feel the grainy texture of the paper. He lifted the corner.

THWIP!

Fog from the beach whooshed around them, adding to the blurry jumble of motion. Addy dropped with a thudding bounce on a very hard floor and bumped up against Wylder's leg. Catnip chirped like an excited bird.

"ADDY?"

Where was Uncle Vim? His voice reverberated in the room like a foghorn inside a jar. Not a room, though. A train car. And not just any train car ... Addy stared in wonder.

Stacks and stacks of golden bricks reached up to the ceiling like a million pounds of butter. She had expected to arrive in the scene with the Red Riders and the gold at the station. But she and Wylder had landed *inside* the armored car!

"Wow!" said Wylder. "It's beautiful. No wonder everyone wants to steal it."

"Um, hello? They're about to think that *we're* the ones stealing it." Addy pointed to the far end of the car, where two officers guarded an open door. Two more were wheeling in a cart loaded to the brim with gold bricks.

"ADDY!"

The Rider guards lifted their guns, aiming at the sky.

Addy scrambled to her feet. Wylder clutched the rolled-up comic book against his chest.

"Where are you?" she called.

At the sound of her voice, the officers at the door swung their weapons around to point them straight at Addy.

"DON'T TOUCH MY NIECE!"

The guards dropped their aim, but they advanced into the car, looking ready to pounce.

"Hands up," the younger one said. "You have some explaining to do." His hat was too big for him and sat low over his eyes.

The older Rider, with a mustache, clicked his heels together and strode toward them, motioning to the other fellow to keep his gun at the ready.

"I think we just blew the story-fixing plan," said Wylder. He lifted his arms above his head, still gripping the comic book.

"Uncle Vim?" Addy raised her hands too. She scanned the spaces not filled with gold. Her eyes went up to a window near the roof—a window so small it was more of an air vent.

"Uncle Vim!"

Peering through the tiny window was a bespectacled and beloved face.

"Fancy meeting *me* here," Wylder murmured.

Catnip, on his hind legs, looked almost as if he were waving at Viminy Crowe.

"*What* did you say?" The mustachioed Rider poked Wylder with his blunderbuss.

"Er, nothing." Wylder looked the way Addy felt—horrified at having a real weapon pointed at him.

"Next time," said the Rider, tugging at the end of his mustache, "say what you mean, loud and clear, Cowboy."

Wylder stared at the officer. Sparkling eyes, cheeky smile, extraordinary facial hair.

"Holy cannoli," said Addy. "I forgot about him."

"Y-y-you're Flynn!" Wylder's eyes were wide open, like a cartoon face of surprise.

"Sssh!" said Flynn. "Officer McNot. Special duty sergeant."

"Special *gold* duty, you mean!" said Wylder.

"We're supposed to be fixing the plot," said Addy. "Not giving it away!"

"THAT'S MY GIRL!" said Uncle Vim.

"And *you*!" cried Addy. "What are you doing here?"

"I FREAKED WHEN I GOT YOUR NOTE, WYLDER WALLACE. I HAD TO COME FOR YOU."

"But how did you—"

"I TRIED THE LADIES' ROOM BUT THAT DIDN'T WORK. SO I FOUND THE DISPLAY AND HERE I AM. SLUDGE! I WISH THIS BOOMING VOICE-OF-GOD THING WOULD GO AWAY. BUT I'M SO HAPPY TO SEE YOU BOTH, I COULD DANCE THE SAMBA."

"Please don't," said Addy.

"HA HA HA HA HA HA HA HA."

Uncle Vim's laughter shook the entire carriage. The Rider with the too-big hat lifted his gun again. The one with the mustache wasn't there anymore.

"Where'd he go?" said Wylder. "The guy called McNot?"

The other guard looked around in befuddlement.

"Um, Officer?" said Addy. "We're in here by mistake. Just let us go, and I promise you'll never see us again."

"I am under orders to apprehend all suspicious persons," said the Rider.

"Then I guess we're going to wreck your day." Addy scooped Catnip into her bag. "Right, Wylder?"

"Right."

THWIP!

Next page. In the train corridor, just as Isadora and Nelly boarded, followed by a Porter ServiDude with four arms carrying suitcases and boxes, and one more holding open the stateroom door. Nelly was talking a mile a minute.

"I *like* this train, Auntie! Did you see those Red Riders? They're guarding something big, I'll wager. I'm going exploring to find out what. Can I? Can I go exploring?"

Isadora smiled. "Not 'can I,' dear. 'May I.' 'May I go exploring?'"

"*May I*, then? And I want new boots. Can I get new ones in Toronto?"

The stateroom door closed behind them.

Wylder poked Addy. "Nelly is based on you, right?"

"Nelly might *look* like me," said Addy, "but actually it's Isadora who more resembles—"

"Nice try," said Wylder.

"Let's find Uncle Vim."

The corridor was nearly empty. The train whistled loudly as it pulled out of the Vancouver station.

CLICKETY-CLACK, CLICKETY-CLACK.

"Can you hear me, Uncle Vim?" said Addy. "Can you see me?"

"I CAN SEE EVERYTHING!"

The voice was loud, deep, scary.

"Where are— Oh, yes." She pointed out the window. Sure enough, a shadowy outline of Uncle Vim's head floated alongside the moving train. Wylder waved and Uncle Vim nodded.

"YOU WERE RIGHT, WYLDER WALLACE. IT'S REAL AS REAL! INCREDIBALLOO!"

"Shhh!" said Addy. "Where *are* you?"

Wylder scanned the page. "His head is in every panel," he muttered. "But I don't see his body anywhere."

"Are you in the train, Uncle Vim?" Addy asked. "Or outside?"

"I AM WATCHING A TRAIN CREW MOVE A TREE OFF THE TRACKS."

"Can you try whispering?" said Addy.

"WHY IS THERE A TREE ON THE TRAIN TRACKS?" Uncle Vim spoke at the same echoing volume.

"Yeah, why is that?" said Wylder.

"The tree was uprooted in the flood. Remember how our clothes were all soaked?"

Jeez, he thought. I fell in the pool and the entire world got drenched.

"We have to meet up," said Addy.

"Do you have your copy of the comic book, Uncle Vim?"

Vim's ghostly head nodded.

A whoosh of air came rushing down the carriage. Outside the window, Wylder saw a tree bend over sideways before straightening back up. A flurry of alarmed cries went through the passengers. A ServiDude zipped past them on well-oiled wheels, arms flapping. It rolled right through the first-class car and banged into the door at the end.

"ASTOUNDISHING! I TURNED THE PAGE AND ZWOOSH!"

"Pretty, pretty please," said Addy. "Will you just whisper?"

Wylder was trying to wrap his brain around the tricky situation. "*Where* are you, Uncle Vim?" Two comic books, open at two different places. A scary balancing act. Like riding a bike on a high wire, the only way off was down.

"I SEE MISS PRISM, MY FOURTH-GRADE TEACHER. SHE GAVE ME A DETENTION FOR RUNNING IN THE HALLS, SO I DREW HER WITH A CANE. HI THERE, MISS PRISM! DOING MUCH RUNNING THESE DAYS?"

Addy bugged her eyes at Wylder, like "How embarrassing could a shouting uncle be?"

Another whoosh of air rushed down the corridor. The ServiDude rolled back past them and through the open door at the other end of the carriage.

"PEOPLE ARE STARING AT ME AS IF I'M SOME KIND OF MONSTER. REMINDS ME OF A HIGH SCHOOL DANCE. HOW DO I GET TO YOU, ADDY?"

She peered at the comic in Wylder's hand. "Turn to page 3, Uncle Vim!" she said. "That's where we are! Third panel."

WHOOSH! Vim turned a page. And another. And another. *WHOOSH! WHOOSH!* Mighty gusts of wind blew new people into the carriage. Some stayed on their feet. Others hovered just above the ground. Where had they come from? A girl floated by. Her face looked just like Nelly's—and Addy's—but she had blonde hair and glasses. Was it Nelly in disguise? No, because *there* was Nelly, creeping toward the door. And there was Isadora—but no, not actually. This woman was taller than Isadora and led a tiger on a leash. A tiger! The beast yawned as it padded along. Wylder squeezed to the side of the aisle, out of its way.

"OKAY, ADDY! I'M IN A QUIET PLACE. I'LL WAIT FOR YOU HERE."

Addy pushed through the crowd to get closer to Uncle Vim's strange floating head, which was still hovering outside the window. His glasses flashed when the sun caught them.

"Tell us exactly where you are," said Addy. "We'll come to you."

"Here he is." Wylder pointed to the comic.

Uncle Vim's answer left no doubt.

"I AM STANDING NEXT TO A TOILET."

28

ylder giggled. Addy shot him what she hoped was a fierce look, but he just shrugged.

"You have to admit, it's kind of funny," he said. "Look at their faces."

Everyone in the train car was staring at Addy and Wylder. As if *they* were the ones standing next to a toilet. Uncle Vim had a way of doing that. Pretty much any time Addy was out in public with him, he said embarrassing stuff too loudly, not thinking about how it would sound to other people.

"Stay where you are!" called Addy. "Don't turn the page! And *please try to whisper!* C'mon, Wylder. Backpack, remember? Jeans. Sheesh, let's get Uncle Vim *now,* before he says anything else."

But the aisle was blocked by dozens of new passengers. In the last ten seconds, it had become so crowded that Addy couldn't budge. And not just the aisle. Two or three people sat in every seat, some right on top of each other.

"Ow!" yelped a scowling man. He snatched a boy's arm. "Is that a slingshot, you scallywag?" The boy looked like Nevins, except that his hair was curly, and he was missing his front teeth. He wriggled away from the injured gentleman's grasp while other passengers tsked.

"Excuse us," said Addy. "We have to get through."

She recognized most of the faces. Mr. Cicero, who ran the Italian market on Queen Street. The postman, who had one time stepped on Catnip. Emma's mom, who drove Addy and Emma to soccer every week. All of them with exaggerated features and wearing steampunk-y clothes.

"Hey, there's a robot made of car parts!" said Wylder. "And look at the one with drill bits for hands!"

Addy remembered sitting in this very carriage before Captain McGurk showed up to shoot his blunderbuss at Catnip. It had been quiet then. She and Wylder had sat together in an empty pair of plush-covered seats. What was going on here?

"Wow!" Wylder's eyes nearly popped out of his head. Addy followed his gaze and immediately poked him.

"Hey!" she said. "Don't look at that!"

He was gaping at a woman whose face was similar to Isadora's, only this one wore a skimpy bikini top that showed off too much curviness, above and below.

"I told Vim that was totally gross and sexist. I made him crumple up that drawing into a little ball." Addy peered at the woman and saw that her skin was faintly creased. A cross-eyed version of Nevins squirted mustard on the lady's butt, and Addy pretended not to see.

"Excuse us, please." Addy wriggled her way between bodies, pulling on Wylder's sleeve to make him stick close.

"There's another one," said Wylder. "Isadora dressed up as a doctor, see? White coat, surgical mask?"

"That's why she could sew Snap's hand onto Flynn," said Addy. "Vim wanted her to have endless cool skills—like doctoring, alongside flying, and fighting humongous reptiles."

"ADDY! AT LAST!"

"What?" said Addy.

"NO, WAIT! YOU'RE NOT ADDY! YOU ARE NONE OTHER THAN NELLY DAY! YOU HAD ME FOOLED IN TORONTO. GOSH, I'M GOOD."

"Aunt Isadoraaaaa!" cried Nelly. "There's a man in the water closet! Talking to me!"

"ON MY WAY, NELLY DAY! ADDY? REAL ADDY? I'M COMING TO FIND YOU!"

The washroom door opened. Addy craned her neck to see through the crowd. She could make out the ragged halo of Vim's wild hair.

"Auntie, where are you?" Nelly sounded frantic. "Come save me!"

"This could be bad." Wylder clenched the back of Addy's vest.

"Yeah," said Addy. "I do not want to witness Isadora beating the sludge out of Uncle Vim with her whip."

"Or *ten* Isadoras," said Wylder. "Plus a tiger."

"He wasn't trying to hurt you, Nelly," Addy called out. "I promise!" She looked around at the bemused faces of the crowd. So many false starts and multiple tries.

"Oh!" she cried. "Lightbulb!"

"I don't understand," said Wylder. "Who are all these people?"

"ALL THESE PEOPLE," said Uncle Vim, "ARE MY INVENTIONS!"

"Exactamundo," said Addy. The answer had come to her in one whole piece. She tossed away being polite and began to shove, chattering at Wylder in breathy spurts. "Uncle Vim is an artist, right? So he draws a million different versions of every character."

A doodling maniac, sketchbooks full of efforts. Every detail on every person and every page.

She pushed past a pair of arguing Nellys, one wearing a sun hat and the other with her arm in a sling.

"Huh," said Wylder. "So when Vim came through the portal—"

"It was like his brain exploded all over the entire comic. Everything he ever drew for the Summer Special came along with him, inside his head. It's all here at the same time."

"Stop that rascal!" A lady with a cane spat like a mad cat.

A Nevins look-alike wearing strange purple kneepads and an eye patch swung from an overhead luggage rack with a pea-shooter between his lips, aiming tiny missiles this way and that.

Addy opened her bag and urged Catnip to run up her arm and onto her head. "Move!"

"*Eep!* A rat!" Alarmed passengers scrambled to get out of the way as Addy dragged Wylder after her.

"PART THE WATERS, GOOD PEOPLE. LET HER THROUGH!"

Uncle Vim's voice cleared the few lingering characters as if he were a snowplow.

"Uncle Vim!" Addy threw herself at him, Catnip sliding down her hair. The crowd held its breath.

Vim went down on one knee and scooped Addy into his arms. Just for a second, the world disappeared, and she hung on to her uncle as tightly as ever a girl could.

"ADDY, ADDY, ADDY," he murmured—if you could call it murmuring when it was more like the roar of a vacuum cleaner. She was crying, but so was he. They looked at each other and laughed through tears, then hugged all over again. Finally she let him go so she could catch a breath.

"HARRUMPH." Vim made a noise into his sleeve. Addy suspected he was blowing his nose and tried not to be grossed out. She disentangled Catnip from her hair.

Vim leaned over to shake Wylder's hand, face bright with wonder.

"ASTOUNDALICIOUS, MY BOY! YOUR REPORT WAS ENTIRELY ACCURATE! THIS PLACE *IS* REAL!"

"It's great to see you, sir," said Wylder. "Uncle Vim. I'm sorry I didn't get a chance yet to fix your comic. You know, to pick up the stuff we left behind. But we've been talking about it."

Ha, thought Addy. If that's what you call me insisting and you caving.

"MY BOY, THREE HEADS ARE BETTER THAN TWO. WE SHALL STRIVE TO DO IT TOGETHER!"

"Are you in deep sludge, Uncle Vim?" said Addy. "With FunnyBones?"

"THE VERY DEEPEST, ADDY-PIE." Vim launched into his tale of woe, filling Addy in on every little detail. In a big, big voice. Magnus Snayle, the FunnyBones prez, was breathing down Vim's neck like a bounty hunter.

He wanted those ten thousand comics, and he wanted them yesterday. But they needed Viminy Crowe's signature to release them from the customs lockup at Union Station. Vim was supposed to have been there … jeez, how long ago? Magnus would be pacing and checking his phone every two minutes in case he'd missed a text message.

"Remind me," Addy interrupted, "to tell you about the VaporLinks."

"They're real," said Wylder gloomily.

"HOW LONG BEFORE MAGNUS SWEET-TALKS THE CUSTOMS FOLKS INTO LETTING HIM HAVE A LOOK?" said Uncle Vim.

How long before he discovered that the story had gone beyond quirky and inventive to the verge of lunacy? How long before Viminy Crowe received word that FunnyBones was withdrawing its investment and never, *ever* wanted to see him again?

"I DON'T KNOW," Uncle Vim went on. "BUT, YEAH, I'D SAY I'M KNEE-DEEP IN SLUDGE."

"If you want to get home right now and see that Magnus guy—" Wylder began.

"No," said Addy. "We have to get our stuff out of the story first. Your backpack and my jeans?"

"AND—"

"And what, Uncle Vim?"

"THINGS WENT WRONG LONG BEFORE THE BACK-PACK GOT LOST," said Vim. "I NOTICED SOMETHING

CRUCIAL WHILE I SEARCHED THE PAGES FOR
YOU."

Catnip leapt from Addy's head to Uncle Vim's shoulder.

"HELLO, LITTLE FELLA! BIG DAY FOR A RODENT,
EH? HOLY CANNOLI! WHAT HAVE YOU BEEN EATING?"

"He *has* kind of grown," said Addy. "He had a couple
of sips of Lickpenny's catalyzer. But what was that you
were saying about—"

"INTERESTING! THE LAB IS EXACTLY WHERE WE
HAVE TO STOP ON OUR WAY TO FLORIDA."

Uncle Vim waved his comic book. A hearty breeze
lifted the hair right off Addy's neck.

"What for?" she said.

He ran his thumb over the edges of the comic, making
a noise like shuffling cards.

"Hey!" shrieked Wylder.

"Stop!" said Addy.

Vim thwipping pages was like an ocean wave slamming into you, knocking you over and holding you
under, with swirling grit and seaweed and the dreadful
feeling that you might not come up again.

29

The stone floor was familiar. So was the steam, the countertop full of apparatus and the smell of old tuna sandwich. Lickpenny's secret laboratory.

"Why are we in the lab?" whispered Addy.

"ONION RINGS."

"Shhh!" said Addy. "We're in enemy territory."

"SORRY. ONION RINGS."

"I thought there was something else," said Wylder, "but ... my onion rings? From lunch?"

He checked the comic, and found the three of them in a panel under the caption *INKHILL MOUNTAIN, 6 MONTHS AGO*. He couldn't see any onion rings.

Uncle Vim was on his feet, humming like an excited bumblebee. Addy yanked him back down.

The heavy door on the far side of the lab screeched slowly open. The three human intruders scrambled to hide behind the table. Catnip's nose peeped out from under Addy's hair.

"Scum-puppy!" Lickpenny shouted through a curtain of steam. "Hurry up with the catalyzer! You good-for-nothing, lazy glob of putrid phlegm!"

This was all the way Wylder remembered it, only "Where are the onion rings?" he wanted to know.

Vim traced the comic panels in his book with his finger. Wylder followed along in his own copy.

"OH," said Vim. "THE ONION RINGS ARE ON THE NEXT PAGE." He licked his thumb, about to turn the page. Addy stopped him.

"Wait," she whispered. "Two comics now, right? Do it together. Don't blow it! Three. Two. One. Go!"

TH-THWIP! Easiest page turn yet, like driving over a speed bump.

"HERE WE ARE," whispered Vim. They were exactly where they'd been—behind the table in Lickpenny's lab—but it was a few minutes later.

"Why are you standing there like an old umbrella?" bellowed the professor. "Prepare the siphon at *once!*"

Nevins, his face glum and resentful, stirred the boiling pot of catalyzer.

"Sludge."

Nevins had spotted the onion rings.

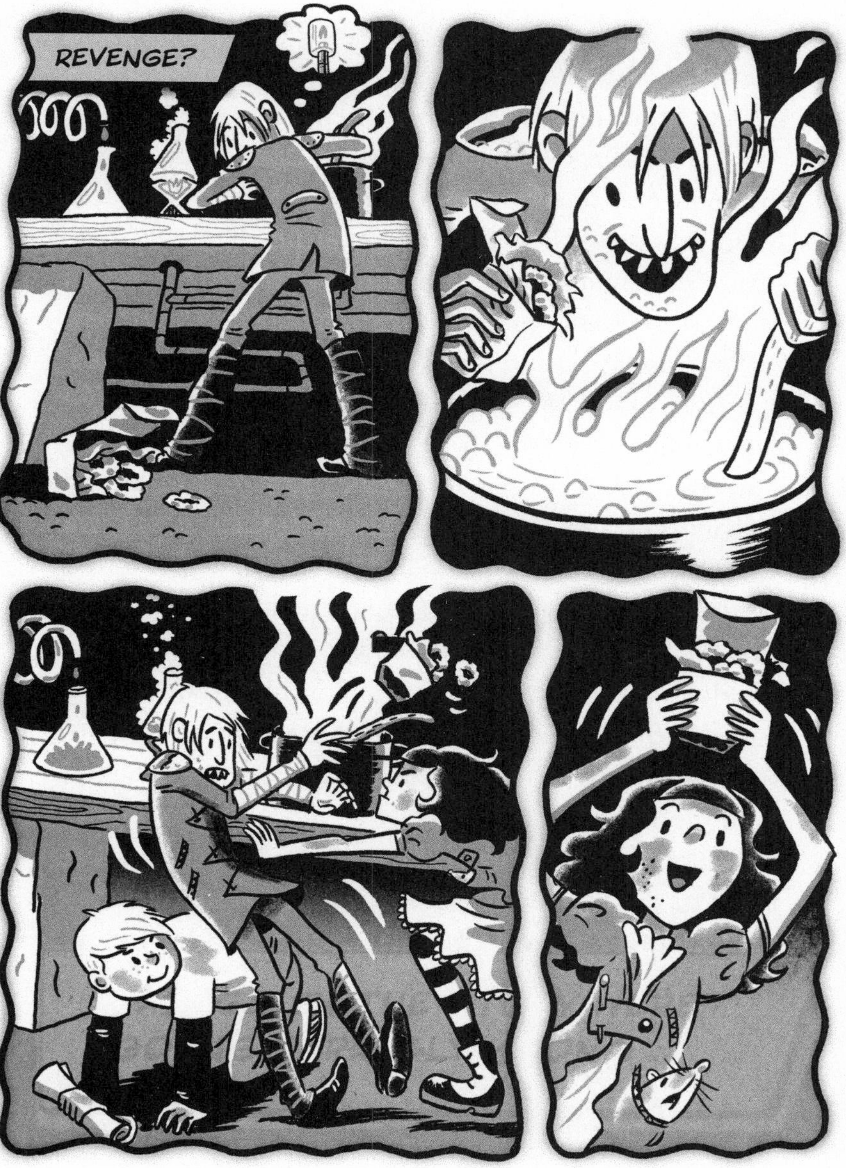
REVENGE?

Addy crammed the box into one of the pockets on her vest and high-fived Wylder. *Whew!* Phase one in fixing the comic plot accomplished!

Wylder thought he understood. He must have dropped the onion rings during the first flashback. Nevins dumped them into the pot, and the strange new ingredient changed the catalyzer formula, making Snap and Krackle behave crazily.

Now the lab was in turmoil. The two familiar robots stomped in circles alongside Vim's early versions of them. There must have been a half dozen—what did Addy call them?—*mechanizmos* altogether, including a monopod, jumping up and down on its giant foot, and a robot with arms like steam-shovel buckets and metal fingers that clamped open and shut. There was even a girl robot missing scraps of her face. Yuck! Wylder shrank away from her. That had to be Poppy, Snap and Krackle's sister. Nevins, on the ground, rolled over just in time to avoid being stomped by the monopod.

"Who are *you*?" Lickpenny worked a controller so that the steam-shovel robot threatened Uncle Vim.

"I MADE YOU," said Uncle Vim. "THINK OF ME AS DADDY!"

"This is no time for jokes!" shouted Addy.

"SORRY!"

"Attack!" cried Lickpenny. "Attack!"

The robot lurched forward, faster than you'd ever

think possible. One of his jointed metal arms shot out to grab the comic book in Vim's hand. There was a ripping, grinding noise, and a papery dust drifted to the floor. Vim let out a startled shriek and jerked his hand away—empty.

"Time to gooooooo!" shouted Addy. They jammed themselves through the door and *ran*.

The three hustled along a hallway that had been carved from the rock of the mountain. The walls and ceiling were rounded. Torches burned in sconces.

"Much worse with all the extra robots!" said Wylder between puffs.

"I DON'T LIKE HOW THINGS JUST SHOW UP WHEN I'VE FORGOTTEN ALL ABOUT DRAWING THEM!"

Vim paused for a second, catching his breath and sighing at the same time.

"MY COMIC GOT CHEWED TO BITS."

"But we got the onion rings," said Addy.

The robots clanked and hissed behind them, joined now by a gang of shouting boys.

Boys?

Wylder looked over his shoulder. "Nevins," he said. "More than one of him."

"Backpack and jeans," muttered Addy. "Backpack and jeans."

They came to a fork in the tunnel. Without hesitation, Vim led them to the right.

"FOLLOW ME."

Totally sure of himself. Well, after all, thought Wylder, Vim was the one who'd imagined the whole setup.

Two minutes later, they reached a dead end.

"Nice one, Uncle Vim," said Addy.

A chilly draft seeped in from who knew where. Wylder shivered. A torch flickered over their heads, making the shadows dance.

"I SWEAR THERE'S A SECRET DOOR HERE THAT WILL TAKE US OUTSIDE."

"Why don't we just turn the page?" said Wylder. "I still have my comic."

"*Your* comic?" Addy raised an eyebrow.

Behind them, a metallic clamor and angry shouts echoed through the tunnel.

30

"**I** meant," said Wylder, "that Uncle Vim could take charge of my ... er, *the* comic book."

"Oh."

"He could turn the right number of pages to get us to my backpack. Or wherever else we want to go."

"I KNOW THIS BOOK LIKE I WROTE IT MYSELF. HA-HA!"

"The story is pretty messed up," said Addy. "What are the chances that—"

"I'D SAY RIGHT ABOUT THE MIDDLE ..."

"Maybe earlier," said Wylder.

He had written it, thought Addy, but it wasn't what he'd written anymore.

"If there's any question," she said, "we should—"

"I AM ABSOLUTARILY CERTAIN."

Wylder pulled the battered comic book out of his pocket and held it in two hands, not quite passing it to Uncle Vim. Maybe he was having doubts as well.

"TRUST ME, WYLDER WALLACE. I DREW EVERY LINE OF THAT COMIC. MOST OF THEM A DOZEN TIMES." Vim pulled a spider web out of his hair, with the spider still in it. He sighed. "I SHOULD GET YOU KIDS HOME. AND FACE WHATEVER SLUDGE I'M IN WITH FUNNYBONES."

A strange bellowing and the clang of footsteps on stone came scarily closer, right around the corner!

"Stop wasting time!" said Addy. "Come *on*! Gator pool, here we come!"

"I agree," said Wylder. "My cell phone's in my backpack. If it's lost, my mom will go purple."

He held out the comic book, and Uncle Vim took it.

THWIP!

Even when the wobbly part stopped, Addy was entirely uncomfortable, with her legs doubled up against a wall and Uncle Vim's armpit over her nose.

"Not Florida." Wylder sounded as if he had a mouthful of hair, which it turned out he did, because Uncle Vim's wild mane was trailing across his face. Disentangling took a couple of minutes, due to the shaking floor and the narrow place they were in.

"WELL, I'M MYSTIFICATED!" said Uncle Vim. "NOT THE GATOR POOL AT ALL! MY CALCULATION SHOULD NOT HAVE CARRIED US HERE. TAKE BACK YOUR COMIC, WYLDER WALLACE. I AM NOT THE PILOT I THOUGHT I WAS."

Uncle Vim stuffed the battered comic into Wylder's back pocket. Addy decided not to argue. Her uncle looked pretty downcast.

"I guess we're back on the train," said Wylder.

"Duh," said Addy. Catnip crawled out of her vest pocket and climbed down to the pocket holding the onion rings. She fed him a string of onion—hardly a ring at this point. He gobbled it down, and every last crumb of the others as well.

"What a useful little guy," said Wylder.

"You're just figuring that out?" Addy carefully folded the empty box and slid it back into her pocket.

Uncle Vim glanced around. "STATEROOM CORRIDOR, FROM THE LOOK OF IT. NUMBER ONE RIGHT THERE, SEE? WHERE THE FIENDISH NEPHEW IS STICKING HIS HEAD OUT."

"Is that one of the Nevinses from the tunnel?" said Wylder. "Did he come with us?"

"That's Lickpenny's suite," said Addy. "He was probably here already."

The hallway outside the staterooms was filling up with people, including a couple of Nellys and more than a few Nevinses.

"OKAY, WE LANDED WRONG. BUT PICK UP YOUR DUDS, ADDY." Uncle Vim climbed to his feet. "SINCE WE'RE IN THE NEIGHBORHOOD."

She scooted over to the door marked with an elegant number 2 and found it unlocked. But when she pushed it open, she closed it again with a swift click. Inside was something more horrible than a slavering alligator.

"What's up?" whispered Wylder. "Go get your stuff."

Addy shook her head and took a step back. Wylder put his hand on the doorknob.

"You do *not* want to go in there," said Addy.

"Why not?" Wylder pulled open the door.

“Oh,” said Wylder.

“I swear this sludge does not happen in the real comic,” said Addy.

Vim's lips puckered in a silent whistle.

"SHE'S REALLY SOMETHING," he whispered.

Addy punched him in the side. "You're being creepy, Uncle Vim. Stop drooling."

Wylder couldn't help noticing all the Nevinses on the train. Short Nevinses and tall ones. Bow-legged, pigeon-toed and curly-haired Nevinses; pimply Nevinses, and Nevinses with extra teeth. All different, but all clearly the same boy. Every Nevins had an evil glint in his eye, and every one was ready to play a prank. One had a bucket of paint and another carried matches; a third tossed a stone in the air and caught it, while a fourth swung from a chandelier. A platoon of impish boys. Wylder was glad he wasn't a nervous old lady.

He jumped when he felt a hand on his shoulder, but it was only Addy.

"We have to get my jeans," she whispered.

"Right."

She pointed at the stateroom door.

"From in there?" he asked, wincing at the thought of Flynn and Isadora locked lip to lip.

"That's where I left them."

They peeked around the corner of the door. The lovers were still at it. Her hat had fallen off, and he was running his fingers through her hair. A blue jewel glittered in her ear.

"The Tooting Sapphire," whispered Wylder.

Addy pointed at a tangled piece of denim in the corner of the stateroom.

"There," she said. "Sneak in. Stay low and quiet. The lovebirds won't even notice you."

"*Me*? They're *your* jeans."

She glared at him.

Uncle Vim sighed. "ISN'T SHE BEAUTIFUL?"

Addy transferred her glare to her uncle and thrust her bag at Wylder. "Hold this."

Addy crawled back nearly to the door and then stood up and leapt the last few feet. She sagged against the wall of the corridor, giggling in a very un-Addy-like way. She tied the legs of her jeans around her waist in a big knot.

"I did it!" she said. "Whoa! Look out!"

Wylder turned to find a little squirt of a Nevins trying to squeeze past him into the stateroom. He looked only about eight, and he had a fistful of firecrackers. Wylder flung Addy's bag back at her and grabbed Nevins by the collar.

"Hey!" the boy squealed. "Let me go!"

The lovers didn't even pause in their smooching. Wylder yanked the kid out of the doorway and pushed him down the corridor. He glimpsed his hero stroking Isadora's face, and as he crept away from the stateroom door, he almost gasped out loud. In the hallway was another version of Flynn and Isadora—and they were kissing too! This Flynn had only one hand. He held Isadora awkwardly, but she didn't seem to mind. She kissed his nose.

"Darling, I love you!" she said.

"I love you more." He kissed her ear. No sapphire this time.

"No, I love *you* more!"

"It's smooching time!" He drew her to him.

Yuck!

"Please tell me the story doesn't end that way,"

Wylder said to Uncle Vim. "With the two of them together?"

"Come on, come *on*!" Addy was at his side. "Get the comic. Ready, Uncle Vim? To the gator pool!"

Maybe there was something to be said for bossiness, Wylder decided. Bossiness got things done.

And then ...

POP! POP! POP!

Nevins! Lighting firecrackers and tossing them!

POP! One landed in a lady's floppy hat. She did a squirming dance, hitting herself on the head.

Another went into the open mouth of one of Lickpenny's robots.

BRAHHWP! It sounded like a gigantic belch.

The next firecracker bounced off the ceiling and right into Wylder's back pocket.

The pocket with the comic book ...

32

"Ah! Ah! Ah! Ah!" Wylder pinged off the wall like a kernel of popcorn in a really hot pan. "My butt, my butt, my butt!"

"WHAT THE DEVIL HAS GOTTEN INTO YOU, WYLDER WALLACE?"

Uncle Vim's roar in the narrow corridor was like someone clanging cymbals right next to your ear. Every character in the carriage, including the naughty Nevinses, froze in place. Even the smoochers stopped smooching. The only thing moving was Wylder. His back pocket—filled with fuel in the shape of a comic book—was now sizzling and sparking like a firecracker. With his bare hand—because what else did he have?—he yanked out the comic and smacked it repeatedly against the wall.

Addy wondered for one second if she could untie the damp jeans from her waist and wring them out to extinguish the fire. About as good as spitting probably.

Catnip kneaded her shoulders with his paws, little tail swishing back and forth.

WHACK! WHACK! Wylder was in a frenzy, whacking the comic so fast and hard that no one could get close enough to help.

"Wylder! You're going to burn yourself!"

But he didn't stop. **WHACK! WHACK!** Sparks popping, smoke puffing, paper curling. His fingers were sooty black, and so was his face. The comic book smoldered. He held it by the spine and rubbed the edges of the pages into the floor.

Addy's legs wobbled. Uncle Vim staggered. The comic book slipped in Wylder's hand and—

THWIP!

DING, DING, DING, DING! An alarm bell rang as smoke swirled about the room. What room? A *big* room! The lobby of the Banff Springs Hotel was in the middle of a fire drill! Or *not* a drill, but the real thing!

"REMAIN CALM AT ALL TIMES," insisted a ServiDude. It was bright yellow, with an enormous nozzle where a nose would usually be. "PLEASE MAKE YOUR WAY TO THE NEAREST EXIT."

A parade of six more yellow ServiDudes rolled past, each with a narrow ladder extending straight up from its firefighter's helmet. *DING, DING, DING, DING!*

Addy saw Wylder drop the comic book, wipe his palms on his pants and scoop it up again. He caught her eye and winced.

"Sorry," he said.

Have you ever picked up a really hot plate? Your fingertips burn, but you can't drop the plate because it has someone's turkey dinner on it. That's how Wylder felt about the smoldering comic book. He couldn't run away and put his hands under the tap because the comic would keep burning, and it seemed more important than anything else not to let it burn!

Wylder's butt hurt too, but not as much. The firecracker had felt like a kick back there, or maybe a hard shot in soccer.

But his fingers—yikes!

Smoke kept pouring from the comic book. He turned the pages, finding the burning bits and rubbing them out. With every turn, the world shuddered, and they went to a new place. Wylder hardly noticed the scenes around him; he was more occupied with the pages themselves.

He coughed a lot, from the smoke coming off the comic book and swirling all around them too. When the comic had fallen into the pool, the whole world had got soaked. Now it was all on fire.

Another *THWIP* and they were on the flatcar of the train, the one with Isadora's balloon, jolting past a railway crossing at top speed. The rhythm of the wheels sounded frantic, out of control. *CLICKETY-POP! CLICKETY-CLICKETY-POP!* With every pop, Wylder bumped closer to the edge of the flatcar. He caught a confused picture of people at the crossing screaming and pointing. Isadora was cutting the ropes holding the basket of her balloon in place. Nelly worked the gas pump as the colorful bag inflated, stamping out flames when they got too close. Her boots were charred tatters.

"How much longer, Auntie?" she yelled. "If fire hits the gas line, we're all going to kingdom come."

Wylder was woozy from all the smoke. A piece of burning rope landed on the open page. He brushed it off. The train lurched around a bend. The wheels shrieked. Wind tried to tug the comic out of his hands. Pages flapped and turned.

THWIP, THWIP, THWIP, THWIP!

Stop. Drop. And roll. That's what Addy remembered from the fire drills at school.

But was that supposed to help if you were burning? Or was it to avoid the smoke? Didn't matter, since she wasn't exactly in control here. She was being rolled from one page to the next whether she liked it or not. The places they'd seen and characters they'd met raced past in a dizzying blur. Addy's head was woozy as she jostled and jounced, faintly aware that Uncle Vim and Wylder were jostling and jouncing along with her.

Until, suddenly, the air changed. The warmth was not only from smoke and fire. This warmth was balmy and sweet-smelling, carried on a breeze and rustling with palm fronds and frangipangi leaves.

Addy managed to shriek despite her mouth being full of what tasted like dust.

STOP! DON'T MOVE!

Wylder's hand froze in midair.

Uncle Vim lay face up, panting like an old dog after a game of fetch. Addy blinked and pushed the hair out of her eyes.

They were exactly where they needed to be.

Wylder heard Addy calling to him as if from a great distance. He was tired and confused and full of smoke. His fingertips tingled and burned.

Was the fire out? Had they got their stuff? Was the comic safe? Time to go. That's what Addy was saying. He shook his head and retched. For a second, his mind cleared.

He turned a page, he hoped for the last time.

THWIP!

"WYLDER WALLACE?!"

The roaring in his ears might have been Uncle Vim, and it might have been the end of the world.

The smell of scorched paper filled the air.

They'd landed—after *such* a bumpy ride!—in a place that Addy recognized, not only from Vim's drawings for the comic book but also from real life. It was Old City Hall on Queen Street in Toronto.

Except its bricks were charred, smoke hung in the air and the steps were full of people who clasped each other as if they might not meet again.

Addy's hair, her skin, the limp fabric of her clothing—all were gritty with smoke. Wylder's face, Uncle Vim's and probably her own were smeared with soot. As was Wylder's backpack, which she found herself clutching. Every person in sight had a smudged face and singed hair. And they all appeared to be as dazed and slightly nauseous as Addy felt. Wylder and poor Catnip both lay panting on the cobblestones.

A storm raged around them. Wind stirred ladies' dresses and tossed men's hats to the gutter. Lightning flashed, momentarily brightening the sky, followed at once by a growl of thunder.

Addy put Catnip on her shoulder. "Please be okay," she whispered. "You're a hero." Her hair whipped her face like a hundred rats' tails.

The mayhem on the street grew ominous as the approaching storm darkened day into night.

Uncle Vim looked up at the sky, turning in a slow, horrified circle.

Addy knelt beside the boy on the ground. "Wylder?" He twitched, so he wasn't dead.

"MY TORONTO!" boomed Uncle Vim. *"HOW DID THINGS GO SO WRONG?"*

"Hey!" Addy gave Wylder a shake. "Hello? Wake up!"

A woman screamed. Addy realized it was Miss Prism. She sure had volume!

The crowd gasped in unison. Addy followed the pointing fingers.

Her breath stopped.

Above their heads, a little higher than the clock tower of the city hall, was a hot-air balloon in distress. Isadora Fortuna—of course it was hers—yanked on ropes as flames licked at the basket.

What thread of the story had put her in this peril?

Isadora clambered onto the rim of the basket and leapt without hesitation into midair. She seemed almost to fly, reaching for one of the gargoyles that perched on the city hall turrets. She swung herself to safety on the statue's back, just as a lammergeyer dive-bombed the balloon, its sharp beak shredding the gold and scarlet stripes.

"WHY IS THAT BIRD EVEN HERE?" hollered Uncle Vim. He looked around frantically, as if someone could actually give him the answer. *"WE NEED A NET!"* he cried. A team of horses hauled a fire wagon down the street, bells jangling. *"OR A LADDER!"* Uncle Vim stepped to the curb, waving his arms at the firefighters.

Wylder began to cough. Addy wished she had some water to throw in his face, but she shook him again instead. He blinked and tried to sit up.

"Wha ... ?" He licked his lips. "Wherezzz ... hmmm?" He licked his lips and tried again. "Why aren't we home?" He had to yell to be heard over bells and sirens and a horde of shouting people. "Are we still in the comic?"

"Yes!" Addy pointed at the threatening sky, dark with clouds. "Near the end, but it's a messed-up end." She tugged the comic, still warm and slightly crisp, from under his elbow. "See?"

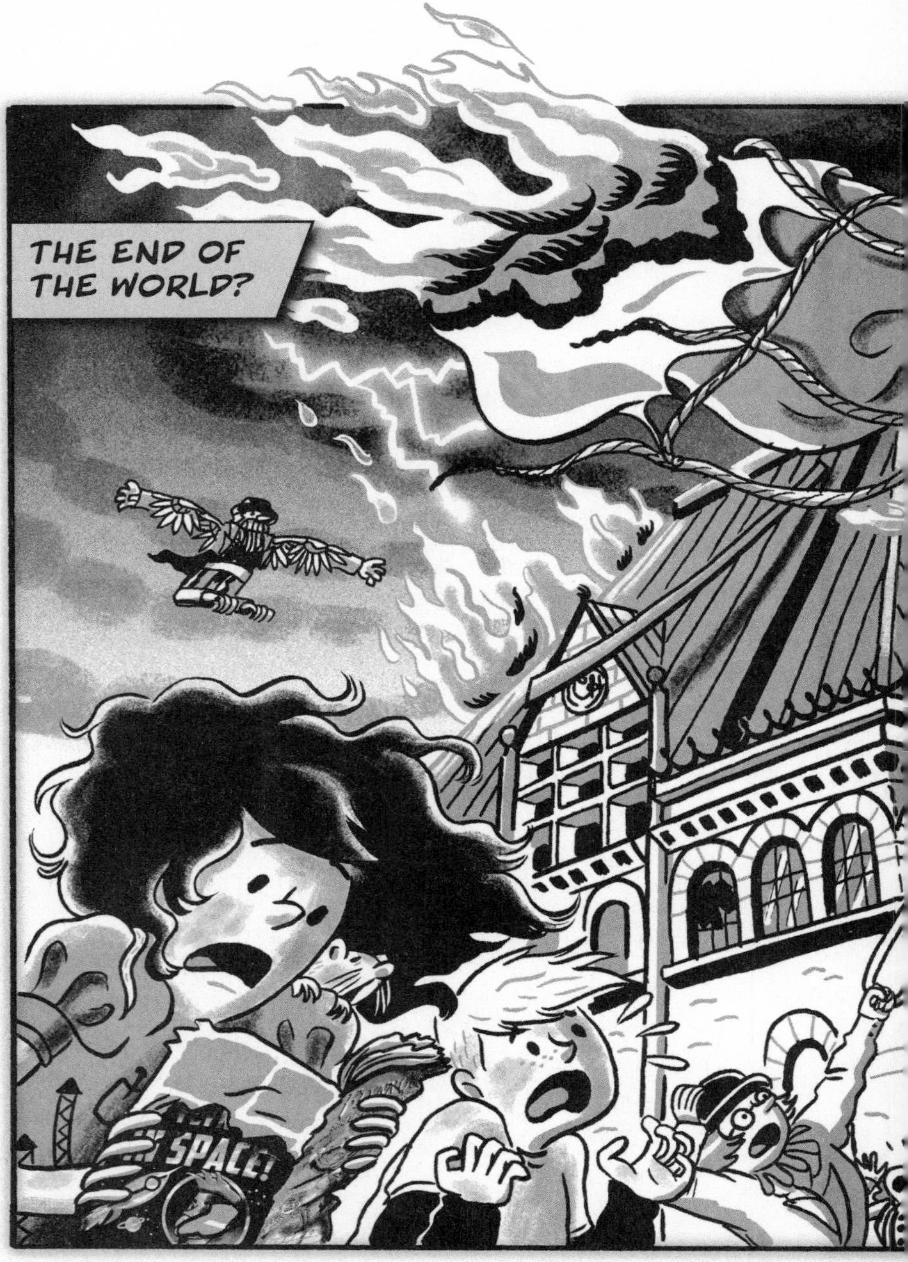
THE END OF
THE WORLD?
SPACE!

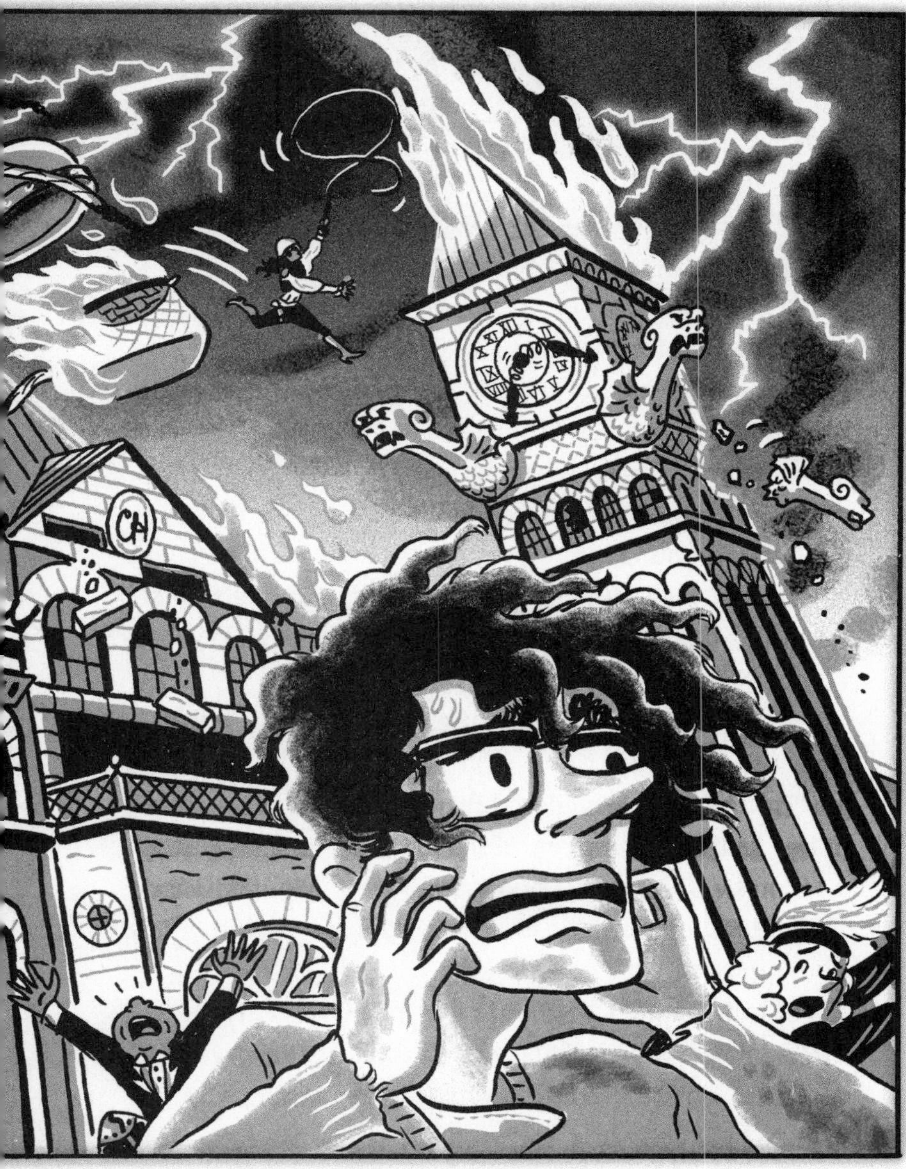

"**T**his is horrible," said Wylder.

"Where's the portal?" shouted Addy.

"At the end."

"This *is* the end! How much worse can it get?"

He took the comic back from her. "This isn't what happened with me and Nelly. Let me look ..."

"Hang on!" Addy dashed away. "Uncle Vim!"

He was in the middle of the street, pointing up at Isadora who clung to the gargoyle for dear life. Carriages and tricycles swerved past him on the road, bells blasting. Addy guided her staggering uncle back to Wylder, who understood what to do.

"The pages are stuck together. The ad for ComicFest is on the back page."

"Then turn!" she yelled. "Turn to the end."

He peeled the page carefully away.

THHHHHHHHHHWWWWIIPP.

Wylder didn't tumble around or lose his breath or fall to the ground.

"Go on!" shouted Addy. "Turn the page! We're still here!"

He stared down. This was the last page all right. There they were in front of City Hall. And there was the inside back cover. But ...

The ComicFest ad was gone. No more portal.

Wylder couldn't bring himself to meet Addy's eyes. He was the one keeping the comic safe, and he'd messed up. "Sorry," he muttered.

"Uncle Vim!" she pleaded. "Think of something!"

But Viminy Crowe was not doing much thinking. He stared at the sky, hands clawing at his face as if he wanted to tear out his eyes. The lammergeyer had grabbed Isadora by her hair and now whipsawed west, its wings flapping in the gale as she struggled to free herself. Uncle Vim watched them disappear behind a church steeple, then plunked himself down on the curb, head in his hands.

And he didn't even know yet all the trouble they were in.

But Wylder knew. "STUPID COMIC!" He flung it away, shaking with rage.

Addy snatched it back up. "Don't you dare!" she said. "This is our only link to home!"

"Don't you see? Our way home is burnt! Stupid Nevins and his firecrackers!"

Workmen hammered and sawed in the city hall plaza. What were they building in the middle of a storm?

"It's all Uncle Vim's fault!" Wylder cried. "Why did he have to come and turn the world nuts?"

Thunder rolled for long seconds. A chunk of stone fell to the street, smashing a fruit cart. Orange juice dripped onto the cobbles.

"And it's *your* fault, Addy! You going to the bathroom at ComicFest made all this happen!"

Hot, scared fury bubbled up inside Wylder, forcing his mouth open. He screamed until he ran out of breath, and when he stopped screaming, nothing had changed except that Addy's face was so close she could have bitten off his nose.

"You want to *blame* somebody?" she said. "Who dunked Flynn in the gator tank? Who grabbed the wrong girl? What good does blaming do? Stop acting like a baby and start thinking how to help!"

She was right. Of course she was right. The screaming had actually calmed Wylder down. He felt better. Stupid, but better.

"Sorry," he said.

"What?"

"I said sorry! You're right."

Catnip yawned and stretched along Addy's shoulder. His eyes gleamed. She turned her head and gave him a kiss on the nose. At least he was breathing easier now.

"Things can't get any worse," said Wylder.

"Things can always get worse," said Addy.

And they could.

"Extra! Extra!" A newsboy with a black-toothed grin held up a paper. "Read all about it!"

The headline read: FLYNN GOSTER HANGS TODAY! MAYOR DENIES APPEAL!

The workmen had been building a gallows! There it stood, on the front lawn of the city hall, a familiar shape even if Wylder had never seen a real one. And here came a cage on wheels, rolling toward the gallows. Snap the robot—singed and smudged, but with both hands in place and a bowler hat clamped firmly on its head—pushed from behind. In the cage, a hunched figure twirled his mustache.

Wylder peered closer. Was it?

It was.

Flynn Goster—his Red Rider disguise in smoke-streaked tatters—was on his final ride, about to be executed right here in front of them! That's what the story had come to: a dead hero. Wylder could only shake his head, and keep on shaking it when he saw that Flynn's jailer—with the big ring of keys—was Nevins.

"Holy cannoli! So who's the mayor?" said Addy.

Right on cue, the front doors of City Hall opened. Captain McGurk led an honor guard of Best Western Red Riders who marched out—McGurk hopped—and fanned away from the entrance in a ceremonial *V*-shape. The officers saluted as a familiar figure strode forward to stand at ease—cigar in his mouth, suit coat and comb-over flapping in the wind, thumbs hooked into his vest and the golden chain of office plainly visible on his chest.

Mayor Lickpenny.

He looked down at his defeated enemy, then transferred his gaze to the ruined city, nodding his head, content to have wrecked everything.

And still the wind rose. The clock tower was rocking. Lightning crackled. Fires burned out of control. Faces pressed against windows, screaming silently. In the distance, Wylder saw a funnel cloud begin to form. The air was full of noise and smoke and terror.

Uncle Vim climbed to his feet, stepped away from Addy and Wylder and raised his arms. *"THIS IS NOT WHAT I IMAGINED!"*

Silence. As if the whole world held its breath.

The howling gale wrenched a stop sign from its post and hurled it—**WHACK!**—at the back of Uncle Vim's head. He fell to the ground, and everything went ...

35

C ompletely, snow-white blizzard blank.

The last panel, the preceding page and, yes—as Addy flipped through with trembling fingers—the *entire comic book* was now as empty as a new journal, waiting for someone's heart's desire to be scribbled across the paper.

"What happened?" Wylder sounded as though he might be choking. "Are we dead?"

Addy was too aware of too many parts of her body to be dead. Her hair was a tangled mass of snakes; her stomach was grumbling with fear and hunger; and she smelled like a giant ashtray.

"I'm not dead and neither are you. But ..."

Uncle Vim lay at their feet. Seconds ago, the ground

beneath him had been the battered cobblestones of a busy street. It was now as white and smooth as a fresh bedsheet. The roar of the crowd, the workmen's hammering, the crash of thunder, the clanking of the cart carrying Flynn to his doom, the cries and the crackle of fire—all had stopped. All sound had stopped.

There was nothing to see. Except each other, adrift in a sea of white fog. Not going anywhere. But not on firm ground either.

Addy had her bag, and her jeans were still tied around her waist. Wylder was wearing his backpack. The onion rings were somewhere inside Catnip.

Addy kneeled—on what, she wasn't sure, but the whiteness was firm where it needed to be—and laid her head on her uncle's chest, feeling the slight, miraculous rise and fall.

"Is he alive?"

She smiled and teared up and nodded at the same time. Catnip crept from her shoulder onto the unconscious man, where he sniffed and quivered his tail before curling himself into the nook under Vim's ear.

Addy gazed down at the funny face she loved so much. His eyes were closed, but he still managed to express surprise. Something about the eyebrows. The left lens of his glasses had popped out of the frame, and who knew where in this fog it had landed?

"Uncle Vim?" she said. "Can you hear me?"

"Chirp!" said Catnip, a whisker away from Vim's ear.

Uncle Vim's eyelids fluttered and stilled. And fluttered again.

THE EFFECT ON THE UNIVERSE WAS INSTANT, LIKE OPENING A SEALED DOOR.

There were faint but clear noises—screeches, crashes, shouts, a deep bell. The fog began to burn away, revealing blasts of color and motion.

"Oh!" cried Addy. Vim's brain was working!

"It's coming back!" said Wylder. "Smell that smoke!" He stomped his feet. They made a ringing sound on stone. "The world is here."

Uncle Vim's lips moved, but Addy could not make out what he was saying. She leaned in close.

"What do you mean, *real*?" she said.

Viminy fumbled at the pocket of his sweater. His eyes closed. The scene around them began to fade. The sounds softened and ceased.

Uncle Vim began to snore.

The world was white again.

"**A**mazing!" said Wylder. "It all went blank when he got clonked. But then he woke up, and his ideas came back to life."

"Sort of the way he starts every time," said Addy. "With a blank page. The story comes out of his head, through his pencil and ends up in here." She tapped the singed comic in her hand.

"So him drawing makes it real, huh?"

"Not exactly. Apart from today, which was a little *too* real. I think it's the other way around. Usually, when Vim is sketching, it's as if he already knows the place. It already exists. And he's inviting you into his world."

Wylder remembered the way he'd felt, wandering around ComicFest. All those writers and artists and fans, all the fun and possibilities.

Addy stared out at the sea of whiteness.

"But he didn't draw this," she said, lifting the corner of a page and peeking in.

"Wait! What are you doing?" Wylder braced himself for the tumble action.

Addy thumbed the edges, showing one blank page after another. But nothing happened.

"All day we were sort of drawing the comic along with him," said Addy. "*Re*-drawing."

"Changing stuff," said Wylder. "But even when we messed up the plot, we were opening doors for the characters, somehow letting them think for themselves."

"Like Isadora having the idea to give Flynn a new hand. Or Nevins dumping the onion rings."

"The catalyzer making Catnip bionic—though I guess that wasn't *his* idea."

Addy ran a finger down Catnip's back. His whiskers quivered as he slept. Life was easier when you were a rat.

"It's cool how the real world sort of overlapped with the comic," said Wylder. "Like when Nelly came to Toronto, she had the idea to steal some guy's wallet."

"What!?"

"Don't worry—I gave it back. But it's the same thing, right? Her deciding to have fun?"

"What if every time you opened a book you actually went into a different world?" Addy looked down at the battered comic in her hand.

"However we got here," said Wylder. "You have to admit that lots of today *was* awesome fun."

Addy flashed a rare smile. "It was," she said. "Part of it. I sure didn't expect to be talking to *you* a whole day after I met you. Or even a whole minute. That's a big fat surprise."

"Let alone helping each other. Being a team together."
Wylder's cheeks went warm.

"But now, seriously." She waved her hand at the blank world. "We have to get out of here."

"Too bad your uncle can't just draw a happy ending."

Addy gave Wylder a sharp look that used to—only this morning—make him uncomfortable. It still did, a bit.

"You're right," she said, surprising him.

"I am?"

"He can't though," she said. "So it's up to us." She stood and began to pace. "I'm going to think on my feet for a minute."

Addy didn't hop like her uncle did, but Wylder could see this was her version, the marching thing. He held his tongue and let his mind whirl.

What if they were stuck here in foggy nowhereland forever? Maybe not as bad as Toronto under Mayor Lickpenny, but pretty soon he'd get hungry, and there was nothing to eat. He'd have to go to the bathroom, and then what? There was no flush factory.

Wylder shook his head. This was not how great discoveries were made. Isaac Newton and Alexander Graham Bell thought about gravity and telephones—*not* about having to go to the bathroom.

Addy stopped pacing. "Are you thinking the same thing I am?"

"I sure hope not," he said.

The colored flecks in her eyes kind of sparkled.

"Lightbulb?" he said. "You have your 'I'm going to make this happen' look."

"What we were saying, about drawing." She poked around in her shoulder bag. "Have you got a ..."

"A what?"

"Never mind. Uncle Vim always has one."

Vim never went anywhere without one.

Addy slid her hand into the pocket of his sweater and pulled out his pencil, a worn 4B.

"Uncle Vim," she said, "wake up. We need you to draw something."

"Sssh, don't!" said Wylder. "Last thing we want is for him to wake up!"

"Holy cannoli, you're right!" Addy imagined the calm, enveloping whiteness split open again. Lightning, thunder, fire, agony and Flynn on the end of a hangman's rope.

She laid the comic book on Uncle Vim's chest, shifting Catnip's tail to make room. The white paper almost glowed against the grubby gray of his sweater.

"So it's up to us," said Addy. "And here we are. Uncle Vim always says this is the worst part. Staring at a blank page."

"I've heard that," said Wylder. "But it doesn't seem that scary to me. It's like writing down what you want to read. Don't you just draw what you want to see?"

Addy knew exactly what she wanted to see most.

But how to draw it? She gripped the stubby pencil and closed her eyes for a second, imagining exactly the lines she would make.

And then she made them.

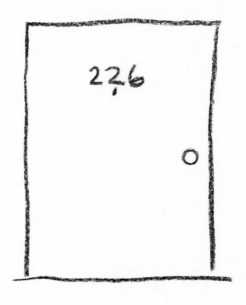

"What's that?" said Wylder.

"The door to my apartment," said Addy. "That's the doorknob. And the peephole. We're on the second floor."

That was all she had time for. The fog whirled in a sudden gust of wind. Catnip scrambled into Addy's vest pocket, Wylder grabbed her elbow and Uncle Vim cried out as the tumbling began.

36

They arrived in a heap on the shabby carpet outside the door to apartment 226.

"It worked!" said Addy.

"We did it!" Wylder lifted his palm, and Addy smacked it hard in a high five.

Uncle Vim groaned and rubbed his temples.

"You okay?"

"No."

Addy relaxed. Uncle Vim was back to his old contrary self. She knew that tone of voice.

"Come on, we made it!"

"How'd we do that?" He shook his long legs and struggled to sit up.

"Addy did it," said Wylder. "She drew us a door."

"Tell me everything. When my head stops hurting."

"I am *so* happy to hear your regular voice," said Addy. "Instead of the Jolly Green Giant's!" She flung her arms around him.

Chirrrp!

"Oops! Sorry, Catnip!" The rat fought his way out of her vest and up to the top of her head.

"Let me see that." Uncle Vim picked up the comic book from the floor.

"I can't believe it," said Wylder.

"I can't believe it," said Addy.

They whammed another high five over Vim's head.

Door number 226 swung open.

"I was pretty sure a ruckus in the hallway meant you guys were home."

"Mom!" Addy bumped her mother into the doorframe with a mega-squeeze.

"*Oof!* Hey, Addy-pie." Addy's mom kissed her. "Your hair is …" She wrinkled up her nose. "Your face is …" She raised her eyebrows. "And is my little brother sitting on the floor for a reason?"

Uncle Vim clambered up. "All in one piece. More or less." He sniffed the sleeve of his sweater. "*Eau de campfire*," he said. "Oh, we've brought home a new pal. This is Wylder Wallace."

"Hello, Wylder Wallace." Addy's mom shook his hand as if he was a grown-up. Addy could see him blushing. "Are you a comic book fan, by any chance?"

"Uh, yes, ma'am."

She laughed. "Ma'am? How about you call me Pippa, like everyone else? And how about we take this party inside?"

The kitchen was warm and smelled faintly of cinnamon. Addy opened the door of Catnip's cage and pushed him through—with much more trouble than usual. He lay down in the shavings and went right to sleep.

"Don't think I didn't notice that you sneaked him out, young lady," Pippa said. "One day on the town and he's *twice* the size."

"It's a long story."

How different the day would have been without Catnip! Holy cannoli, what a difference a rat makes!

"Not sure about the jeans-as-belt, Addy," said her mom. "But cute costume. Even though you're all kind of filthy!"

"Wild times, wild times," said Uncle Vim.

"Whose boots are you wearing? What happened to your high-tops?"

Addy stared at her feet. "I, uh, left them ... er—"

"You brought her home without her *shoes*?" Pippa's voice was suddenly a lot sharper.

"They're somewhere," said Uncle Vim. "It's been ... one of those afternoons. My glasses got broken, see?" He poked a finger through the air where the left lens should have been. "We left in a hurry, didn't we, kids? I forgot my jacket too!"

"Why does that not surprise me?" said Pippa. "Seriously, her *shoes*?"

"It's not his fault," said Addy. "And truthfully, they might be ... well, missing. Kind of forever. There was a mix-up ..."

Addy didn't often lie to her mom. Pippa had Viminy as a little brother, after all. She was used to strange truths. But what they'd done today? How to explain *that*?

"Well, your uncle can buy you new ones," said Pippa, "out of all his riches from the Summer Special. Riches that oughta be pouring in any day now, right? Before the next rent is due?"

Uncle Vim grimaced and ducked his head.

"Oh." Pippa's voice went very quiet. "Was the launch ... um, did it go badly today?"

Addy nearly laughed. Did it go *badly* today?

"Not at all! Not at all!" bluffed Uncle Vim. "It got postponed, that's all. Big party tomorrow." He slipped an arm around Addy's shoulder. "Riches aren't everything anyway. Right, kids?"

"Right," they said.

"Rent would be nice," said Addy's mom.

"I have to go." Vim buttoned up his sweater. "Right now. I'm going to check on some things." He tucked the comic book into Addy's bag, but his face told her nothing. "I'll just nip downtown," he said. "FunnyBones business. Back in a flash."

Pippa's fingers snagged on a tangle in Addy's hair. "Oh! And find the guy who has been trying to reach you. Is your cell phone off?"

"Dead," said Vim. "What guy?"

"Um, Bernie? A security guard?"

"Ernie," said Wylder.

Addy raised her eyebrows at him. Who was Ernie?

"There was an *incident*," said Pippa. She said "incident" the way Ernie must have said it—very solemn. "One of your crazy fans."

"What kind of *incident*?" said Vim.

"You know the big cutout train display? Some fan tried to steal it. He was all dressed up like Flynn, with a mustache and riding boots, and he started dragging the Gold Rush Express through ComicFest, shouting 'Fancy meeting *me* here!' and twirling a sword. Ernie claims he chased him and tried to tackle him. The guy tripped and went crashing down the escalator, right on top of the display. It got all jammed up, and now it's totally wrecked."

"Holy cannoli!" said Addy.

"Oh, jeez." Wylder sighed.

Uncle Vim was quiet for a moment. "I liked that train," he said. "But maybe it's better this way." He looked almost wistful. So did Wylder, come to think of it. Huh? Had they already forgotten just how *real* it was on the other side of that portal?

Vim patted his pockets. "Wallet?" he said. "Keys?

Where's my pencil? I'm just going to make sure that everything is set for tomorrow. Why don't you order a pizza? On me. With dipping sauce. I bet I'm back before the Gino's delivery guy can get here."

He paused at the door to look straight at Wylder. "Don't *think* about going *anywhere* till I get back."

And off he went.

"Your uncle is so cool," said Wylder.

"Yeah," said Addy. "He totally is."

Her mom ordered a pizza right away. Pepperoni, green peppers and pineapple. And two dipping sauces.

"I have to go to work at eight," she said. "Evening shift. I'll get changed while we're waiting."

"Boo," said Addy. "You always have to go to work."

"Don't remind me, honey." She lifted and dropped her shoulders with a big fat sigh. "Someone has to keep this family's feet on the ground."

"May I please use your phone?" asked Wylder. "I'd better call my mother."

"Tell her you're staying for supper," said Addy. She pointed him to the phone on the hall table. "Use the landline."

Wylder sighed and picked up the phone. He tapped the number slowly.

"Good luck!" said Addy.

"Hi, Mom," he began.

Addy could hear the muffled torrent of words from the other end of the phone.

"Mom …" said Wylder. And again, "Mom …"

He didn't say another word for as long as it took Addy to get a glass from the cupboard, add ice, fill it with water and deliver it to him.

She poured water for herself and opened her bag. The comic book was buckled from how it had dried after being in the gator pool, as well as singed and battered from its other adventures.

"Hey," she whispered. Gooney to be talking to a comic book as if it was something real. But, after all, wasn't it? More than paper and ink, more than Uncle Vim's brain full of ideas, it was a whole world. And she'd been there. She might not ever go again—not that way!—but she had a feeling there were other places where books might take her.

And the cover was back to normal! Addy traced the lettering: SUMMER SPECIAL! FLYNN GOSTER AND THE GOLD RUSH EXPRESS! FLYNN IN LOVE?

So far, so good.

Did she dare to open it?

Deep breath.

"Mom," Wylder said. "Mom! I didn't *see* you at ComicFest! I'm sorry if—"

The Red Riders were loading bricks of gold.

OPEN INVITATION TO TRAIN ROBBERS, IF YOU ASK ME, said one of the officers.

Exactly what he was *supposed* to be saying!

Addy hesitated a second before flipping ahead. She didn't think she'd ever be casual about turning a page again. After all, who knew what lay around the next corner? You always had to be ready to think on your feet.

"Well, yeah," Wylder said. "At first there wasn't any reception. But then—try not to get mad—my cell phone got wet."

Addy's finger followed Nelly along the train corridor. Into an *empty* washroom. Out again to creep after Nevins and eavesdrop when Lickpenny told his nephew the plan for stealing the gold.

"And if you want all the bad news at once," said Wylder. "My clothes are kind of ... extra dirty. From this adventure game. Kind of like LARPing."

Flynn, disguised as the master of ceremonies, dove into the gator pool to rescue Isadora Fortuna. **FANCY MEETING ME HERE,** said his speech bubble. He used *two* hands to wipe water from his mustache. Isadora, her lips close to his, murmured, **MY HERO!**

Hope bubbled inside Addy like ginger ale as she kept turning pages. It was all here. The yucky romance, the breathless battles, the gadgets and tricks and vengeful twists ... all in place.

Until the end.

"I'm sorry you had such a bad day, Mom," said Wylder. "Mine was ... *incrediballoo.* Best day of my life." He took a deep breath. "I'm staying for supper at my friend Addy's house … *Please* don't worry. I have money left over from my allowance, so I'll take a taxi home. Yes. You too. Bye."

He didn't move for a second, his hand still gripping the phone.

"Holy cannoli, Wylder. I'm impressed. You just stood up to the mom who sent one hundred and ninety-seven VaporLinks."

"One hundred and ninety-seven last time anyone *checked*," he said. "Which was a few hours ago."

"Double that by now," said Addy.

"I guarantee."

They laughed. Together. Who would have guessed, eh? Still talking to Wylder Wallace at the end of the day. Might even see him tomorrow.

"So." He nodded at the comic book in her hand. "Did it all work out?"

"Depends on your point of view," she said. "For some of them it did. Even if we missed something."

"Who gets the gold? Flynn or Lickpenny?"

"Mmmm."

"What do you mean, we missed something?"

"Let's just say we know what happened to my high-tops."

"But is there a happy ending?" Wylder said. "Or is it full of smooching?"

"See for yourself …" Addy turned the page.

SHE HELD THE COMIC BOOK SO WYLDER COULD LOOK TOO.

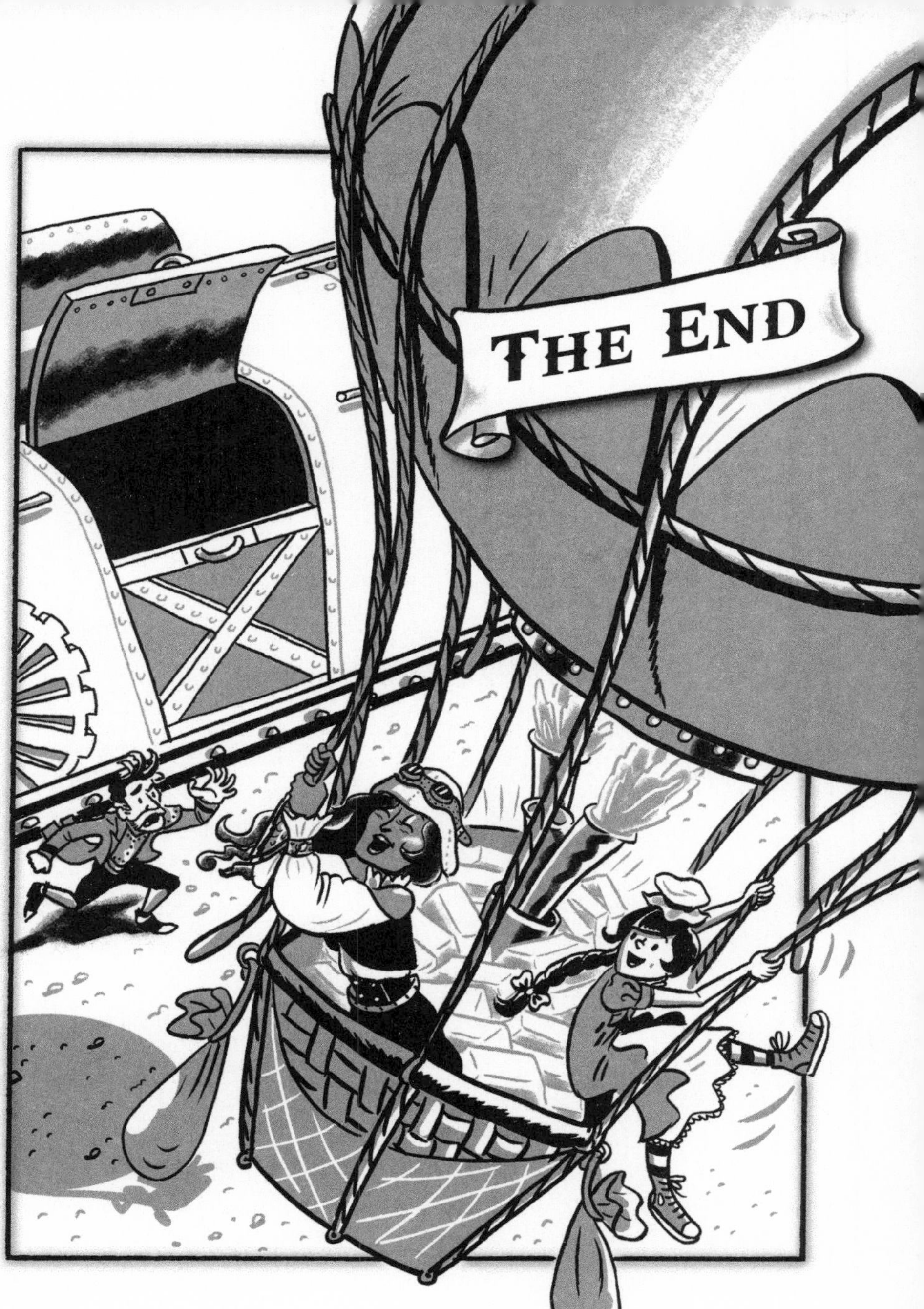
THE END

ACKNOWLEDGMENTS

Usually you try to acknowledge everyone who helped, from your agent and family to Mr. Finnegan's seventh-grade class who picked the title to the dry cleaner who took extra care of your work clothes. Not this time. The book you are holding exists thanks to our editor, Tara Walker. No one worked harder, inspired better or cared more. Thank you.

MARTHE JOCELYN has written or made pictures for more than thirty critically acclaimed children's books. Her YA novels include *How It Happened in Peach Hill*, *Would You*, *Folly* and, most recently, *What We Hide*. Her middle grade novel *Mable Riley* won the inaugural TD Children's Literature Award, and she was the recipient of the prestigious Vicky Metcalf Award for her body of work. Marthe lives in Stratford, Ontario. Visit her at marthejocelyn.com

RICHARD SCRIMGER is the author of almost twenty books for children and adults and is widely regarded as one of Canada's funniest writers for kids. His first children's novel, *The Nose from Jupiter*, won the 10th Annual Mr. Christie's Book Award, and *From Charlie's Point of View* was chosen as one of the "Best of the Best" by the Chicago Public Library. Richard's latest novels for young readers include *Downside Up*, *The Wolf and Me* and *Zomboy*. He lives in Toronto, Ontario. Visit him at scrimger.ca

CLAUDIA DÁVILA is the former art director of *Chirp* and *chickaDEE* magazines, and is the author-illustrator of the award-winning graphic novel series The Future According To Luz and the picture book *Super Red Riding Hood*. Claudia was born in Santiago, Chile, and now makes her home in Toronto with her husband, daughter and son.